The Age of the Outer Kingdom

The Age of the Outer Kingdom

Elyse F. Gathy

In memory of my dog, Bender.

Table of Contents

Chapter 1

I lay down on the dusty cotton blanket lazily placed on the bed. I stare at the ceiling in my room, spacing out. After school had ended, each day had gotten more tiresome. The world of learning about trades and cooking was over. Now most of the kids in my school have the summer for fun and playing. All of the other teenagers in my class would be working for the summer. My choice of work was either an apprentice with my father or mother. Neither of which I wanted to do. I glanced over at my bookcase; one of the few things that was not dusty in my room. I pulled myself up and off the bed and plucked one of the few books I owned off the top shelf.

"The Story of King Bartholomew," I read the title to myself. Reading was all I had to do when I was bored, so the same books began to get repetitive. However, I did not mind the monotony, since the books were so enjoyable. I lie back down on the bed and slowly open the cover, turning one of the worn-out pages. A familiar tapping noise came from my roof. I looked out my window and noticed rain beginning to shoot down from the sky like arrows. I looked back down at the book and read out loud. Reading out loud to myself was something I liked to do. My friends at school say "it's just weird" but, then again, my entire class consists of only 20 other 16-year-olds.

"Once upon a time there was a big kingdom; this kingdom was called the Outer Kingdom. And in that Kingdom lived King Bartholomew Drandor. A great ruler loved by all of his subjects. That is, all but the ogres; uncivilized brutes that lived like vermin in a kitchen. One day the ruler of the ogres, Renhi, sent an ogre to make a demand to King Bartholomew to be granted king of the Outer Kingdom. The King denied his request and said the land would continue to be ruled by a Drandor. Renhi was furious and declared war. King Bartholomew stood his ground and swore that the Outer Kingdom would be safe. So, Renhi went to war against the king of the Outer Kingdom and his army."

The rain pelted down harder. I picked my head up and scanned the room. The room was fuzzy at first until my eyes adjusted to the light. I looked over at the dusty bureau next to my bed. A candle flickered sending shadows dancing around the room. My eyes fell over my bookcase again. A few other books were left on it. Although it sometimes seemed that I owned little, I knew my family was very fortunate.

"The King was furious; the ogres had burned down houses, taken villagers hostage, and killed some of the King's subjects. The King and his royal army marched bravely into battle. A gruesome battle played out for many days. The ogres could not beat King Bartholomew and his gallant army of heroic soldiers, so they eventually surrendered. The defeated ogres were banished to live in a large cave deep inside the Swamp Forest. King Bartholomew and his army returned to Trisanburg victorious."

I closed the book. In school, we learned about King Bartholomew Drandor all the time. The King is still alive today and has a son, Prince George. When the war between ogres and humans happened, I was not born yet, and the King was only 19. I could not imagine having to lead an army into battle at that young age.

The Outer Kingdom's royal history was my good friend Byron's favorite subject. As a result, I know a lot about it from listening to him talk all the time. I climbed off my bed and walked over to my bookcase, gripping the book in my hand. I slid it on the shelf realizing how much I needed to clean my room. I always seem to wait to clean until it is absolutely necessary. My dad always says that a clean house belongs to a high-class family, so we always have to keep ours clean. Ironically, our small piece of the Outer Kingdom was far from high class. Brendsworth was one of the smallest regions in all of the Outer Kingdom so, no one paid attention to us. It is so small that there is only one town so, everyone refers to Brendsworth as both a town and region.

One of the only interesting places in Brendsworth was the marina, where travelers from abroad come and it serves as a marketplace for fish. What I found particularly fascinating about the marina was the various oddities the foreign merchants would bring into port on busy days. My house is closer to the market than to the marina so, I go there more. I rolled off my bed with a sigh and lazily walked down the stairs to the main floor of my house. The room was buzzing with hungry customers and the scent of fresh baked goods.

"Liam, is that you?" my mother asked.

"Yes, Mom!" I replied.

"Could you look outside? I think the mail is here and I'm really busy right now," she rummaged around the kitchen, tending to the customers.

"Okay."

My mother owns the most successful bakery in Brendsworth. Well, that is, the only bakery in Brendworths but, nonetheless, she is still the best.

I walked outside to fetch the mail. The Outer Kingdom has letters delivered one day out of every week to one or two specific regions. Our letters come on Thursdays. The rain was ceasing, leaving droplets on the grass and puddles dotting the ground. A letter was placed on our doorstep. Our neighbor ran outside; he must have noticed the rain stopping too. Thomas, the boy next door, held a wooden sword that he got for his fourteenth birthday. The sword looked disproportionate to his body. He had obviously outgrew it because, like me, he is sixteen now. Thomas started to violently swing it around.

"What's up, Liam! Jealous of my skills with the sword? I bet you are!" Thomas yelled, shooting a dirty look. I hated his dumb fancy-sounding accent.

"Oh, come on! Leave me alone, I'm not jealous of you! In fact, nobody is!"

"Oh!" Thomas sneered, feigning offence. "That *really* hurts me, but at least I don't look like a donkey!" he retorted snobbishly. I felt my face flush with color at his snide remark.

"Really? That's the way you're gonna take this? You are like a child! I hope you fall in the mud face first!" I snatched up the moist letter and marched back inside. The sound of Thomas laughing at me grew fainter as I closed the door and strolled into the kitchen. Thomas and his friend, Jim, are not the nicest people in our school. My best friend Byron tells me they just say that because they are jealous of me. I doubt that. Sometimes, I feel like he is perfect compared to me.

Thomas was taller than me, had ebony skin, and perfect short black hair. Every girl in school reminds the other boys constantly how "cute" he is. However, none of them would ever be interested in him. Although he had good looks on the outside, on the inside he is a jerk.

"Who is that for?" my mother asked. I looked at the letter. The ink was smudged, but it was still readable.

"Eleanora Rocklen of Brendsworth," I mumbled, still angry at Thomas.

My mom took the letter out of my hand. She scanned over the letter.

"Here, go put it on the table, and then go clean your room! I swear, if you put your hand on that floor, your hand would be covered in dirt."

I sighed and followed her orders. Slowly, I grabbed the broom out of the closet and pulled a pail and sponge along with it.

"And don't forget to clean the mirror in the hallway!" she shouted up the stairs.

"Okay."

I brought the pail outside to the small well behind our house. I looked around at our beautiful property. Our house was two stories tall and was dark brown color with light brown shingles. I was lucky to have such a nice house. We, thankfully, were not a poor family, as wealth goes in Brendsworth. The richest family in Brendsworth was the Lord and Lady. Each region has at least one Lord and Lady that sees over it. Their job is to report to King Bartholomew in person twice a year and help better the region. A lot of people don't like Lord Dougel and Lady Fiona because they do not contribute much to

Brendsworth. I pulled the heavy bucket of water out of the well and filled up my pail. Heading back inside the water sloshed around getting my pants and boots wet; I don't care though. I trudged upstairs with my equipment into my room. Loud noises came from downstairs. I suspected my mom was still busy. As soon as I reached my room, I hastily swept the floors.

Outside, two boys were playing a game of pirates and merchants. I watched as I rubbed my window clean. I longed to be a kid again and have no responsibilities.

Watching them having fun reminded me of the Winter Festival. Each year, everyone in my class looks forward to the Winter Festival. Everyone in my class has known each other since we were kids, and we have done the same thing every year at the winter festival. We eat pound cake and then play games of tag and hide-and-seek. It is the only time of year during which I feel complete happiness and bliss. The more I thought about the festival, the sadder I felt.

After a while, I stopped sweeping and got ready to wipe down the shelves and bureau. The repetitive movements of scrubbing made me reflect on my life.

"The same friends every year, the same boring summer every year, the same school every year. Every year is the same." I mumbled. Quickly, I changed my train of thought. I wished I were the son of a lord, so I would never have to clean again. However, if I were, I would never have the opportunity to go and become something great. Suddenly, the thought of Thomas bragging about his skills with a sword popped into my mind. Maybe I should practice fighting with a sword?

I doused the sponge with water from the pail. As my hand touched the moist sponge; my arm grew tired just from the thought of continuing to wash my bureau. As I dragged the sponge across the surface, it left a trail of dust free wood behind it. The noise of pots and pans from downstairs echoed throughout my room. My hand guided the sponge across my bedframe. I picked up the pail full of murky gross water, satisfied with the work I had completed. I looked over the room once more. It still appeared plain and boring, but at least it was clean. Sadly, I sit in my room alone almost every day. Over the summers, I have read every book that I own more than one hundred times, and the only excitement I get is from sitting outside and watching the trees move back and forth. The other time is spent cleaning or at school. Of course, every once in a while, I spend time with my friends but, other than that, my life could be explained in a few sentences. It is boring and uneventful compared to the stories I read in my books.

What am I doing? Will my whole life be behind the boundaries of this town? I go to school starting at the end of fall and ending at the end of winter. That is not even half the year. What will I do the rest of the time? I gazed down at myself in the murky water of the bucket. Was I wasting my life?

I hopped I would accomplish something incredible before I died. Will my whole life be spent here? Going to school and learning how to cook or clean or trade, so I can go practice that same thing here for the rest of my life? Cook for my family, clean my house, and trade for better items? The words cook, clean, and trade haunted me. Will I just get a small trade, like a cobbler or a carpenter? Am I always going to be remembered as just Liam Rocklen, the carpenter or the baker? Will I grow up to be just like every other kid in my grade?

No! I will not live like that. I will be known as Liam Rocklen, the dragon slayer or the knight! Everyone in my class will remember me as the kid that went out and made something of himself! My confidence built up inside me. I rushed to the window and threw the water out into the grass. If I was going to make this dream possible, I had to start preparing for it now. I'm going to learn how to use a sword.

Chapter 2

I walked down the stairs, determined and confident. My mom was behind the counter in the bakery, counting the money she earned for the day. I put the cleaning equipment back in the closet. She quickly put away the money and rushed into the kitchen. Smoke emerged from the doorway. Mom was waving away a cloud of smoke from the garlic bread. She frowned at her pitiful creation.

"The bread is only burnt a little," I said, attempting to make her feel better, but the bread was actually scorched.

"I usually am more careful with filling the wood fire oven with too much kindling; I have just been a little distracted by the new taxes and such."

"Mom, can I ask you something?"

"What? Is it about the bread? I refuse to make another one! I just don't have the time!"

"Umm no, not that. I want to learn how to use a sword, like Thomas. But not a wooden one."

"You mean the young man next door? And that was not even a question."

I rolled my eyes. She was off when she said Thomas was a young man: he was more of a baby if anything. Also, I could tell this might not have been a good time to talk to her because she seemed stressed.

"Yes mom."

"I am sorry Liam. I am just so busy! I will think about it. You know it would be hard to get a sword if your father was not a blacksmith. Your chances are better because he is-" she was interrupted by the sound of an opening door. A man walked inside the room.

"Ugh, what do those neighbors burn to make it smell so gross?" he said with a smile.

The man had a big brown mustache and brown hair that grew close to his shoulders. Ashes and soot covered his face from a hard day at work.

"Hi Dad. We were just talking about you."

Dad had been at work since the crack of dawn that morning, working hard on a new sword that a merchant had ordered.

"Good day at work?" My mom walked over and kissed my dad on the cheek.

"It was long. How about here? Looked busy when I left."

"We sold a lot of bread today…and we got a letter from him," my mom and dad exchanged a look. I looked at them puzzled by their strange actions.

"Who?" I asked.

"Well then, why don't I fetch dinner?" My mom headed into the kitchen. Looks like my question was ignored.

"I have not had very many orders for swords lately. All day I spend time making hooks and random metal things people need. It has gotten boring at work, which I thought I would never say! Anyways, you said you got a letter?"

Curiosity started to bubble up inside me. What could the letter have been about? If they are keeping it a secret, it must be about me. I started to stare at Dad. He did not notice at first, but when he did, I could tell he felt uncomfortable. I tried to keep my suspicious expression, as best as I could, but the thought of the answer coming out of him made me want to smile. My mom walked in with a plate of steaming boiled potatoes and some bread.

"Oh yum! I have been waiting all day to get some of my wife's cooking! Where is the salt?"

"I ran out today. I can have Liam pick some up at the market tomorrow though. We can manage one night without salted potatoes, right, Liam?"

I had zoned out for a while after my mom had said market. The market is my favorite place to go. You can find the strangest things that traveling merchants bring in. However, the best part was that new merchants came every week. So, there is always something new. Additionally, there is a tree in the market that is perfect for climbing. Since I was a little kid, I have climbed that tree and filled up the bird feeder that rests at the top of the tree. The market was truly the most interesting place to go.

"Liam?"

"Oh…oh yeah, sure."

We all ate our meal in silence. The potatoes were soft and well cooked, but they were bland and flavorless. I walked up to my room and got ready for bed.

It was hard to fall asleep. Not because of the crickets making a symphony of noise outside, but the excitement of going to the market tomorrow. After a while, the fact that I could not fall asleep annoyed me. I stared out my window at the night sky. It was like a big cloth dotted with bright yellow specks. Suddenly, I remembered I forgot to ask my dad about the sword. I could hardly wait. I almost jumped out of bed to go ask him, but I knew it was too late and I had to sleep.

As I sat in silence, it finally became clear to me what I am really passionate about. I wanted to save lives by defending those who can't defend themselves. I wanted to feel adventure. It felt like what I was born to do. I started to conger up a dream of me being declared a royal knight. The dream sank into my mind, and I slowly fell asleep.

I woke up to the sounds of spring. Morning doves called out to other birds wishing them a 'good morning'. Today is the day! Without waiting, I pulled on my tan pants and dirty black boots. With haste, I threw on my green long-sleeve shirt and black belt. I was so excited; I almost forgot to put on my brown vest. When I got downstairs, the bakery was flooded with people.

"Where is Dad?" I asked.

"Your father is outside at the well. He already left for work. You can catch him if you're quick enough."

"Got it! Thanks Mom! I will be right back!"

I quickly sprinted out the door and to the well, not far from the house. A minute later, I found my Dad still by the well, which was in a beautiful meadow area. The wheat grew up to my knees and tickled my legs as I galloped through the field. I breathed in the cold early morning May air, which burned my lungs. The sun was barely shining through the grey clouds.

"Dad!" I shouted.

He looked up. I skidded to a stop next to him. He took another sip of the well water.

"Anything wrong, Liam?" He offered me a sip of the water from his canteen.

"Thanks," I wheezed.

The cold water felt like snow in the dead of winter in my mouth. The water felt satisfying to my throat and tasted refreshing. The well water was safer than water from a river or a pond, so everyone in town used the same well.

"I wanted to ask you if you could make me a sword," I gasped, still exhausted from the run.

"A sword? Well, are you sure you want to take an interest in this? You know that they are not toys. Besides, you should not be thinking about new toys, you need to be considering a career. I don't want to see you sit lazily around this summer."

"No, this isn't some toy. I want to pursue a career as a knight. So, I need a sword so I can spend my summer preparing for that."

"A knight? Well, that is not an impossible job. You have to work very hard though."

"I know."

"Is this really what you want? I don't want to make it an then have you change your mind a day later," He sternly said.

"Yeah, I am sure. And besides, it would be good for self defense, you know?"

"It is going to have to be one made for young adults. You're not ready for a real big one yet. Also, treat it like a weapon, not a plaything. And most importantly don't try to stab anyone with it!" my dad said as he strode back toward the town and to his blacksmith forge. It was a "yes!" I jumped for joy.

"Thanks dad! Also, what would give me the urge to stab someone with it?" I laughed.

Finally, I am going to have something new to do instead of wasting my time away. Now I am one step closer to becoming a knight. I should go and find books to learn from and invent my own style of fighting with a sword. There are so many things I can do now with a sword of my own.

Chapter 3

The bakery was bustling with people buying freshly baked breads, muffins, and bagels. I swiftly maneuvered my way through the crowd of people. My mom always complained about how small the bakery was for the number of people we bring in.

"Alright, so… the half loaf of bread? Is that all?" My mom asked the woman who was first in line.

"Yes. Oh, do you happen to have any cakes?" the woman said with enthusiasm.

"No sorry ma'am, not today. That will be two bronze coins."

I liked how my mom talked so cheerfully and polite around the customers. The woman reached out and handed the coins to my mom. She waddled around the people behind her toward the exit. I knew of that woman. Her name is Mary-Kate Rubard, and she works at the Lord and Lady's home. As a smaller region we only have a Lord and Lady, while, some of the bigger regions have Earls and Barons. Earls and Barons are wealthier citizens who commonly discuss the region's problems with the Lords.

"Mom, I am going to be out in the woods today. Dad is going to make me a sword, so I want to create a spot where I can practice with it. Is that okay?"

"Practice what?"

"With my sword. I just told you, Dad is making me one."

"Wow, that's great Liam! Well, go on then- I can help who is next."

"See you- oh, hi Mrs. Bekwood- later Mom!"

"Remember to be careful!" She called over the noise.

"Yes, yes, I will make sure to walk away with every stranger that I see and go say hello to each creepy person that walks by me! You know how people are in Brendsworth!" I called out to her sarcastically.

"Liam! I'm serious!" She got the joke but was not too happy.

I waved and then ran out onto the street toward the woods. I could not help but wonder why she was so worried. Travelers rarely come to Brendsworth, and if there were bad people around, they would be at the only tavern in Brendsworth: The Termites' Nest.

I was always allowed to roam around freely as a child. However, now that I am older, I learned of the murders and kidnappings that happen in more populated regions and towns in the Outer Kingdom. They rarely happens though because the Royal Knights that patrol the towns and cities keep the area safe.

The trees rustled as they swayed back and forth in the cool spring wind. I walked on the Main Road: the long dirt road that went straight through the center of the town. If I follow it long enough, it would lead me straight to our kingdom's capital, Trisanburg City. Located in the region called Trisanburg, surrounded by wheat fields, is a thriving city called Trisanburg City. Every school year since I was young, we learn about every region in the kingdom. A boy in the class bellow me named Padro used to live in Trisanburg City. He spoke of how big it was compared to Brendsworth and how many shops there were. I have always wanted to go to Trisanburg City and see the magnificent royal castle.

My mind shifted back to my task at hand. Now, I need to find a spot where I can practice with my sword and also a book to teach me. I had seen Thomas do his fighting stances so many times that I have a sense on what to do. As I ventured into the woods, I thought more about the infinite possible moves I can practice.

The woods were a little colder than the yard or the field, but there was a magical glow to it. The way the sun shone through the branches made a pattern on the dirt path in front of me. Squirrels and birds seemed to show themselves more often in the woods than in the town because they are hidden under the safety of the trees.

My favorite part of school was learning about the millions of creatures that live in our world. In fact, my favorite author and my personal hero, Sir Frederick, writes books explaining what creatures are dangerous and what creatures are helpful.

Suddenly, I saw a clearing of trees not too far off the dirt path. Hurdling over the broken tree limbs and rocks, I ventured toward the clearing. Loose sticks and small piles of leaves scattered the ground. The spot was perfect.

I hunched over and began the process of picking up the leaves and sticks to clear the area. My back ached from bending over for so long. In addition to the clear secluded area, the trees surrounding were perfect to whack at. Unlike Thomas, I have a target and now an advantage.

After spending the whole morning clearing the space, I headed back home. A line was sticking out of the door of the small bakery. The morning rush must still be happening, I thought to myself. Our house was not the only one in town to have a business on the bottom floor, with bedrooms on the top. Our teachers taught us this is how most buildings are in the Trisanburg City.

I decided to wait for the people to leave before going back inside, and take a walk instead. It was a perfect day for a walk anyways. The streets were now more crowded. I took in my surroundings. Three other houses surrounded my house until you reached the edge of our town and the woods. The houses continue in the other direction until you reach the market square where tons of vendors go to sell their goods. I walked in the direction of the market. Kids ran through the streets playing games and horse drawn wagons pulled various goods. From the market, four other roads led off to different areas of Brendsworth. One of the roads was the Main Road, which led straight to Wodarn and then onward until Trisanburg City. Wodarn was one of our neighboring regions and it was famous for its skilled fisherman and the Elizabeth River. The Elizabeth River was named after a famous Lady of Wodarn. I noticed Byron coming down that road. Byron was one of my best friends since my first year in school. He is a very laid back person unless he is on his farm working.

"Hello, Liam! What have you been up to? I just started my summer job with my father, again. The life of a farmer is hard work," Byron said.

"Yeah, sounds like fun, sort of. Anyways, so far this summer, I have been preparing myself to learn how to use a real sword. Not like a fake wood one like Thomas's," I bragged.

"What! No way! Now that's awesome, man! I wish I had time for that, but I need to learn how to be a bean farmer like my dad and mom. You know what they say, 'If it ain't beans it ain't farming."

"I hope I never hear you say that ever again. But, literally, I don't think I can see myself as a bean farmer. I would rather grow something cool like squash," I said attempting to make him mad.

"You take that back! My grandma would be rolling in her grave if she knew I was friends with a squash man."

"Oh, I almost forgot, I have decided that I won't become a baker or blacksmith like my parents," I revealed.

"Really? That's surprising, not many people would give up an interesting job like that. Don't worry though, a lot of people don't do what their parents do. I mean there are lots of other jobs here that are great. You can always work for me," he suggested with a cheeky smile.

"Not a chance. You would probably work me to death. Not to mention, I am planning on getting out of Brendsworth and going to become a knight or something."

"Really? You remember Grace? She graduated last year and went to train as a knight in the Dorgan," Byron said.

"Yeah, and then she flunked out after the first week, and now she is a seamstress. I know that happened to her, but I am not her! I am going to pass no problem if I practice enough here."

"Good luck with that, man. You will need it!"

"I am serious! I will! There is no way I am flunking out."

"Byron!" His father called from down the road.

"Okay, I've got to go. My dad is waiting. Good luck with all that," he said as he walked away.

I waved to his father and then went back to my walk. The other two paths were dead ends and had only houses and businesses. My father's blacksmith forge was down one of those roads. The school was also on that road. I wanted to avoid school as long as possible, so I decided to take the road toward the marina. The farther I walked, the stronger the smell of seawater got. Three ships sat in the harbor. Each ship was being loaded or unloaded with goods. The Termites Nest was one of the buildings surrounding the marina along with tackle shops, houses, and inns. My favorite thing to do at the marina was sit on the boxes of cargo and take in the ocean and the salty air. I had only been on a boat once; it was not the best experience for me because I got seasick. Sitting on shore and swimming was what I preferred. I looked out at the hill overlooking the harbor. On top the hill sat a large manor. That is Lord Dougel and Lady Fiona's house. When I am older, I want a pretty house overlooking the ocean.

"Howdy Lam'! How is your day!" a teenage girl called up to me. I recognized her immediately. She is in my class. I rolled my eyes. No one likes her because she is so annoying, but I try to be nice to her anyways.

"Umm… pretty normal. How about you, Sandy?"

"Oh, you know, I have been starin' at these here sailors carrying them boxes. I wanted to go over to em' and try to ask them some questions, but I am just too darn shy! I wish I was bolder and talked more, but ya know I am scared of being too talkative! I can't have any of yall thinkin I can't shut my own mouth! You know, I was wonderin if you could ask Byron out for me? He is your best friend right? I could get lost in those deep blue eyes, and I bet his hair is as soft as a hay barrel in July! I can't wait until school starts again; it will be so fun! It would be so great if we could all stay friends in school forever!

Don't y'all think that would be nice?" She continued to talk, but I zoned out and didn't catch the rest. I tried so hard to smile and nod like I was interested in what she was saying, but I couldn't take it anymore. How could she be that oblivious?

"Yeah, that sounds great, but I have to go! See you later!" I said, waving.

"Yeah, see ya real soon! Bring Byron with ya, okay? Or even better just have him come without ya! Bye now!"

"How about no..." I said under my breath. I briskly walked back to my house to find the bakery was less full.

"Mom, I'm back!"

"Liam! Can you do something for me? I need you to go get salt at the market."

I was not excited to go back to the market, but if it means I get salt on my dinner, then I will. My mom handed me four bronze coins and a gold one. I loved the power I felt when holding them. I can go buy anything with them.

"Remember the salt, Liam. And if you find anything there you might like."

I sprinted to the town square before she could finish. I already knew she was going to tell me I could get something special for myself.

The market was alive with people bargaining and selling their products. A girl and her mom were sitting at their booth yelling "Get homemade beeswax candles right here!" One familiar cart quickly distracted me.

"Abigail! What's up?" I shouted.

The woman at the cart turned her head toward me and smiled. The wooden cart was covered top to bottom in trinkets and potions. The trinkets looked like ordinary junk, but I knew they must have magical properties to them.

"Ey, hello Liam! I have not seen you since last fall." Abigail said.

I gave her a hug. She was about the same age as my mother and her best friend. Her sunset orange hair glistened in the sunlight. Her skin was pale and dotted with freckles like the stars in the night sky. However, the thing that made her stand out the most was her height. She was at least six feet tall. I barely reached her shoulders. She adjusted her long blue dress and her black cloak as we pulled away from the hug.

"How is your mother? Is she well? What about the bakery?" Abigail showered me with questions.

"She is doing okay. The bakery is also good. How have you been?" I said distracted by the exotic items on her cart.

Abigail was my mother's best friend growing up in Wodarn. My mom would tell stories about her friend. She told me that once during the school year my mother and Abigail's friend Eloise had been made fun of by two of the boys in their school. They would make fun of her old hand-me-down dresses. My mom told them on her own to stop being unkind to her, but they started to say that my mom had a stupid name. The next day at school Abigail said "If you don't stop making fun of Eloise and Eleanor, you will regret it and I will do something the whole school will never forget!" The two boys did not listen, though; they told her that they would keep doing it. Then, they would learn that they made a bad choice by adding that Abigail had ugly red hair. I have learned over the years that Abigail has a big temper and loves her long red hair.

The next day at school Abigail had kept her word. Using her magic, because she is a witch, Abigail had made a potion that would turn someone's hair green if drunk. With the help of my mother they made cookies with the potion baked into it. Eloise had brought them to eat at lunch, but she would not eat the cookies herself. Once the two boys had seen their chance to make her upset, they stole the cookies. As soon as they swallowed them, the boys' hair turned a disgusting color of yellow-green. "Who has ugly hair now?" Abigail had yelled. The school had erupted with laughter. Those boys had gotten what they deserved. They pleaded for her to turn their hair back, and she did eventually but, only because they agreed not to make fun of anyone ever again. And she made sure they didn't.

"So, anything I can interest you in?" She gestured to her cart.

I went over to take a closer look. The first shelf had potions on it such as medicine or phony potions that claim to grow back hair in five minutes. None of it interested me. I scanned over the row below it. There were strange magical items like a bracelet, a stick, and a jar. One item on the row caught my eye. It was a small wooden dragon that was painted over in a base color of purple and stripes of blue and yellow curled around its body. The small dragon was about the size of my palm.

"May I pick it up?" I asked, pointing to the dragon.

"Sure. You know everything on this cart is very rare."

"What is it? It's very cool looking. I really like the design," I said, holding out the dragon.

"Yeah, isn't it? Dragons are a pretty cool species. I wished there were more of them. It's too bad they are endangered. But the figure you got there is pretty special too. It's an Enchanted Wooden Figure."

I turned it around in my hands as she explained what it was.

"When I was up in the forests of Arone, I came across a clan of fairies. They were amazing; you should have seen them! They all had different color hair from spring green to ocean blue! And their clothes matched their hair color; it was so cute. Ya know, I see many interesting magical creatures when I travel to sell goods around the Outer Kingdom. Oh! And the best thing of all is that fairies had magical abilities like me! Ya see, fairies practice magic called fairy magic. Good name, right? Few witches are lucky enough to be taught it. But, guess what! They taught me! The more powerful fairies, who had magical powers almost as strong as mine, made the Enchanted Wooden Figures out of simple tree wood!"

"How?" I asked.

Abigail snatched it out of my hand. She was so lucky to go anywhere she wanted and see so many interesting things. I wish I could go and find magical fairies.

"So, they would go to the special kind of tree that only grew where they lived; it was called a Willistera. Where they lived, there are about twenty trees, but those are the only ones in all of the Outer Kingdom. So, like the fairies, the Willistera is going extinct. Anyways, the trees grow tall above the ground! Even for me!"

"Taller than the pine trees here?" I asked. She was opening my eyes to a whole world that I can only imagine.

"Yes!" She pointed to a pine tree nearby.

"Anyways, and their branches went up, but curved down with the leaves falling downward. And they explained that only in the winter do they blossom. They said the trees have big purple and pink flowers!" Abigail said barely stopping to take a breath.

"And the fairies taught me how to make the Enchanted Wooden Figures. They cut down one branch off the Willistera tree to form the figures. They have a rule, though, that you have to plant another Willistera tree for every branch you cut down using the seeds the blossoms release. You see, the fairies collect them."

I longed to travel outside of Brendsworth and discover magical worlds in the Outer Kingdom like the one she is describing. I have never been out of Brendsworth, not once. I could not wait to become good at using a sword so I have a chance of maybe going to the knight school in Arone.

"Then you use a knife to carve out your figure; the fairies take a long time to make them, though. I was only there a couple of days. Then you create any animal you want, but you have to have a scale or hair of the animal, and you can't do a human because the fairies say the magic does not work well with a human hair for some reason. Or mice hair, strangely. Luckily, I had gotten a dragon scale I found in the mountains of Arone laying in the dirt. And when I was in Dorgan the hills were so pretty and covered with wild flowers; I collected tons of them that I gave to the fairies as a way to say thanks. I was so grateful to have met them. They taught me more about fairy magic than any other witch could."

"Wait, isn't that near all of the prestigious schools in the Outer Kingdoms? Like the knight school!"

The hills of Dorgan! The mountains of Arone! How did she get there? And, how can I get there? Whenever she would visit us I would hear the most amazing stories about her travels. It makes me want to travel.

"Ugh, those schools there are just filled with snooty brats. Not any one of them would care about the beautiful hills that are surrounding their schools. Anyways, then, you use a special spell to make the wooden figure enchanted with the spirit of the animal you carved! Then, we painted it. And you don't need to feed it or take care of it all the time! Just bring it to life whenever you feel like it!"

"Bring it to life?"

"Yes! The fairies' magic is basically; they use spells to transfer magic into objects. It's not used for more than a fun toy but it's still beautiful. Do you want the dragon?"

"How much is it?"

"Just one gold coin. I would usually charge four, but I heard someone had a birthday in early March. You're practically a man now, 16 years of age! And it's the least I can do for my best friend's son."

I was happy she brought the price down for me, but it was still a bit much. However, if it can come to life, then it must be worth it. I handed over the coin. She grabbed my wrist and placed the dragon in my hand. Then, directed my finger toward the head of the wooden figure. Next, she mumbled a spell. Her eyes were shut, and her mouth moved quickly. Abigail was clearly a powerful witch.

"What is its name?" she said.

The question came too quickly. I could hardly follow what was happening. I needed more time to think. She mumbled words quickly under her breath. I don't want to ruin the magic; I have to think of one now! Think! THINK!

"Scales?!"

A small spark came from her hand, and I felt something weird travel up from where she held my wrist to my finger.

"DONE!" she flung her hands off me.

"What?"

I looked down at my hand. The dragon shook his head. It was moving. The wings came out from the body, and Scales flapped them. He flew up to my head and sat in a bed of my soft brown hair. It was like having my own little pet. My parents had never let me have a pet because my dad is allergic to cats and dogs. Now, that won't be a problem because it's made of wood!

"Wow. Is this what it feels like when moms see their babies after labor?"

"Ha ha, I am sure it's not the same thing. All you have to do, now that I have made a magical bond between you and Scales, is to place your finger on his head when he is "alive" to make him become wood again. Just put it hold your finger on its head again when you want him to be enchanted."

"Thank you, Abigail!"

I admired the new "pet" I have. Each hour of the day seemed to be getting better and better. I could not wait for what will happen next.

Chapter 4

I could not wait to play with Scales. I ran upstairs away from the noise of the bakery. In the quiet safety of my room, I enchanted the dragon following Abigail's directions. A small light flashed on the dragon's head when I enchanted it. The small creature shook its head as if waking up from a long nap. It hopped playfully around my palm. As if it were a dog or cat, the dragon leaped around and chased its tail. An idea sprung into my head. I took Scales over to my writing desk and placed him gently on the hard surface. Scales stayed in place while I studied him. Maybe I could train it? As soon as I stood up to collect some things, he began hopping around again. I came back with two pencils and a bookmark. Bending and piercing the bookmark, I fashioned a small hurdle.

"Okay Scales! Let's see if you can do some tricks! Try to jump up and over this."

I attempted to teach Scales how to jump over hurdles. The small dragon curiously inspected the object that I placed before him. Scales stretched out his wings and flew over the bookmark hurdle. I completely forgot he could fly. I tried again by gesturing the jump with two fingers. Scales followed my instructions. With ease, the dragon hopped over the hurdle. I sprung up and cheered. Then, I began to experiment with more tricks. Soon, I had built an entire obstacle course out of the objects in my room.

"Alright, Scales, first you must jump over these two different sized bookmark hurdles. Then, climb up the book ramp and slide down the "Sir Frederick's Adventures" book. Next, climb up with stack of books where you have to carry this quill in your mouth, and fly it back here into this pool of ink!" I exclaimed.

"Okay! On your mark!" The dragon hopped up and down.

"Get set!" Scales flexed his wings.

"GO-"

"Liam! Liam, you father wants to speak with you!" My mom yelled up the stairs.

"Aww, darn it. I guess we have to continue this later... wait a minute! I almost forgot about my sword!"

I sprinted down the stairs almost falling twice. Dad was sitting at the table eating a piece of bread. My mom was bringing over dinner; more cooked potatoes.

"Dad! Do you have it?" I asked.

"Have what?"

"You know my sword?"

"What sword?"

I felt my excitement slowly deflated. He forgot. I had to wait another day until I could begin my training. The whole next day's plans went out the door.

"You don't remember? I asked you this morning."

"What do you mean?" He looked confused.

Sadness turned into anger. How could he forget? I had run out to the well just this morning.

"Are you serious?" My tone showed my anger.

"Calm down, Liam! I was just tricking you!" He started to laugh.

"That was not a very good trick. It was a little rude..." I mumbled.

"Oh, hush up Liam, let your father have some fun," my mom said.

Out of his satchel, my dad pulled a sword wrapped up in a white cloth. I reached out and took it. I had underestimated how heavy it was. I quickly unwrapped the cloth. It felt like the most important moment in my life. The sword was shorter than an adult's sword, but the tip was thin and sharp. If I wanted to, I could pick my teeth with it.

"Liam! Not in the house. You are only allowed to use it outside, I don't want anyone getting hurt," my mom scolded me.

"I was not going to swing it around!" I said in defense.

"It's a fine sword, and it will do you good against any attackers."

"Honey, who is going to want to hurt Liam?" My mom questioned.

"Probably no one but, it's good to have just in case,"

"Thanks, Dad! Mom, I promise I won't hurt myself- oh, I just remembered I forgot to get the salt today…" I revealed feeling guilty.

"Just eat dinner without it then. You can get it tomorrow," my mom said.

Soon after I finished dinner, I took my sword up to my room, anxious to use it. Sadly, I would have to wait until tomorrow to use my new sword.

I woke up the next day, ready to use my new sword. With a skip in my step, I ran downstairs. The sun shined brightly through the bakery windows.

My mom was setting up the bakery for the day.

"Liam, where are you off too?" She asked as I stuck my foot out the door.

"I have this cool spot for me to practice in so, I am going to go try my new sword out," I explained.

"Be careful! I don't want you coming home with any cuts! Oh. Come to think of it, maybe you should ask that nice boy next door if he wants to go practice with you. That way if you get hurt he can run back and tell me."

I could not believe that even came to her mind. I would rather I drink a gallon of soul milk.

"That will never happen," I said, leaving.

"Goodbye! Be careful!"

"Bye Mom!"

With the sound of the door shutting, I took off down the road. The woods were very quiet today. Only the sounds of an occasional bird or the rustling of the trees could be herd. The sun tossed shadows of trees onto the road ahead of me. I retraced my steps and made it back to the clearing I had found earlier. I breathed in the fresh spring air.

Carefully, I unwrapped my sword and felt the cold handle. I took off the rest of the rag revealing the metal underneath. It shined in the sunlight, almost blinding me.

I held it in my hands, just like how I saw Thomas hold it. Okay, this is not that hard, I thought as I followed each step he had made.

Forward, I lunged my body with my arm outstretched. My left arm was close to my body, and my right arm gripped the sword tight, holding it in front of me. I think I got the hang of it. My mom always said I was a fast learner.

As I moved back, the sword moved back with me. I completed this stance over a hundred times, so it was stuck in my mind. As I went along, I tried to add some new moves. Sometimes I would slice the air when I went forward and pretend like I was in a duel.

"Okay... okay, I think I got the basics."

Now, I felt more confident. I tried spins, jumps, and blocks. I was a natural. Now, it was time to hit a target and not just the air.

I stood next to one of the trees. Then, I struck. Again and again, I practiced my new moves as I pretended I was in battle. I had never felt so connected to an object. It was as if I was meant to have this sword. I loved the sound it made when I hit the trees and the feeling during each swing of my blade.

Sweat dripped down my face. I looked up; the sun was high in the sky. It was about noon; I had been doing this for more than five hours. It was time to head back.

I gave my training area one more look before leaving. Every tree surrounding the clearing had cuts in them and the dirt had spots showing where my feet had been sliding on it.

I knew I would be back. It would take more than just swinging the sword to become a strong knight. I would have to run every day to build endurance, lift heavy objects and my body to build strength, and it would not hurt to make an obstacle course to build agility.

Hours of the same routine turned into days. Each day, I started with a run around the span of Brendsworth; then, I lifted the heavy bags of sand in my dad's forgery; next, I did push-ups and curl-ups outside my house in the trees. Two hours out of each day was spent practicing with my sword, and the rest of the day I spent reading books on fighting and building my skills.

It had been one week of my new routine. I found that I enjoyed exercise more than most people. I had just finished my sword practice and returned home. The house was quiet when I got back.

"Mom!" I called out. No answer.

"Dad!"

No one was home. I flopped down into a chair at the table. Minutes passed as I sat. I had hoped that I would be able to spend the rest of the afternoon reading a new book on swords but, without my dad here, I can't read it. My dad told me not to go in there and take his books without permission. I really didn't want to break his rule but, I also didn't want to waste all this time I have for reading. With that in mind, I gave into temptation and went upstairs, and without a sound I opened the door to my parent's room.

The room was dark because of the closed curtains. I wanted to go open them, but my heroin in his book "Sir Frederick's Adventures" said, when trying to go somewhere unseen and not get caught, it is important to not tamper with the way the room looked originally. Keeping that in mind, I memorized the way the room looked.

The bookshelf was located in the corner of the room. I tiptoed over and looked the titles. One caught my eye, "The Guide to Being a Knight." I felt like I had just found a million gold coins, but I had really just found the perfect book. My dad told me about this book. All the best warriors and knights used the moves in it.

I opened up the book. It had an old book smell, which is my favorite smell. I flipped to page one. There were drawings of a man holding a sword. It was a step-by-step book.

I flipped past the basics that I already knew until I reached the more advanced moves. There were ones in which you block another sword from hitting you, and then another picture showed a person jumping and then smashing the sword on their enemies' heads.

After a while, I felt extremely guilty about taking the book without asking. My dad's books were his treasures. I felt the same way about my books. I know that if I had waited and asked, he would have let me read it. However, I also know that I will become way more advanced with the sword if I read the book now and practice the new moves tomorrow. Maybe he won't notice? My dad's rules on books were not going to keep me from becoming a knight. I took the book and rushed downstairs to read at the table in a brighter room.

In no time, I began to read almost the entire book. Information seeped into my brain with each page I flipped. Suddenly, I heard the faintest sound of my dad's voice. I rushed to the window to see him strolling down our road. I had to get the book back where it was before he came. He opened the door.

"Hey Liam! Anything interesting happen today?" he called out.

It was too late; he saw me. Quickly, I shoved the book up the back of my shirt. Maybe he wouldn't notice? I stood awkwardly leaning on the table.

"Interesting? I don't, don't think so, not that I know of…" I said talking quickly.

"What are you doing there, Liam?" He looked me up and down.

Oh, no. Just stay calm. He might not notice the strange square that I developed in my back during the time I saw him this morning to now.

"Practicing a new way to strengthen your biceps, you just uh... lean on the table like this... and move your arms in a push-up position and just go up and down!" I said, doing the worst push-ups I have ever done.

"Hmm, never seen that before. Just make sure that you are cleaned up in time for dinner," he walked inside.

That was close. Unfortunately, I still had to get it up the stairs, in his room, and on the shelf without him noticing. That couldn't be too hard. Right?

As soon as began my stressful mission, my dad decided to suddenly have another conversation.

"So, how's that sword working out for you? Did you get down the basics?"

"What sword?" I tried to get out of the conversation.

"The... one you're holding?"

"Oh, that sword. It's fine! Just terrific and I am so great at it," I said, slowly drifting toward the staircase.

"Great! Why don't you come over here and show me a few moves?"

I cringed at the thought of him watching me perform my stances with a book under my shirt; especially the book that I stole from him.

"Okay...sure." I got in a stance that requires little movement.

"So...take a swing!" He watched with anticipation.

I make a small movement in my arms, and then smiled like that was it.

"Come on! You can't be that bad!"

"Oh, I guess I am," I started to walk toward the stairs again.

"Liam! Come on," he gave me the 'stop fooling around' look.

"Okay…"

At that moment, I decided never to take a book from my dad ever again. I got in my stance and started to take a few swings. The book bounced around in my shirt. It was slowly slipping down. I looked at my dad; he was still not pleased.

"Okay, can I go now?"

"Give me a few jumps and dodges, I want to see if your old man's agility genes were passed down to you!" he said, laughing.

Well, this could not get worse, I thought to myself. I did a dodge and then tuck jump. Right at that moment the book slid into my pants. Now I had a strange square butt.

It just got worse.

"Very cool! So, how is your friend Byron?"

"Good. Great. You know I need to go and do something…"

"I heard his parents are giving him a job on the old bean farm again. Making you think about any jobs?"

He kept the conversation going. I felt the book pull my pants down. I grabbed my pants right over where my butt to keep it or my pants from falling down.

"Uhh, Liam, are you okay? Do you need to use the bathroom?" my dad said with an uneasy voice.

Yes! This was my chance! I slowly moved up the stairs.

"No…I'm just going to go upstairs…"

"Well I think I have work to do out back near the well… keep yourself out of trouble." He walked quickly to the door, most likely feeling uncomfortable.

"Okay," I said as he left the house out the back door.

As soon as I made it up the stairs, I pulled the book from out of my pants.

A sigh escaped my mouth. I gathered my strength and continued toward the room. Some of the floor creaked as I stepped toward his room making me shudder. It looked exactly like the way I had left it. Quietly, I tiptoed in fear that my dad would not come back in the house and hear me. Then, without any regret, I put the back the book.

Then, I crept back down the stairs. My dad was still gone. I let out a sigh of relief. In order to avoid talking to him again, I decided to go on walk in the town.

I was so glad it was spring, which means no school until fall. I still had five months of vacation before school started again. However, for most people in the Outer Kingdom, it is no vacation. Most kids spend the time outside school working on the family farm or business.

I walked away down the main road. Two little girls ran past me with two dolls that resembled a princess and a fairy. One of the girls jumped up and down as she yelled "I am a fairy, so I can fly!" Her brown braids flew up and down as she jumped. I felt my face grow red as two boys that were in my class walked past me. Adrian and Jeremiah walked past deeply engaged in a conversation. I tried to act like I did not see them, hoping they would not notice me. I prefer not to see most of my classmates outside of school, with the exception of Byron, of cource.

"Jeremiah, please, you know that Prince George is engaged to Lady Jules's daughter Cordelia. Cordelia is by far the prettiest girl in the Outer Kingdom, no question. Rumor has it that she is looking for a husband and that is gonna be me," Adrian said.

"What? That is ridiculous! Why would she pick you? She doesn't even know you exists!" Jeremiah asked.

"Because," he showed off his full head of messy, brown hair, "I have brown hair and she like guys with brown hair. Why else would she be interested in Prince George?"

"That is the dumbest thing I have ever heard! That is totally not true," Jeremiah said.

I rolled my eyes. They could not really be talking about this.

"She also likes green eyes! Which I have and you don't so, that is two points for me and none for you," Adrian bragged.

"What logic are you using?" Jeremiah questioned.

"Well, Cordelia like Prince George. Prince George has brown hair and green eyes. I have brown hair and green eyes. Therefore, Cordelia likes me."

"Okay, let me explain this to you: first of all, Jason Maximah started the rumor that Cordelia is even looking for a husband. Besides, your logic is completely flawed. Why would she like him only for his hair color?! She probably likes Prince George because he is a prince. Unlike literally anyone else in the Outer Kingdom," Jeremiah explained.

"WHAT! No way! How is that not true! All of the facts say it's true. And how do you know- oh hey Liam!" Adrian waved.

Jeremiah waved too. I waved back feeling happy they said hi, even though we were not good friends. Byron was my only best friend, however I still had some friends who I talked to in class.

I could still hear them arguing about the two rumors as I walked away. My boots kicked up dirt as I strolled down the road. The dirt puffed up like a tree and then drifted back down onto the road.

I looked at where my dad's shop was. Memories flashed past me. I began to remember the first time I went to my dad's shop. He pointed out the houses of people he knew and talked about when he was a kid living in Brendsworth.

Every time we had entered his blacksmith forge, I recalled the feeling of smoke and dust stinging my lungs and eyes. Sparks of light shot off the metal like lightning during a storm. Like a god, my dad hit the hot metal with his hammer, making him seem practically unstoppable. Sometimes, he would ask if I wanted to have a try; I was young and scared of the hammer back then, so I rejected it. Now, I am always eager to use the hammer. Additionally, my dad would explain how the fire becomes hotter when you use the handheld bellows. Although it was not as exciting to me as the hammer was, I listened anyways so he would not get upset. I love the feeling when he says 'Liam, why don't you give it a try!' He would hand me the hammer, and I would feel the weight, the power. With my arms raised above my head, I would feel stronger than ever. The strength used to bring the hammer up would be released as the hammer came crashing down. BANG! It was the sound of satisfaction.

I noticed three girls in my class were walking down the street. UGH! This was worse than seeing Jeremiah and Adrian. I wished that I could just disappear. Panna, Gwenda, and Marybeth were all walking together. Calm down, it's not like they're going to say anything.

"Do you think that my hair should be short, or should I grow it out long?" Panna asked her friends.

"It looks perfect right now! I wish I had your hair! Maybe I could get like a witch to dye my hair black like yours!" Marybeth said, pulling at her short frizzy brown hair.

"Marybeth, are you crazy? Do you remember what happened to Gina? She said that brown hair was overrated and did exactly what you say you're gonna do! We all know what happened to her," Gwenda warned.

"You don't have to tell me this story! It scares me..." Marybeth complained.

"Oh, come on! I love when she tells stories!" Panna said.

"See, Panna wants to hear it. So, Gina went to a witch that said she was going to help her hair. Gina wanted her brown hair to be colored red. You know what happened!" Gwenda held out her blond braid and made snipping motions with her fingers.

The girls were being so loud I could hear them from where I was walking. The story Gwenda told was one everyone was familiar with, and I knew what had happened to Gina's hair.

"The witch shaved her head clean off! Leaving Gina bald! This was because the witch was actually a BAD WITCH!" Gwenda yelled.

Marybeth squirmed at the end of her story because Gwenda poked her in the ribs. Panama laughed with Gwenda at their scared friend. Marybeth quickly clutched her brown hair and started stroking it, as if to keep it safe.

"On second thoughts, I will keep my hair," Marybeth said.

The girls walked closer to me, and my palms began to sweat. If I did anything dumb, they would have surely gossiped about me like they do Gina. I would hate to be the laughing stock of the class.

"I think Gina deserved it; she was so stuck up," Gwenda admitted.

"Yeah," Marybeth added sadly.

"I can't believe that she said brown hair is dumb and red hair is better! I think brown hair is cool!" Panna said, trying to make Marybeth feel better.

"Did you guys see that Marilyn has a new dress? It is like so pretty!" Gwenda said, trying to change the subject.

"Oh, yeah! I have been trying to make a new yellow dress because my dark skin looks so good with yellow," Panna said, holding out her arm.

"You should totally be a model for a traveling salesperson," Gwenda said complimenting her.

"Right!?"

The girls drew closer. My eyes met with them as I walked past.

"Liam! Long time since we saw you! It was like, what, a week!?" Panna said jokingly.

"Yeah… hi," I mumbled, walking faster.

"Nice boots Liam! Did you buy them in the color dirty?" Gwenda laughed.

"Nice one," Panna high fived her.

"Yeah…you really got me," I said sarcastically.

"Yeah! Where did you get your hair cut? The bad hair cutters place?" Marybeth tried to poke fun at me.

Panna and Gwenda shared a disappointed look.

I walked father away and left the sound of laughing behind me. I didn't really have any feelings for any of the girls in Brendsworth. All of the girls here care about being famous or rich. Besides, I had zero interest in making any permanent relationships with anyone in Brendsworth because my plan was just to leave. The only permanent relationship would be my friendship with Byron and my parents of course. I sat in the tall tree in the market and watched all of the hagglers and shoppers in the market square. I noticed my mom wandering around. She saw me and came over.

"Liam? I thought you were in the woods?"

"I was."

"How did it go?"

"Fine. I can tell you about it on the way home."

I began to tell my mom about the experience using my new weapon as we walked back home. Today was defiantly the start of a new life.

Chapter 5

The next day, I spent the whole morning in my special training spot. From spending so much time there, I was getting very good with my sword. Also, I learned that my practice area was not only a good place to work out, but it was also a good place to sit and think.

I took a deep breath and lifted up the hay barrel that I had brought here two days ago. I shuffled over with it to the middle of the space. Yesterday morning, I had practiced one of the first moves labeled as "Extremely Difficult" in my dad's book. After stealing the book, I decided that asking for it was easier. I had the book open in front of me open to the page. Three thieves surrounding a knight in a stable was the scenario the book presented. Just like in the book, I placed multiple hay barrels in my training area.

One thief is behind the knight and two in front of him, a haystack is on the ground in the middle, and a couple feet between the knight and the thieves separates them. The knight then runs at the two thieves in front of him. Using the haystack in between them and quick maneuvers, the knight stabs his sword into the hay. Using the acceleration you got from running, you swing your legs up, kicking the first thief. Then, as the force brings your body around, twist your hands, so you continue to swing around toward the second thief. The next image shows the knight kicking the second thief. Lastly, the book instructs you to continue your swing back to the start where the third thief will be approaching you. I went through the move in my head.

"Okay, just stick the sword in and pivot. Sounds easy…saying it out loud…" I said.

I jumped up and down to warm up my muscles. Then, without giving myself a moment to think, I sprinted at the hay barrel and shoved my sword in the middle. I jumped up for the kick but came right back down. My fall tipped over the hay barrel and I fell to the cold hard ground.

"Ow…that did not go as planned," I stood up and wiped off the dirt, preparing to try again.

This time, I got more of a running start. I then stabbed my sword into the hay, leaned my weight backward, and swung up. Once again, my body fell right back down on the ground.

"Darn it! Maybe it's my hand position."

I ran at it again with my hand positioned backwards. I stuck my sword in the hay and swung my body around and landed on top the hay barrel. Annoyed, I shook my head and tried again a few more times. After a couple more falls on my butt, I decided to give up and head home.

As soon as I got home, I sat down and relaxed with Scales and a new obstacle course I created out of kitchen appliances. I was peacefully relaxing until suddenly, a knocking sound came from the door. I jerked my head up. I turned to the window. There was a man knocking on the door. I rolled my eyes.

"SORRY WE'RE CLOSED!" I yelled so he would hear me through the glass. He shook his head and walked away. I was too busy not making eye contact that I totally missed what he looked like.

"Stupid travelers," I said, making Scales wooden again.

Later in the day, when my mom came home from the market, I told her about the new obstacle course I made for Scales and the new move I tried learning with my sword.

"That move sounds difficult indeed!" Mom said from the kitchen.

She came back with a whole baked chicken that was seasoned with salt and pepper. Odd. We only eat chicken on special occasions. Anytime I saw the crispy tan lightly peppered skin on a chicken or tasted the warm meat on the inside, it felt like a special occasion, like my birthday. She then came back with some sliced tomatoes.

"Mom, what's all this?"

"Dinner."

"You know that but why are we eating baked chicken and tomatoes? Isn't that a special thing?"

At that moment my dad walked through the door, along with someone who looked familiar to me.

"And the look on his face!" the man said.

"Priceless!" My dad laughed.

The man looked almost identical to my dad. There was only a difference in his hair. Unlike my dad, he had black wavy hair that reached down to his shoulders. Also, he has a black handlebar mustache on his face that he would curl every so often. However, the similarities between strong bone structure in their faces and hazel brown eyes were peculiar. They could not be related? Right?

"William, we had some good times back then, didn't we?" my dad asked.

"Yes, yes we did. Hello Eleonora! Mmmm…that chicken smells good!" William said.

Could this man be...

"Liam, I want you to meet your Uncle William!" Dad said smiling.

"Hi," I said awkwardly.

"Liam, it's so nice to finally see you. Last time I saw you, you were a little naked baby! Ha ha ha!" Uncle William laughed.

My face grew red. It was so embarrassing to hear that. I could not help but feel mixed feelings about having my Uncle William here. It was cool to see my uncle whom I had never really met, but I didn't know anything about him. I don't know why he never came to see me in between my infancy and now as a 16-year-old kid.

"What a good smelling meal! Now, how about you tell me a little about yourself and your hobbies, Liam, over this delicious meal! We have so much to catch up on!" he said cheerfully.

"Okay..." I cautiously replied.

"When I was a young lad, I had been into making weaved baskets! Of course, my father wanted me to be a blacksmith like my brother... is that one of his creations?" he said pointing behind me.

I had not even realized my sword was leaning on my chair. My mom shot me a dirty look.

"It is. I have actually been practicing for the past few weeks. Sometimes, I really wish I had an adult sized one, but Dad says this will do for now. I think that it's a really cool weapon," I said shyly.

"Now, that is something we both have in common! I still have my sword from my youth. The one I have today is much bigger than that one, though. However, your father did not make any of mine; I had my sword made from a wise nomad in the mountains. He also made wind chimes!" Uncle William explained enthusiastically.

"So, do you make baskets for a living?" I asked.

"Oh, no! That was just a lost dream! In fact I work at the palace! It's a very nice job. I am in charge of all of the workers, and I help Queen Emily on a regular basis. It is very rewarding."

"The royal palace?! That is actually pretty cool," I said in awe.

"Your uncle here was telling me earlier that our great uncle worked in the palace, so one could say it runs in the family!" Dad explained. We began eating dinner.

"So, Liam how was your day?" Mom wondered.

"Ehh, pretty boring," I answered, focusing on my meal.

"So, sounds like you're going to be a little bored this summer?" Uncle William asked.

"I guess…"

I noticed his voice was deep and sounded like a roar of a bear. It was not so deep that it was annoying though - it was kind of peaceful. In a way it was also powerful. Having a voice like that must be helpful for his job.

"Well, I have been thinking and I think you should come stay at the palace with me and take up a job as a servant!" Uncle William announced, curling his mustache with one hand.

I stopped chewing as soon as the words entered my ears. My dad choked a little on his bread, and my mom dropped her fork. Other than my dads coughing, the room was silent.

"You can come to the palace and experience life in the big city. You will have a small but very fulfilling job as a servant. Don't worry though; I am the palace reeve. I supervise the work so, you won't be too far from me. We would even stay in the same room, and all you would have to do is clean some things. We could go around Trisanburg City and explore the town and the cool shops! The palace is also quite lovely and the people are so friendly. We would have the best time! And don't worry about school or travel! You will be back in time for school, and my good friend Roman will give us a ride in his wagon!"

"William? I thought we would not discuss this until later?" my Dad said frantically.

"Oh, please Alderic, we don't have time!" Uncle William called out.

"Time? That does not matter!" Mom stressed.

"Yes, indeed it does! I am leaving tomorrow, and I need to know tonight."

"Tomorrow? What?! You just got here though! Why are you leaving so fast?" Dad demanded an answer.

"Well… in the letters, it may have come across that I was staying for a long visit. The truth is that I came to bring Liam back."

"So, you didn't think to ask his mother first? Ugh! William, you can't just spring these things on us! I mean you just came back!" my mom stressed.

"I agree! You are not just going to come and take my son," said my dad.

"He needs to prepare himself for the real world!"

They argued back and forth. I hated how torn they were. I could not contain my feelings about this any longer.

"Excuse me.... EXCUSE ME!"

Everyone stopped talking and gave me their full attention.

"I think maybe I should give my opinion. I would love to go to the palace! It would be a good way for me to get money. And I don't want to sit around all summer! Like Uncle William said, it would prepare me for the outside world." I explained.

They were all deep in thought. Maybe Uncle William being here was a sign. Maybe I am supposed to go with him and see the world! By going out into the world, I can see new creatures and meet new people! This can also help my chances of being a knight! It was like fate!

"Alderic, the boy says that he wants to go. It would be a good opportunity, and I promise he will be back by the end of August. And besides, the money he earns can help him prepare for the future," Uncle William said stating his case.

"Please," I pleaded.

My mom gave my dad a look like she was saying 'I am okay with it if you are.' My dad sighed.

"Lucky for you two, we have given something like this some though. You better not be lazy when you're there, and don't give the palace workers or your Uncle William any trouble," my dad said.

"Really?! I get to go to Trianburg City!?"

My heart jumped for joy. Byron will be so jealous when I tell him. I could not wait to meet new people in the city and make new friends. This was even better than getting a sword!

Chapter 6

The birds chirped harmoniously out my window. I woke up with a smile on my face and a skip in my step. I was so excited to go to Trisanburg, the capital region of the Outer Kingdom. I could not wait to see Trisanburg City and the giant castle that overlooked it. Everyone in my school is going to be so jealous of me. I would without a doubt be the talk of the town. Trisanburg City is the place that everyone wants to go visit on vacation or see before they die. Some people even want to get married there!

I grabbed a leather satchel to hold my few belongings, taking with me "Sir Frederick's Adventures" and all of the clothes I owned. When got to the bottom of the staircase, my mom greeted me with muffins and bread to take on the road. I thanked her for the food and in return gave her a warm hug. Packing took less time than I thought so, I quickly ran down the road to Byron's house and knocked on the door.

"Oh, Liam, what you doing here this early?" Byron asked with tired eyes.

"You will not believe it! So, yesterday my Uncle William came to visit, you know, the one who I haven't seen since I was a baby. Well, he is talking me back with him and I am leaving for the summer! I will be working as a servant in Trisanburg City at the royal palace! My Uncle William is the palace reeve there!" I bragged.

"Ugh, it's too early for pranks. You're messing with me right? I know when you are lying," he said rubbing his eyes. I was startled by his reaction but he has been skeptical like this before.

"Do you not believe me? I am dead serious. I am going to be gone all summer. Don't worry though, I will be back in time for school."

"Oh, come on Liam. I refuse to fall for your pranks."

"Fine. If you want to reach me this summer, you have to send your letters to the royal castle," I said getting annoyed.

"Nice try, buddy," he said, closing the door.

I shook my head. I had a feeling he would think I was lying. Byron has always been a cautious person. I wish I were there to see him when he realizes I was telling the truth. My mom was waiting in the road.

"Liam, you behave yourself when you are in Trisanburg. I'm gonna miss you so much," my mom said, giving me a hug so strong I thought she would not let me go.

"Goodbye, Liam. Goodbye, William. Take care," My dad said hugging us.

"Oh, Liam, if you ever run into trouble, that sword won't fail you, because I made it."

I chuckled wiping away my tears. I was excited to go to the castle, but I did not want to leave my parents. This will be the first time I travel outside of Brendsworth.

A wagon drawn by a dark brown horse pulled up to our house. A tall large man sat in it with the reins in his hands. He scratched his head of curly black hair and then stroked his large mustache. I gazed up at him. Never in my life have I seen someone so intimidating.

"Ah, Villiam. Good to see you," Roman said with a thick accent.

"Are you ready to go?" Uncle William asked me.

"Thank you so much for the ride, Roman. This is my nephew, Liam."

"Hello," I said shyly. He gave me no more than a wave.

I quickly moved to the back of the wagon to load my things. Quickly, I had shoved Scales into my bag, so I could have something to do on the very long ride to Trisanburg.

I jumped into the wagon and got comfortable. Uncle William sat next to me.

"Well, this is going to be exciting! Are you ready, Liam?"

"I guess so."

Roman cracked the reins and the horse trotted away from Mom, Dad, and home. I had not realized how fast this morning had gone by until now.

"Goodbye!" I called out.

"Goodbye, Alderic! Goodbye, Eleanora!" Uncle William yelled.

We made our way down the main road toward the woods. My smile slowly turned into a frown. My stomach turned and my mind began to race. Suddenly, I changed my mind; I want to stay. What happens if I need something from my parents while I am gone! What will I do if I am in trouble and Uncle William can't protect me? What if I was making the worst mistake of my life? I made up my mine. Who needs adventure? I took a look backward. It was too late. It looks like I will have to accept the path I chose and wait to see what will happen next.

I quietly watched as houses turned into trees. We were on the main road that cut straight through the woods. Looks like I will be doing what I had dreamed of after all. There was no turning back now.

52

I watched as the trees and shrubbery flash by as we rode down the dirt path. Maybe this change will be a good thing.

One half hour later, I was already bored. I thought traveling on the open road would be more exciting. The only thing that has happened was a cart full of barmaids and drunk me came racing up the road. I assumed their wild caravan is either currently crashed into a tree or stopped by a pair of Royal Knights.

"How much longer…?" I moaned.

"It will be four day ride. Castle is in center of Trisanburg City. We will camp out at night," Roman said. He kept his sentences short and straight to the point.

My dad always told me that Trisanburg was only 3 days away, or less, going at a normal pace. However, four days sounded accurate for us seeing as the horse was slower than molasses. I practically had to hold myself back from complaining about the speed.

"I'm bored!" I announced, flopping onto the bags.

"Little boy always complain like dis?" Roman asked Uncle William.

"I hope not," He mumbled in response.

I scowled at him and he laughed.

"Hey Liam, why don't I tell you a little history about Trisanburg and the royal family, so that way you know a little of the facts for when you work at the palace?" Uncle William offered.

"Sure, I guess. I mean I already know some of the information but I'd like to learn more."

"They may have already taught you this in school so this is just a refresher. The history of monarchs in the Outer Kingdom is a long line of rulers from different noble and powerful families. There are four different dynasties: the Jalence, the Ports, the Turner's, and lastly the Drandors. The first recorded king of the Outer Kingdom was King Jake Jalence," Uncle William explained.

"Oh, I remember this one. King Jake had a son named Frederick Jalance who had no kids so the line ended," I recalled.

"Yep. Then the throne went to King James Ports who married Queen Terry Ports and had a son and a daughter. King James is responsible for the peace between witches and humans. That was something that was already established in most of society but without King James, we would be nowhere close to the technology of today. He and his wife created the systems of farming and food manufacturing that witches and humans practice today. Not to mention, he began to educate people on the three types of magic," Uncle William explained with excitement.

"What are dis, again? The three types of dis magic?" Roman asked.

"I believe the three are rudimentary magic, elemental magic, and fairy magic," I answered.

"Right! I don't know more than the basics about it but I know that only witches practice elemental magic, which is very difficult to learn. And I believe fairy magic is practiced by the fairies and only some witches who have learned it but, the fairies are dying off so, the fairy style of magic will too," Uncle William explained.

"Oh, my mom's friend Abigail practices fairy magic. She learned from them while in a forest in Arone, I think, I can't remember. But she said it is kind of useless but, you learn how to transfer your magic into things," I said.

"Yes, I heard of dis! Dis fairy magic is rare but, more for making toy for de little children," Roman said.

"Right. Then lastly there is rudimentary magic. Witches, mermaids, and fairies all practice this magic. Basically, potions are what rudimentary magic is. It is how they make medicine or poisons and grow food or create bread quicker. I think it involves like mixing things together and creating stuff that could, let's say, increase the growth of plants, for example. If you ask a witch they would know a lot more than me. I don't even know a single thing about magic besides that. And then there was wizard magic which was extremely powerful but, they are extinct so, no need to stress over that," Uncle William tried to remember.

"Huh...I actually didn't know that about magic. That's pretty cool. Okay, so what about the Ports dynasty?" I asked, becoming more intrigued by the subject.

"Well, the daughter was first in line for the throne and she became Queen Veronica. Fun fact about her, Queen Veronica held duels and competitions in the fields surrounding the castle during her rule. Watching jousting competitions was her favorite. Anyways, King James Ports son, Millem, never married. However, Queen Veronica had two children, Mary and Will. But sadly they died at a young age due to an illness. That was how the Ports dynasty ended," Uncle William said.

"I actually did not know that. What happened next?" I asked.

"Next came Turner," Roman added.

"Right! King James Turner was probably my favorite king. He was the king that helped create the strong army and navy we have today. He also instituted the Turner Academy," Uncle William said.

Turner Academy was a school that I dreamed of getting into. It is where all of the Royal Knights go and train. However, it is very hard to get into. You either shadow a knight as a squire to get in or come from a rich family that can buy your way in.

"After King James came his son, King James the second. Then Queen Ariel Turner and her son King James the third, he died before he was able to have a child and ended the Turner dynasty," Uncle William finished.

"Wow, that is a lot of monarchs. Let me guess, next came King Andrew Drandor?" I asked.

"Correct. Followed by his three sons. Carlos, Jackson, and Harry," Uncle William started.

"Oh, I remember this! Carlos was the first inline and died soon after he was named king in a storm out at sea. Then it went to the next brother who was King Jackson, he ruled for a long time until dying in a battle with pirates who had been plundering the ships that distributed goods to the Outer Kingdom," I began.

"That is a good memory, keep going," Uncle William encouraged me.

"Then the last son, King Harry, he never boarded a boat while he was king because of what happened to his brothers. He married Queen Mary and had their daughter Queen Peniel. Queen Peniel created a fleet of naval ships for the Outer Kingdom Navy so there would be more protection on the coast. Also she helped fund the creation of almost all the modern medical potions that have been curing almost all of the diseases," I said.

"Yes! Then she had two kids do you remember their names?" Uncle William asked.

"Cornelius was the one who became king and Bartholomew's father but, I don't recall the other kid," I confessed.

"That was Mary the second," Uncle William said.

"Oh yeah! Right! Then he had King Bartholomew who married Queen Emily and now the last of the line is their son, Prince George," I said, almost out of breath.

"Looks like you are ready to be working at the castle. I don't know who or why anyone would ask you that but, it is good to know about your kingdom," Uncle William finished.

Uncle William began to talk about the rulings of King James Turner III again, while I studied Scales. I sat watching Scales fly around my head and lightly landing on my hair. It was interesting how complicated magic was. How it is possible this small cute little dragon was once a piece of wood. It was magical!

Soon, day turned to night. The sun started to set, painting a range of colors from pink to yellow across the sky.

"William. We camp here for de night. Its getting dark out," Roman advised.

We parked the wagon on the side of the road.

"Liam, do you mind going into the woods and finding some large sticks for the fire?" Uncle William asked.

"Okay," I mumbled.

I trudged into the woods. My head was pointed down to the ground, scanning it for sticks. I watched as bugs, leaves, and grass passed by with each step I took.

"Bugs…leaves...stick! Grass...more bugs…more leaves…"

My eyes began to blur and blood rushed to my head. I had been staring at the ground for too long. I kept my head up high for a while. By doing this, I lost sight of the ground. I listened to the sound of leaves crunching beneath my feet and gazed up at the sky; it was still a beautiful canvas of reds and oranges. Suddenly, the leaves disappeared from under me. I threw my arms up in the air causing the sticks to fling out of my hands. Abruptly, I rolled down into a deep pit. The wind had gotten knocked out of me.

"Oh no… what just happened?"

Everywhere I looked, I was surrounded by dirt. WHAT JUST HAPPENED!? My heart beat faster as the fact I am stuck in a hole rushed over me. I spun in circle's, searching for some way out. Only if I tilted my head up, could I see grass that I had been standing on moments ago. Could this be a hunting trap? How did I not notice this when I was walking?!

"Hello? Uncle William! Anyone? Help!"

No one could hear me. This was just what I needed! To be stuck in a hole! I frantically clawed and grabbed the dirt with my hands, attempting to climb out. The feeling of the dirt in my fingernails made me cringe. The earth crumbled underneath my hands. It was no use. I did everything I could think of that could get me out of the pit. All that was left was to keep shouting, "help".

"Hey, look! We just set that trap yesterday, and it already has a catch!" an excited voice called out from above.

I could hear horses approaching the pit. Thank goodness. I wouldn't be stuck here for long.

"Hello? Hello! Help, I'm trapped in this hole!"

I backed up to get a view of my rescuers. I looked up to find two odd-looking men. They both had no shirts on and only a quiver around their chests. Not to mention, they were surprisingly hairy men.

One of the men had beautiful brown flowing hair that grew from his head to his back. The other man had hair that was long and black in dreadlocks. I could not help but notice that both men had a side of their head with their hair shaved off.

"Ha! A stupid human got himself trapped in our deer pit," the man with dreadlocks laughed.

"Come on and help him up," said the second man.

A hand reached down. He had thick black hair growing on his arms and knuckles. I hesitated before grabbing his hands. Who were these strange men wearing no shirts in the middle of the woods? I imagine these were the type of strangers my mom doesn't want me to be around.

"Come on, I don't bite!" he laughed.

I took his hand and he pulled me up with ease. I flung forward a little as my feet hit the familiar grassy ground. He was surprisingly strong for a weird shirtless forest guy. Suddenly, I noticed something even weirder about my rescuers. They did not have normal legs! Instead of human legs they had horse bodies! My jaw dropped. I had never seen anyone like them. Both men had the body of a horse from the torso down and from the torso up had the body of a man.

"What? Never seen a centaur before?" the centaur with dreadlocks laughed.

"Ugh, I hate these humans. They are so dumb. They can't even educate their kids on the types of creatures there are. I wish we could just be rid of them," the other one spat.

"Hey! Humans aren't dumb!" I said, standing up for mankind.

"Why were you in that hole anyways?" the centaur looked down on me, ignoring my statement.

"I fell into your pit. Why would you even put that so close to the road?" I ask.

"Ha! He fell into such an obvious hole. Try watching where you are going, human," he said in a snobbish tone.

They took off running with their bows in hands and hair flowing behind them. I could not believe what just happened.

"Well that was rude," I said to myself.

I have to tell Uncle William about this! I sprinted through the woods back to our camp.

"Uncle William! Uncle William! You won't guess what just happened! The craziest thing! I just met two centaurs!" I burst with excitement.

"What is dis little boy talking about?" Roman said emphasizing the word "little" with his accent.

The two were setting up tonight's meal of mashed potato's.

"What? What is it, Liam?" Uncle William said not listening the first time.

"I saw a centaur!" I said catching my breath.

"That's nice," he said acting like it was no big deal. He continued to wash the potatoes.

"Well, there were two," I stated.

"Okay," Uncle William said.

Maybe seeing a centaur was no big deal. I thought I had just found something new and exciting. Guess I was wrong. They must not be uncommon.

"Uncle William, what do you mean by just 'okay'? Are centaurs like normal?" I asked. There was no chapter on centaurs in Sir Frederick's book.

"Centaurs are pretty common to see out here in the woods. They all have clans. Well, there are two clans. Did you happen to notice the sides of the centaurs heads?"

I thought back to when they pulled me out of the trap. They both had one side of long hair and one side short, with a symbol shaved out of their hair.

"Yeah, I think there was a symbol of a letter F on the sides of their heads," I recollected.

"So, little boy did not get sticks? That's okay. I go get them for fire," Roman walked away, interrupting our story.

"Okay Roman. Anyways, back to the centaurs. That means the ones you saw are from the clan Farneris. The centaurs have been here in the Outer Kingdom just as long as humans. Obviously, there are far more humans that centaurs but, those two were from the clan Farneris. The other clan is called Wardiran, which has territory in the western parts of the kingdom. Back when I was a young boy, the centaurs would have horrifying battles for territory. They have hated each other only because they worship different goddesses. The Farneris clan worships the forest goddess Farner. The Wardiran clan worships the river goddess Wardin. It's quiet interesting actually," Uncle William explained.

"Are there still battles today? Like between the two clans?" I wondered.

"No. Usually, they stay on their side of the kingdom. There was a treaty signed. That's funny; we were just talking about the monarchs. King Cornelius Drandor had them sign a treaty saying 'All of thy from Farneris shalt stay on the eastern side, and thy of Wardiran must stay on the western side of the Outer Kingdom,'" He quoted.

"Wow, you still remember that?"

"I'm back. Here is wood," Roman strolled back into camp.

"Eh, that is just a small snip of the actual treaty. I see a lot of them every day when I work at the palace," Uncle William said starting the fire.

"Wait! I will get to see that treaty hung up on a wall?"

"The king is very...how do I put this...well, he is very proud! Most of the monarchs are. In fact, a lot of the treaties and important historical documents are hung up around the palace."

"Wait. Who signed the treaty again?"

"His father signed it. King Cornelius," Uncle William reminded me as he plopped the potatoes into the boiling water.

Then the sun set lower and the night sky tucked it in below the horizon like a blanket. After enjoying our small meal, we sat around the campfire watching the flames grow as Uncle threw wood into it.

The embers sparked off the burning wood. Staring deep into the flames, I began to wonder what new things I will discover tomorrow. Uncle William began whistling to the crickets. My eyes grew heavy and my head flopped downward.

"Liam! Get up! Time to go!" Uncle William said cheerfully.

I stood up groaning. The sun was just peeking over the trees. Roman was already sitting in the wagon with his hands on the reigns. My eyes were half open as we rode down the rocky, dirt path. I finally gave into my body's urge to keep sleeping and fell asleep again.

Suddenly, our wagon hit a bump. I opened my eyes abruptly and woke up. We were in the woods still. I had hoped that we would have been closer to the castle by now. I watched the trees one by one as they slowly passed by me. The horse walked at turtle speed down the road. I wished we could go faster. Roman did not seem rushed at all.

"Uncle, where are we?"

"We are in the woods."

"That's not what I meant."

"Why don't you take a look at the map and figure it out?" he asked, chuckling.

I followed his suggestion and pulled the map out of his bag. I unfolded the fragile old paper revealing the map of the Outer Kingdom. The shape of the entire kingdom stared back at me. I had no idea how to tell where we were. I wished there was a small drawing that could indicate where I was going at all times or maybe a voice to tell us where to go next. Oh well, that is stuff of myths and legends.

I returned the map back to its home and leaned back into my bag to watch the sky. A bug fell from the trees onto the edge of the wagon.

I watched it crawl around from the corner of my eye. The bug attempted to crawl off the wagon, but stumbled onto it's back when we hit a bump. My attention was then drawn back to the sky. Various shaped clouds floated along like boats forever lost on the endless blue sea. Birds serenaded us with song from deep inside the woods. I turned over to look at the trees pass by once again. To my surprise, I spotted a female deer in the distance, not too deep in the woods. It was strangely standing, looking directly at the tree that was in front of it. What did it see that I didn't? I continued to watch the deer. It did not move. What did I not see? Could it be looking at something that might put us in danger? I had to investigate. The wagon moved farther away.

"Hey Uncle William…"

There is the possibility I could be making this all up in my head. I ignored the thought and told Uncle to stop the wagon.

"We not there yet, little boy," Roman said.

"I need to use the bathroom," I lied, hopping out of the wagon before they could stop me.

"Okay, we are going to go park the wagon up ahead," Uncle William called out after me.

 I crept closer to the spot where I saw the deer.

"Where are you?"

I looked left and right until I saw it. The deer was standing in a grassy magical looking spot full of flowers and sunlight. It was amazing. Wildflowers dotted the ground and butterflies fluttered around the trees. I cautiously crept closer to the deer. At first, it seemed like something out of the fairy tales like Snow White and Sleeping Beauty, but now I am getting a little suspicious. I hid behind the trees, moving from one to the other. Most deer's would have heard me and ran away by now but this deer continued to stand still, looking at the tree. Either the deer was dumb or I still can't figure out what she is looking at. I walked up to it, waiting for the moment when it would spring up and gallop away. Now, I was so close that I could take two steps and touch it's soft fur.

Finally, it moved.

Very slowly, its head turned toward me. I stood as still as I could. Trying not to move quickly, I reached for the handle of my sword. If I was not careful, the deer could run into me and break one of my bones. Or worse, it could kick me straight in the stomach and break my ribs. I shuttered at the thought. The deer was now looking straight at me. It felt like its cold black eyes were piercing through my heart.

The deer's head turned slowly in the other direction. What could it be looking at that I still don't see?!

Then, my stomach turned from what I was watching. The deer's head did not stop turning. It's head turned all the way around in a full circle. I felt vomit rising in my throat from the traumatizing scene. This was no deer; it was some kind of crazy demon! The deer turned its head twice all the way around until stopping. It was as if the head was unscrewing. I was frozen in trauma.

Strings separated from the neck as the head began to come off the deer's body. I began to doubt everything I knew about nature and life. Could this be an illusion? Is this deer being held together by strings!?

"What the..."

I poked the deer with my sword. Is it dead? As if I cracked open a beehive, small devilish creatures gushed out the empty carcass. I immediately recognized them. Their small, gangly bodies, disproportionate big heads, and pointy ears gave it away. These were worse than bees. Their wings flapped quickly and they flashed their pointy teeth at me.

These were imps.

I have gone against all the warning I was told as a child about not approaching these terrible creatures. Thousands of imps came flying out of the deer's neck, the head now dangling on the side of the deer, held up by a few brown strings. Now I was in trouble.

"HOLY SH-!"

Sword in hand, I sprinted away from the limp deer carcass, deeper into the woods. I hoped and prayed I could loose them in here. I hurdled over fallen trees and big rocks, leaping without thinking where I was going. I bounded through the woods with only one thought in mind: get away from these crazy imps. I do not want to find out what being eaten alive by a thousand imps is like.

Suddenly, I came to an obstacle. I was at the top of a huge hill and very far away from the Uncle William and the safely of the wagon.

Then, at the very bottom of the hill, I spotted through the trees what looked like a road. The chances of it being the road we were driving on are very high. I peered down the steep hill.

Quickly, I looked behind me for other options. The swarm of imps flew toward me like children to a candy vendor. They covered the sky like clouds of dark soot from a chimney.

I looked left and then right. They were coming from all directions but one. It looks like the steep hill is my only option.

I flew down the hill, running at a high speed. My legs were now moving just to keep up with my body. Frantically, I gazed back over my shoulder over and over again. The imps were closing in on me. If only I had wings!

Suddenly, something hit the back of my head. They were throwing rocks at me!

I tried to gain more speed by pushing myself further so my legs would move faster.

In a second, my face began to fall down toward the dirt. I already knew what had happened. I tripped and now my body was being thrown all the way to the bottom of the hill. Repeatedly, I tumbled over myself, down the hill. I struggled to stop myself from falling any further. Grass was in my hair and dirt was on my clothes; I hit the bottom with a thump. The imps were right behind me still. I jumped up and stumbled down the road. Calls for help began to escape me.

"HELP! HELP!"

No one responded. The only noise I could hear was my heavy breathing and the buzzing of the imps.

It was no use. The imps reached me and immediately swarmed around my body. Two were on my face biting at my nose. Others joined them and started biting at my legs and arms. Blood dripped into my mouth. They were going to eat me alive! Is this how it ends!? Death by imps?!

I flailed my arms like a tree during a storm, whacking the ones around me and throwing some down to the ground. I grabbed the ones on my nose and threw them far off into a tree. I had to keep running away. I then sprinted down the road screaming. I prayed that someone, somewhere would hear me.

To my surprise I got an answer.

"LIAM?" a voice cried out.

I ran faster than I had ever run before. I had never been in more fear of my life. Uncle William and Roman must be up ahead. The wind stung the cuts and the bite marks that covered my body.

"Come on, Liam! Run!"

"I can't even say how happy I am to see you," I panted, reaching the wagon.

"Hurry, Roman! Get that horse going!"

"How did you find me?" I asked hastily.

Roman pointed to the cloud of imps flying toward us.

"Little devils very easy to spot," Roman said encouraging the horse to move faster.

I jumped into the wagon, as it was moving. Even though our horse was finally moving fast, the imps kept coming toward us and throwing rocks. We will never be able to get rid of them!

"Liam! I need you to throw something at them!" Uncle William shouted over the buzzing of the imp's.

"What do I throw?"

The imps drew closer. They became so close that you could practically see the fleas on their heads.

"Anything!" He cried out in fear.

I grabbed the closest thing to me. It was the food. Uncle William did tell me to throw anything. I chucked the food straight at the swarm of imps.

Not only did it hit some of them but the smell of bread, potatoes, and muffins caught their attention.

"Yes! We did it!" I called.

Roman gave a smile.

"Spot on, Liam! Wait a second. Is that our food?! Liam! Why did you throw the food?!"

"You told me to throw anything! Besides, it caught their attention, and now they won't eat us. They are eating that instead," I argued.

"Ugh! Well, now we are going to have to stop and get food!" Uncle William said with his head in his hands.

I felt my heart drop. That was a dumb thing to do. I decided it was best to sit back in silence for the rest of the ride. I had caused enough trouble already.

We rode into a town that was in the middle of nowhere. Hunger pains began to hit us. I needed food, and fast. I wondered how people with little food could survive. Uncle William had been telling me that in some parts of the Outer Kingdom, people went days with only a few loaves of bread. I had never known that there were parts of the Outer Kingdom in such poverty. In school, they always taught us that each and every region in the Outer Kingdom is flourishing. I guess they were not telling us the whole story.

We entered the village. Although it was small, it was still filled with life. People walked around buying food, selling items, and socializing. Three little boys ran past us playing a game of chase. I noticed two girls that looked to be about my age walking next to us on the road. I smiled and waved at them. They giggled and waved back.

We pulled up next to a pub called "The Shrinking Goat." A picture of a small goat was painted on the sign that hung outside the building.

"Uhh… where are we?" I asked.

I had hoped we would get food from a local bakery or market, not a pub filled with drunkards.

"We are going to get something to eat while Roman gets the horse some water and food."

"Villiam, get me mutton," Roman said walking the horse away.

"Will do!" replied Uncle William.

When I stepped into the smelly pub, and I immediately regretted my decision. There were only two people in the whole pub. One was a man at the counter was spit cleaning a glass, and the second man was drunk, passed out at a table. I looked in disgust at the pool of drool surrounding him. I looked at Uncle William, who, to my surprise, was not put off by the place at all.

"Umm…let's go now. There are other places to get food, I think…" I whispered to Uncle William.

"Oh, just come on."

Uncle William walked right up to the counter. No! What is he doing!? Why can't Uncle William just listen to me and leave?

"Hello, sir, do you offer any food at this establishment?"

"We offer food here, yes," the man behind the counter, said. The man had a huge baldhead, giant hands, and a large overall stature. He was so big he was practically a giant! I have never been more intimidated by someone. My legs were shaking as I watched Uncle William talk to the man.

"Ah! Liam, come over here! This man can offer us some food! Sorry, sir, what is your name?"

"Bone Cracker is what people call me around here," he cracked his knuckles. I flinched at the sound.

"What a lovely name! Is that a family name?"

My eyes bulged out of my head at his comment. We were going to be beaten up; I can just feel it. What was Uncle William thinking? Bone Cracker is going to use his giant fists to beat us up, for sure.

"No."

"How about a drink?" Uncle William suggested.

I felt like slapping my forehead. Uncle William can't be serious. I hated being in this musty dirty pub. Surprisingly, Bone Cracker poured him a drink. I could not tell what it was, but it looked thick and grey Uncle William accepted it and without question, drank the strange concoction.

"What about you, boy?" Bone Cracker asked, pointing a mug at me.

I suddenly froze. I was so scared I could not move. I had hoped he wouldn't notice me and leave me alone. That clearly was not the case. I gave him a nod, and he poured me a drink.

"Do you have any mutton?" Uncle William asked.

"No."

"What about chicken?"

"No."

"Beef?"

"No."

"Potatoes?" Uncle William said, getting irritated.

"No."

"No?"

"Yes."

"Oh, so you do have potatoes?"

"Ugh! No," Bone Cracker said, spitting into a mug.

Uncle William tried to put on a smile again. I wanted to remind him that there are other places and we should just leave, but I was too scared to ask a second time.

"Then what do you have?"

"We have beets."

"Beets?"

"Yes, beets."

"Then, I will have three bowls of beets!"

My mouth dropped. Beets! I hate beets! My mom had to put sugar on beets when I was younger to get me to eat them.

Uncle William gestured for me to sit down at the bar. Looks like I have to stay. The stool I sat on felt gross and sticky. It is gonna suck having to go the whole trip with these sticky pants.

I waited for dinner while watching Bone Cracker pull out a bucket of ice from under the counter. Inside were bowls of already cooked beets. The beets looked boiled and bled a deep dark red color.

"Here ya go."

Bone Cracker handed us the beets without cutting them or any preparation. They were just boiled beets. I had no idea what to do. He did not even supply us with forks.

Bone Cracker picked up a beet from one of the bowls and took a bite out of it like an apple. I cringed watching him. Uncle William looked at me and shrugged.

Next thing I knew, he was eating it the same way. I held the cold beet in my hand and watched the red juices stain my fingers. Cautiously, I took a bite out of the beet and was shocked. It was delicious! It was sweet, soft, and healthy tasting all at the same time.

"What brings you travelers here?" Bone Cracker said. We told Bone Cracker about the imps who had attacked us.

"Oh yeah, we get a lot of those pests in this area," he said, shaking his head.

Bone Cracker left the bar area and grabbed the drunk man that had been passed out on one of the tables. He picked him up and exited the bar. Through the windows, we watched as Bone Cracker placed him on the ground and grabbed a bag out of the man's shoe. I could not believe what I was watching. Bone Cracker then took three silver coins out and placed the sac back in the drunk man's shoe. After he came back, we looked at him, waiting for an explanation.

"Got to clean up for the night shift," he said whipping his hands on the rag.

Through the window you could see Roman walk by the man without giving him more than a sideways glance. He sat down next to me and let out a tired sigh.

"Where is my mutton?"

"We got you beats instead," I said, smiling. He sighed and began eating along with us.

"Can I get you a drink?" Bone Cracker asked.

"Vodka."

Bone Cracker poured him a small glass. After we finished our "meal", Uncle William paid Bone Cracker five silver coins for the food and drinks. Bone Cracker looked outside.

"Looks like a storm is brewing. Rain should be coming around the morning time."

"We will camp out here tonight and then start again in the morning," Roman said, like the storm was no big deal.

"You don't want to try and ride tonight to get away from the rain?" I asked.

"No."

The next morning, small drops of rain woke us, delicately landing on our heads. The humid air smelled tropical and the sky was calm. Nature waited in anticipation for the storm to start. It only took a few minutes on the road for rain to sprinkle from the sky.

Now, an hour later, the sound of rain pounded in my ears. Roman encouraged the horse to keep going through the downpour. We covered all of our bags with a blanket that Roman had bought from the market in the last town. My hair was soaked, and my clothes weighed my body down like armor. It was raining so hard that I could hardly open my eyes. Uncle William began singing a song that sounded like he was yelling at the rain.

"You pound on the land! You rise up the sea! Searching for death to bring upon me! You wash out the dirt! You kill all the plants! Soaking me from my hair to my pants! I dare you rain, keep on pouring on me! I dare you rain, keep on pouring on me..."

The song was familiar, but it was hard to tell by his shouting. He wasn't angry though. It seemed like he was trying to cheer everyone up, and to be honest it was working. I found myself humming along to the tune. Uncle William explained that the people of the coastal side of Arone wrote the song and they would sing it out at sea during storms. He explained it was a classic song that sailors learn.

The rain began to subside after a few hours. The sky cleared up right as we reached the next rest stop. We drove into a village named Traven. Roman pulled into a horse stable.

"Viliam, I am hungry. You and dis little boy get me food," he ordered as he led us to the street.

A big crowd of people swarmed the village square. People were talking about the latest news and gossip. A group of kids were kicking around a ball and splashing in puddles. Most people were shopping at the many clothes and food shops. The village reminded me of home.

Uncle William told me to stay in the square while he searched for food in the shops. I sat down in the grass and watched all the people as they went about their day.

Suddenly, I noticed a small group of people forming a circle around something at the other end of the square. As I walked closer, I noticed that it was someone, not something.

A dirty old man wearing a barrel was jumping up and down in the center of the people. His bloodshot eyes and five remaining teeth were very off-putting. The old mans hair grew out long, and you could tell he had had no access to a hairbrush in a long time.

"The end is near! The end is near! Everyone will suffer soon!" He yelled.

I dodged the villagers to get up closer. Even from the back of the crowd you could tell he was spouting nonsense.

"We will all be in ruin!"

"What is this guy talking about?" A man shouted.

"Go back to the sewers, ya old rat!" A large woman shouted.

"Yeah!" A young boy shouted.

The crowd erupted with laughter after the mockery. I started to laugh along with the crowd. He was just a crazy old man. Then, his expression changed to anger. He walked over to a little girl in the crowd and grabbed her shoulders.

"Little girl, you must listen! LISTEN! The end is near!"

Her mother ripped the girl out of the old man's grasp and slapped him across the face. He crawled away from her whispering 'the end is near' to himself. This man was insane!

He made his way back to the center of the circle the crowd had formed. He scanned the crowd. Oh, no. My palms had become sweaty as his eyes fell on me. No. He crawled toward me. No, no, no! Why did he have to choose me?! My mind told me to run, but my legs were too scared to move. His face came so close to mine that I could smell his horrible breath. I gazed into his bloodshot eyes.

"Boy! The end is near! You all will perish!"

I was scared to death. Four Royal Knights rushed over and apprehended the crazy old man. As he was dragged away, he was screaming the King's name and failing his legs.

Uncle William grabbed my shoulder and pulled me away from the scene. My mouth was wide open, and I could not believe what had just happened. Why would he say such terrible things? If I said something like that at home, my mom would not give me my dinner.

"Uncle...Uncle William? UNCLE!"

Uncle William did not even flinch when I yelled his name. He was ignoring me. Uncle William was pulling me back to the wagon. My sleeve was in his left hand, and a bag of corn was in the other. I could not understand why he was ignoring me. Why is he mad? It's not like I agreed with the old man.

"Uncle William, what's wrong? I was just seeing what the crowd was-"

"Liam, be quiet, and let's just leave this village. This man is clearly insane!"

Roman cracked the whip as soon as we got into the wagon. The horse pulled us away from the strange town. As we drove away, I saw that the old man was placed in a pillory. They clamped down the wooden bar on his wrists and head. He was still shouting, "the end is near". Someone in the crowd threw a tomato at him. He flailed his head around, covering his beard in tomato juice.

I shuddered. Nothing like this ever happened in Brendsworth. I wanted to ask Uncle William so many questions, but I could tell that no one wanted to talk.

We rode into a large field that continued on for miles. You wouldn't even believe it had rained earlier this morning based on the hot weather. The sun shined brightly down on us as we rode through the big field.

"How much further?" I asked.

"Well, this field goes on for a pretty long time. It should be no longer than two days," Uncle William answered.

Sweat poured down my face. The sun burned my skin. Flies flew around our heads, annoying us with their constant buzzing. The flies reminded me of little kids trying to get our attention.

I felt like I have never hated the sun more than right now. However, the meadow was not that bad of a ride. Sometimes, the meadow was nice when a gust of wind blew through it. The grass flowed with the wind like waves on the ocean, and the breeze almost made you forget about the scolding heat of the sun. Sadly, the breeze was rare. This whole trip was the most exciting and educational trip of my life. I have seen things that I never would have seen living in Brendsworth. There weren't even large meadows like this one in Brendsworth. This summer will be like no other.

Even though I have to spend my summer working in the palace, I am not complaining. This way, I will get to make some money and have something interesting to do every day. I could not wait to meet new people and make new friends. However, I still missed my friends and family back in Brendsworth.

My heart ached to see my parents again and my best friend, Byron. A part of me wanted to be back to Brendsworth. I remembered smelling the fresh baked bread every morning and going to see my dad at his blacksmith forge during the day. However, the other part of me wanted to be out with Uncle William, having adventures, meeting new people, and seeing new sites. I was torn. I wish there was a potion that could let me do both at the same time. I wondered if Uncle William could help solve my problem.

"Uncle William?"

"What is it, Liam?"

"I am kind of torn between two things, and I can't figure out what to do."

"Really? Hmm… well, you know, life is all about tough choices. You have to make your own choices in life in order to be successful."

"I guess…" I said, thinking over what he said.

"Did that help?"

"I'll have to see."

Nightfall came, and we parked the wagon in the field and set up camp. The sounds of crickets shook our ears and the stars lit up the sky. Miles and miles of fireflies stretched out in front of us. It was the most beautiful and happy sight I have ever seen. This was defiantly worth leaving Brendsworth. Uncle William untied the horse from the wagon and walked it over to me.

"Roman, what is this horse's name again?"

"Chanson."

"Liam, wanna take old Chanson out for a ride?"

"Wait, what? But it's not my horse," I said looking at Roman.

"Little boy can ride horsey," Roman said with a slight nod.

I was hesitant at first. I haven't been on a horse since I was ten. That was six years ago. From what I remembered, I was not too bad at it.

Uncle William helped me get up on the horse. I grabbed the reins and felt the soft hairs on the horse's head.

"Okay," I said nervously.

Suddenly, my muscle memories kicked in, and before I knew it Uncle William and Roman were far behind me.

The sound of Chansons hoofs hitting the ground was like music to my ears. I was so happy to finally be moving fast for once. The tall grass tickled my legs as we pushed through the meadow. The wind blew through my hair and puffed up my shirt. The cool night air was nice compared to the heat of the sun. Each step Chanson took, fireflies fled from the grass and out into the sky. It was like a burst of light followed behind us. I felt free. I could ride through the fields forever. Out here riding through the grass, I understood what bliss and inner-peace was. All of my worries from before had melted away.

The fireflies began surrounding me as if the stars in the sky had fallen down to the earth. I slowed down the horse and brought our speed to a gallop. Gazing out at the dark field, I spotted a large weeping willow off in the distance. I made a clicking noise and hit the horse's side with my feet. Chanson began to gallop toward the tree. It seemed special since it was out in the middle of an open field. As we approached the tree, its long leaf-covered branches floated with the wind and brushed against my back. I hopped off the horse to get closer.

The truck of the tree reminded me of an older person. It had knots and grooves creating a pattern all around the tree like wrinkles on someone's face. I touched the trunk and felt the rough bark. The wind blew again, the branches and grass all blew in unison. I walked backward, out of the cover of the tree. Chanson began neighing and walked toward me.

"Ready to go back?" I pet his soft fur on his face.

As we rode back to Uncle William and Roman, we left a trail of fireflies behind us. I made a clicking noise to encourage Chanson move faster. The wind picked up blowing my hair in all different directions. My shirt was filled with air. Chansons mane flew back in the wind. It was as if we were flying through the field.

I reached camp to find Uncle and Roman standing around a fire. We were greeted by friendly smiles.

"What does the field look like up ahead?" Uncle William asked.

"There was a super cool tree that was out in the middle of the field. It was like a willow tree kind of. Chanson can actually go pretty fast, Roman," I said, hinting that we could be traveling at a much faster pace.

"Little horsey will get tired quick," he said without giving it any more thought.

"If you say so…" I replied, shaking my head back and forth. I decided that fighting Roman about his horse was a lost cause.

That night we slept under the stars. It was so peaceful that I didn't have to read "Sir Frederick's Adventures" to get me to fall asleep.

Chapter 7

We got up early the next morning and tried to cover as much ground as we could before it got too hot for the horse. We passed by the tree that I saw last night. I smiled, watching the branches as they swayed in the same fashion. Uncle William informed me that we would make it to the palace by late noon.

My stomach filled with butterflies. I was so nervous. What if I mess up? I won't even know where to go when I get there or what to do! I took a deep breath and calmed myself down.

Soon, I could see a wall in the distance.

"Uncle William, where are we?" I asked.

"We passed by the Tri Edge a few miles back. It is the point where the borders of Trisanburg, Aron, and Jarvally meet. That was a very important battle spot during the Ogre wars," Uncle William told me.

"Don't you mean Tri Borders?" I said correcting him.

"No, you're talking about the second spot where the other three regions meet. You did learn about the regions in school, right?" he asked curling his mustache.

I rolled my eyes. "Of course, I did. There is Arone, Trisanburg, Dorgan, Wodarn, Brendsworth, Pineswood, Jarvally. Oh, yeah, and the swamp forest."

I smiled knowing that information was locked in my brain. It felt good to show off my knowledge.

"Very good. The Tri Borders is the border of Trisanburg, Dorgan, and Pineswood- wait; did you say the swamp forest? That's not a region! That's just a section in Arone where they dumped all of those god-forsaken ogres," he corrected me.

"Oh, whoops," I frowned at my mistake.

"Oh, look! Up ahead, the city gates! How exciting!" Uncle William pointed up ahead.

"Did you know there are three gates; they are the only way in and out of Trisanburg City, by land that is. A big wall surrounds the whole city. Basically, there is no way in or out expect through the gates. Even the marina requires special clearance to get on shore. Trisanburg City is impenetrable! Not even those darn ogres could penetrate it during the war!"

Surprisingly, I didn't know that.

We finally reached the wall. The closer we got to it, the bigger it looked. I gazed up at the big, wooden gates. Up on the top of the tower, two Royal Knights stood guard. I was in awe just from the sight of them. Being a knight is my dream! What if one day that was my job? What if one of those knights was my friend or my boss? I could hardly hold in my excitement.

The knight's metal armor glistened in the sunlight. Each held out their spears with confidence. However, the thing that stood out the most was the emblem that was on their chest plates. It was hard to make out the details, but you could easily tell it was identical to the big crest on the gate that stood between the city and us.

The crest that was painted on the door had silver lining with the Trisanburg elk in the center and a backdrop of yellow. A guard who had been standing outside the wall walked up to the wagon.

"Good morning!" Uncle William greeted him.

"Good morning. What business do you have in this city?" the guard demanded, glaring up at us.

"We are employed servants for the King's household, sir. I am William Rocklen," Uncle William began, and gesturing towards me, "this is my nephew, Liam."

Roman straightened himself as he addressed the guard. "And I am Roman, chef of His Majesty's household."

The guard glanced briefly at us and then back down at his roster.

"Quite all right, then," he admitted gruffly before directing the other guard to open the gates.

"Welcome to Trisanburg City. Be on your best behavior, and you won't run into trouble."

The big wooden gates opened revealing a dirt road leading toward the city.

"Look, the castle!" I cried, unable to hold in my excitement.

As we drew closer to the city, the castle appeared bigger and bigger. We had made it! I was blown away. The castle towers were so tall they practically touched the clouds! And the city stretched out so far and wide, it was like a forest of brick and wooden buildings.

Our wagon moved across the cobblestone road. A woman waved to us from outside a tiny wooden shack. I smiled and waved back. I wondered if people were this friendly in the city.

Suddenly, the dirt road ended, we had arrived at the edge of the city. I could not choose where to look because every direction had something amazing to look at. Tall brick and stone buildings surrounded us. Clothing lines hung across and above the street, and almost every building had birds sitting on windowsills or the roofs.

Few houses had balconies, but the ones that did were a spectacle. Only the wealthiest could afford those houses. A man had a stand full of handcrafted jewelry and was yelling at the top of his lungs calling people to buy his items. My mouth watered as a baker was offering free samples of his sweet bread. Another man with a large black beard and turban came up to our cart with assorted fruits in a basket.

"You look like hungry travelers! Three of my delicious fruits for only five silver coins! Fill your stomachs in seconds!"

We kindly declined his offer. Another man walked out of his sweet shop with jars filled to the top with honey. Kids swarmed around the man, practically worshipping him. The large man patted the kids' heads and told them to run along. I had never seen so many people in one place! Shoppers walked up and down the sidewalk, shopping and talking to neighbors. It felt so crowded that if I stepped out of the wagon, the crowd would whisk me away like the current in a river.

All types of shops surrounded the town square. The shops were set up in a way that made an oval around a fountain in the center. The fountain was a stone sculpture of an elk. Water poured out of its horns and filled up the fountain. It was in the traditional Trisanburg elk pose, with its head held high.

I looked to my left and noticed a bookshop. I bet they have "Sir Frederick's Adventures" in there. I wanted to stop and go into the shops, but Uncle William said we had to head up to the castle.

We left the market through a path between two shops. The path led up to a small hill. Excitement rushed through my veins as soon as the castle came into a closer view. The magnificent castle was built on top of the hill, surrounded by endless grass covered grounds. We learned in school that Queen Emily had grown a large garden around the back of the castle. We also learned many other secret facts like that there is a secret giant wine cellar below the castle. I was so excited to see everything!

"Here we are!" Uncle William exclaimed.

As we got closer, the castle appeared even bigger. The only way you could see the top of the towers was if you tilted your head all the way back.

We rode right past the main doors toward the back of the castle. I could smell the sweet scent of flowers from the Queen's garden, but sadly, still could not see them. Some say the most exotic and beautiful flowers grow in her garden.

"Go through servants entrance," Roman said, pointing to a small wooden door at the back of the main building.

Roman tossed our few bags into our arms and cracked the reins. Chanson slowly walked to the stables. Uncle William and I entered through the small wooden door into a room full of mops, brooms, and buckets. The exterior and wall were made of cobblestone while the floors were made of wood. Uncle William continued on walking through another door. The second door led to a room that had five people in it. One was a grown man who was hauling a bag of items into another room that looked like the kitchen. Two other men followed him. The last man was a cook behind a counter making what looked like bread. The last person in the room was an older woman.

The woman squinted at us through her small spectacles that sat delicately on her nose. Based on the eggshell white apron she wore over her grey dress, this woman must be a servant or something. I was slightly off put by her disgusted expression and wrinkled face. Her grey and brown hair was placed in a tight, neat bun on the top of her head.

"Ugh…I could have sworn I told Jeremy to take out the garbage. I guess he didn't."

The woman gestured to Uncle William. Her voice was raspy and sounded like it would belong to an angry cat. If I didn't know better, I would say this woman was a dark witch.

"Well, well, well, it's been a while since I have seen you," Uncle William said with his hands on his hips.

"Not long enough," she said, crossing her arms.

I could only assume by this not so warm welcome that Uncle William is not her favorite co-worker.

"Ms. Woodround, meet my nephew, Liam."

"You know you're late, William."

"He is going to be a servant."

"What?! I don't think so! I refuse to hire another Rocklen!"

"You don't have a say in it. I do the hiring around here."

"Of course I have a say in it!"

"As a reeve, I supervise the work; that includes your work!" my Uncle stated loudly.

"It does not!" countered Ms. Woodround.

"Go ask the king himself if you think other wise."

"Ugh, the housekeeper is a higher position compared to a reeve!" she hissed.

"Not in a million years! Go ask him I dare you!" snapped Uncle William.

"Why don't you go ask the king?" Ms. Woodround said snottily.

"Pfft, I don't need to hear it from him!" Uncle William said dismissively.

"You should! He is the king!" Ms. Woodround said.

"Umm am I interrupting?" a boy from behind us questioned, causing their argument to come to a halt.

I was so caught up in the fight that I did not notice a boy had come in.

"I was told to come in here to talk to the people in charge. Can one of you tell me where I am supposed to be? Or what I am supposed to be doing? I'm Charles Brockfur, by the way, one of the new servants. Are you the reeve? I think I heard you say...er...shout it."

My mind did backflips. This was great! I will not be alone! Another new servant who can help me figure out what I am doing.

"Oh, yes, I am the castle reeve. Sorry about that; that was very unprofessional. Please call me Mr. Rocklen," Uncle William shook his hand.

"I am Ms. Woodround, the housekeeper," she said, pushing Uncle William aside and holding out her hand. Charles cautiously shook it.

"Here, come look at the room chart, and we can get you situated. Oh, looks like you're in my room with my nephew, Liam!"

Charles looked at me and smiled. I smiled back and gave a weak wave. Charles was much taller than me, and his skin was white, but much tanner than my skin. I was a little jealous of his perfect short curly blonde hair and sky blue eyes. My hair is just brown, flat, and boring compared to his.

"Shouldn't you show your nephew and this servant to their rooms?" Ms. Woodround asked, with a disgusted look on her face when she said 'nephew.' I wanted to say something to her for that, but she is one of my superiors. I needed to just 'turn the other cheek'.

"So. Are you saying that I have more authority, and therefore should show them to their rooms?" Uncle William said, smirking.

"Wait! No!" she said, crossing her arms.

"Right this way, boys."

Uncle William led us through another door and into a long hallway that was lit by torches. There were a total of seven rooms in this hallway. The room Uncle William led us to was at the end of the hallway.

"Here ya go!"

"This is a nice room," Charles said nodding with a smile.

The room was about the same size as my bedroom at home, but with less open space. Four beds were placed in each corner of the square room. Each bed had a slab of rock above it, imitating a shelf. One window was directly in line with the door, providing light for the entire room.

"Wow, the window has a perfect view of the field! I bet we can see the Royal Knights practice!" I said pointing at the window. I almost screamed; I was so excited. I would now be able to watch and study the way real knights train and fight. This would help me improve by so much!

"We can also see the stables. I have a couple of horses where I live in Jarvally" said Charles.

"I get the bed closest to the door," Uncle William announced, setting his bag down.

"Wait, you're rooming with us?" I asked.

"Of course! You're both rookies and need me to look after you. So, you are going to room with me."

"Well, Liam, I guess you get your pick of those two beds," Charles said.

I chose the one next to Uncle William. Charles went to the bed near the window and began unpacking. I started to empty "Sir Fredrick's Adventure's" and Scales from my leather satchel. They both sat on the shelf above my bed.

"Cool statue! Is it a dragon?" Charles asked.

I transformed Scales in order to impress him.

"Whoa! That's incredible! Where did you get that?" Charles said, laughing as the dragon ran across his arm.

"A witch in the Brendsworth market."

"That is so cool. My dad has actually been to Brendsworth market to sell our carrots."

"Yeah, we see a lot of merchants," I said.

"So, how old are you, Charles?" Uncle William asked.

"I am sixteen."

"Me too!" I said, transforming Scales back to wood.

I could already tell that I would get along with Charles, which was good since we would be spending the whole summer together.

Charles asked where we were from. I explained to him that I live in Brendsworth and how Uncle William came to bring me back with him.

Charles explained he was from a farming village in Jarvally. His parents' family farm has a variety of food grown on it from carrots to apples. Charles said that the farms in Jarvally mostly belong to witches who, over the years, have become the Outer Kingdom's top farmers.

"You see, witches use their magic for all kinds of food production jobs. Their magic can make farming much easier and they produce high quality food. The potions that the witches are able to create help with the growth of food that can feed so many people. Additionally, it leaves other jobs like carpentry, shoe making, and book publishing available for all of the people who no longer need to be farmers. So, as a result, the Outer Kingdom is flourishing with all the food and items that are created. I personally like the system we have here," Charles explained, demonstrating his knowledge.

"Well, in the very early days of the Outer Kingdom, the witches did not live in harmony with the humans. People typically didn't trust them, mainly because they did not understand magic. After we formed a bond of trust and understanding with them, the Outer Kingdom experienced a booming economy and people had never been happier. I could not even think of a world without both witches and humans.," Uncle William said.

"Well, it would be nice to get rid of the dark witches," I commented.

"Oh, yeah. Dark witches don't care for peace with the rest of the Outer Kingdom. They are just evil and dangerous women that attack humans and other creatures, even other witches who want peace with the humans!" Charles said.

"Yeah, I would rather they were not in the Outer Kingdom," I restated.

"In my village, there are lots of witches. My neighbor is a witch. Her name is Kara, and her husband's name is Richard. They grow peppers on their farm and are super nice people. They only grow one vegetable though because that is all they need to grow in order to live comfortably. Due to her magic potions, the peppers grow faster and with almost no imperfections," explained Charles.

"That is so cool! The only witch I know sells magic trinkets made by fairy magic. She made me the dragon that I have. We only have witches come and go in our town because of the market. If it were not for the market, I bet we wouldn't see any witches," I added.

"It is just amazing how they can make food grow so quickly! Not to mention how interesting it all is," Uncle William said.

"Yeah, like the law of magic," Charles said.

"What is that?" Uncle William asked.

"The law of magic states that you cannot create, nor destroy matter, you can only change it into new things. The potions that the witches use on the produce require some ingredients. Most require simple things, like certain herbs and salts. Kara has to use pepper stems and seeds in her potion. She is required to soak the pepper stems and seeds for three days in sea salt, rare magic herbs, and water. Then, she puts them in the ground and enchants them. The peppers will be fully-grown in less than a few weeks. It would usually take them at least two to three months," Charles explained.

"Wow. I had no idea it was that complicated. So, each spell requires something in return?" Uncle William asked.

"Yeah. I only learned a few of these things from my mom and Kara. I am sure an expert knows more," he said.

My teachers hardly taught us anything on magic. They assume we won't need to know it. They expect us to stay in Brendsworth our whole lives, which limits our potential.

Uncle William stood up abruptly.

"I have to get back to meeting the new workers. Lucky for you two we got back in time for the new marking period. That means mostly everyone will be assigned a new work shift group. Anyways, I got to get back. I can't let them think that Ms. Woodround is in charge around here!" Uncle William said, laughing.

"Oh yeah, that woman seems kind of rude," I said cautiously.

"Hey, watch what you say about her! She will eat you two for breakfast if you don't listen to what she says. She is going to be your boss," he said and smiled as he was leaving.

"Wait what?" I said.

Charles looked at me with his jaw dropped to the floor. I could not believe it. That monster will be telling me what to do all summer?

Maybe I should not judge her just yet. Mom always said to give people another chance. Maybe Ms. Woodround has a reason for being harsh with my Uncle. Who knows, she could have had her tea spill on her lap today? What do I know?

I looked over at Charles's shelf and noticed he also had "Sir Frederick's Adventures".

"You read 'Sir Frederick's Adventures'? I love that book!"

"Pfft, of course I have! Every kid in the Outer Kingdom has! His stories are the best! I want to meet him so bad!" Charles exclaimed. Soon we were engaged in an in depth conversation about the book. Charles began telling me about his favorite chapters.

"Mine is the one on Wizards. It's fascinating how their magic was not passed down like witches. They say it is a receptive sex-linked ancestral trait. Basically, magic can only be passed down to females. But that is what made wizards so cool! They received a mutation or something in their traits to make them have it. Not to mention they were ten times more powerful that witches," Charles explained.

"Too bad they are basically extinct," I said.

"Well, I have heard some cases where people that have had wizards as their ancestors have some magical abilities," Charles said with hope.

"Yeah, maybe," I said.

I was very impressed by how much Charles knew. I mean anyone who read "Sir Frederick's Adventures" was smart. However, I would not jump to say he is smarter than me.

"Hey, so, what are we supposed to do for the rest of the day?" I asked.

Charles got up and stretched his arms and back.

"Let's go and explore the castle!" Charles said, waving for me to come with him.

I hesitated. It didn't feel right walking around without Uncle William giving me permission.

"Let's go explore the servants' hall instead. We can see who we will be working with. It doesn't feel right to be going out on our own in the castle just yet," I admitted.

"Awww, come on Liam! It will be so cool!" Charles pleaded.

"Charles, I just think we should keep out of trouble on the first day. Come on lets go this way," I said pointing away from the stairs that led up into the throne room.

"I guess you're right," Charles said, walking down the hallway.

There was nothing interesting to look at in the servants' hallway and decided to see if all the rooms were the same as ours. Neither of us wanted to be missing out on any perks. We opened the door to the room that is next to ours. It had four beds with shelves. Just like ours. The next room we looked in was full of four workers.

"Whoops, sorry we did not know anyone was in here," I said, embarrassed.

"Pfft, newbies," One of them gave us a dirty look.

"Oh, sorry," Charles said closing the door.

"Wait, don't be so rude, Madeline. Do you guys have any questions? Are you lost?" One of the other workers asked politely.

"Actually, yes. Do you know where the rest of the workers are?" Charles asked them.

"Everyone is working but, their shifts should end by dinner," one of the men answered.

"Oh, okay. Thank you," Charles replied leaving.

"Thanks, again," I said closing the door carefully behind me.

"Wanna just go hang out in our room? There is clearly nothing else to do," he said.

"We can read some of 'Sir Frederick's Adventures' or something? What ever you want," I suggested.

"Yeah sure,"

"Wanna read out loud? That way we are still like talking and stuff. I personally like to read out loud," I suggested.

"Okay, sure! That just means I won't have to do any work," he said smiling.

I opened up the book to a random chapter and began to read off the worn out pages.

"Sir Frederick walked through the woods. He swung his sword back and forth, cutting down briars and weeds that grew in his way. Sir Frederick was searching for the shore. Suddenly, he came across a cliff on the edge of the ocean. There would surely be some type of creature here. Sir Frederick walked up to the edge of the cliff. He pointed to something down below. 'Aha! Now, see there is a mermaid down there. Mermaids are both fierce warriors and elegant beauties. There are four types of mermaids. One type is the northern mermaid. Northern mermaids are very kind and shy creatures. They have lived the longest out of all the mermaids. As a result, they have a vast knowledge on everything in the sea. However, it is hard to acquire the knowledge that the mermaids contain because they are very shy and won't talk to people unless you earn their trust. Blimey! This mermaid here is a southern mermaid! Southern mermaids are devilish liars and would go out of their way to trick innocent people for fun. Sailors have told stories about how the southern mermaids point the sailors in the wrong direction and try to get them into trouble. Some of the southern mermaids would even go as far as to try to kill the sailors and eat them. Unlike southern mermaids, eastern mermaids are brave and trustworthy. They train every day and are great and fierce warriors. Us humans have fought battles against pirates with the help of the eastern mermaids. The last type of mermaid is the western mermaid. The western mermaid possesses powerful magical powers. They practice making potions using the rare ingredients found in the ocean. Sadly, they only have the abilities to practice rudimentary magic.' How does one tell these mermaids apart? 'There are four symbols that represent what type of mermaid a mermaid is. They carve the symbol on rocks that they wear as necklaces, bracelets, sashes, or belts. This helps to inform people and other mermaids on what type of mermaid they are. However, most mermaid types are found in their territory in the Outer Kingdom.

The symbol for the western mermaid is a circle with seaweed in the center of it. The southern mermaid symbol is a circle with a seashell in the center of it. The eastern mermaid symbol has a circle with a tidal wave in the center of it. And the northern mermaid symbol has a circle with a starfish in it. The mermaids' symbols date back to the clan of the very first mermaids ruled by four separate families.

Now, every hero should know that the best way to deal with southern mermaids is to leave them alone. But if you find yourself in a situation where you can't get away from them, seek dry land as fast as possible.' Sir Frederick slowly walked away from the cliff and back into the woods to continue his adventure."

I closed the book. Charles started clapping in a joking way.

"Wow, you're pretty good at reading out loud! You didn't stumble over a single word. Is that like your hidden talent or like special skill?" he asked, surprised.

"Thanks! I mean it's not that special of a skill. I would not even call it a talent. I just like hearing the story out loud I guess."

"That's cool though," he said.

"Have you ever seen a mermaid?" I asked.

"No, but my friend Jessica's dad has. I think she said the mermaid was a northern mermaid. I don't think the mermaid spoke to him though," he recalled.

"That is still pretty cool. I want to at least meet every type of mermaid before I die," I admit.

"Same. I wonder if there are any mermen?" Charles asked.

"Oh, I actually read a chapter on mermen in 'Sir Frederick's Adventures'," I said.

"Wait, really? I totally forgot there was a chapter on it. What did it say?" he asked, intrigued by the subject.

"There are mermen, but they are not part of the four different mermaid groups. They are like lone wolves that constantly swim all around the Outer Kingdom's oceans. The only time they stop is to hunt or mate with the mermaids. They are kind of always alone," I said, trying to remember what Sir Frederick had wrote.

"That's kind of sad. They don't even get to have a family?" Charles asked.

"No. They leave the babies with the mermaid group. And what is ever crazier is they have more than just one mate. Which is completely weird," I said.

Voices echoed from down the hall. Right as I was about to suggest we go investigate, Uncle William entered the room with another worker.

A bald man with a large belly followed him into the room and put his things down on the fourth bed. He gave a big smile and shook each of our hands.

"Hello, hello, hello, my name is Samuel Wu. I am the royal carpenter! Your uncle told me you are both servants here. Ms. Woodround's organization of the rooms is so weird, I mean, why not just put all the maids in one room and all the carpenters in another–oh, wait, I'm the only carpenter. Clumsy me! William, which one is your nephew? The blonde one does not look like you, so I am assuming you are Liam? It is so very nice to meet you!" Samuel said, talking so fast that I could hardly keep up.

"Yes, Samuel, that is my nephew, Liam."

Samuel and Uncle William began talking about the recent repairs made in the castle. I could hardly wait to start work and see all the amazing sites here. However, I was still a little nervous since Ms. Woodround would be my boss. I guess I should just give her another chance at a first impression.

"It looks like it is getting darker outside. Why don't we go get some dinner?" Uncle William suggested.

"Oh, good! I love dinner!" Samuel said clapping and then rushing to the door.

"Now that is my kind of attitude. Let's go get some dinner! Gonna get my grub on! Who knows what will be there?! Probably bad tasting food but, lets go eat some garbage!" Charles cheered jokingly.

I burst out in laughter. Uncle William shook his head but I noticed him crack a smile. This summer will not be as bad as I thought.

Chapter 8

We walked back through the hallway and into the servants' hall to eat our meal. We were served a bowl of plain greens. I looked down at my dinner and frowned. How am I supposed to feel energized from a few leaves? I then noticed I was not the only one disappointed with the meal. Uncle William was furious at the fact they supplied us spinach and mustard greens and no other vegetables or proteins. I looked over and noticed Ms. Woodround walk in through the door and grab a bowl of vegetables. It was like night and day compared to everyone else's bowls. Hers was vibrant with different types of vegetables and nuts.

"Hey, Uncle William, why does she get carrots and tomatoes in her salad, and we don't?" I ask angrily.

"She has always received special treatment from the cook," Uncle William sighed.

"Why?" Charles asked.

"Well, she has been leading the head chief on for years now, if you know what I mean. That poor old man, Chief Taron, thinks that she is actually interested in him. Besides, Ms. Woodround believes that she is superior to everyone. The worst part is that my position is superior to hers, yet I'm still eating these nasty greens," he said with disgust.

I can't believe that something so unfair goes unnoticed.

"So, have you heard the elf race is going extinct?" Uncle William created small talk with Samuel.

"Oh, yes, yes. That is very unfortunate that that is happening. However, they are kind of stuck-up people. That doesn't mean that I would like them to go extinct. Some are very wise but oh so very proud. It feels like we won't have any elfs or fairies left at this point," Samuel said, talking almost too fast for me to understand. We finished our bland greens and headed back to our room.

Everyone had fallen asleep but me. My worries about the day to come kept me awake. I twisted and turned in my bed, trying to find a comfortable position. The stone shelf above my head caught my eye. I reached up and grabbed "Sir Frederick's Adventures" off the shelf. Quickly, I flipped through the chapter on magical potions. I began to read through it, using the moon as my source of light.

"Magic is the most mysterious thing in the Outer Kingdom. Witches and scientists combine powers to help us better understand magic and its association with our ancestral traits. Generations of families pass down an ancestral trait that allows a woman to have magical abilities. This trait is very rare in males, and there are no known wizards in the Outer Kingdom anymore. Still, the full power that witches have is amazing. Witches are the only species that can practice elemental magic. Using air, water, earth, and fire, witches use their power to change the states of these elements. Creating elemental magic is difficult to learn, and only few witches can master all of these elemental changes. The most common and easiest element to learn and manipulate is water. Some witches are able to master fire, the second hardest, and earth, the third hardest. No known current witches can master air because it takes years of dedication and skill. However, if air is achieved, the witch becomes very powerful and strong.

The most important thing to take away is all magic must come from an already existing object whether it is mastering elemental magic or practicing rudimentary magic and using simple ingredients like flour and eggs to quickly make bread."

My parents told me that there are no cases of magic in our family, but it would have been cool to have that type of power. My mind moved on to thinking about tomorrow. It will be the first day of my first job ever.

I ran scenarios through my head about what could go wrong. My nerves built up. What if I trip and fall, or even worse, I could get lost in the castle! Most of all, I am afraid that I won't be good enough to work at the palace. I calmed myself down, and finally, my eyes closed.

I woke up to a blinding light shining through the window. Uncle William was already walking out the door. Quickly, Charles and I dressed and got ready for the day.

I followed Charles away from the servants' hallway. We climbed up a small staircase into the biggest and brightest room I have ever been in. I was in awe at the sight of the throne room. Torches lined the large stonewalls and beautiful tapestries hung from the ceiling. Every single tapestry was golden or blue with a traditional Trisanburg Elk on it. At one end of the room was a large door identical to the one we saw at the entrance to the city. A long red carpet led from the door to the other end of the room where three thrones sat. One throne, in the middle, was bigger than the other two. One could only assume that chair was the King's throne. Behind the thrones was a stained glass window almost the size of the whole wall. The window was made of an assortment of colors from blue to tan. It was a traditional image of the Trisanburg Elk standing tall in the woods.

"Oh…wow, that is amazing!" Charles said.

A large group of people formed a cluster in the center of the room. We joined the group whom all seemed to be looking at Ms. Woodround; she was standing on the step below the thrones tapping her foot. Her arms were crossed, and she glared at each and every one of us. Then, she cleared her throat.

"I hope everyone is here because I am not waiting for anyone else."

Everyone either sighed or rolled their eyes. No one seemed to like her. They whispered back and forth, and her name was thrown around amongst it.

"Now, listen up, because I'm only saying it once. Each week, I will place a piece of parchment in the servants' hall with your group's assignments for the week on it," she began.

Ms. Woodround rummaged through her papers that she held. She adjusted her spectacles and started to read.

"Here are the groups and your assignments for the day. Keep in mind this will be the only time I will read this to you. Oh, if there are no assignments written, that means King Bartholomew does not want any one of you peasants around the castle that day. Also, you will have a minimum of four assignments each day if I'm feeling nice. Today, I am, so there is only one. That's only because the King does not want you low level commoners walking around spreading your filth," she spat, looking over her paper at us.

"Question?" a man who stood next to me said.

"Does that mean he doesn't want you walking around the castle?" he said and then broke into a laugh.

The man next to him laughed, and the woman on the other side did the same. I cracked a smile. Ms. Woodround frowned and stomped her heels on the floor to regain their attention.

"I have a real question," an older girl in the front said. "If we ever see a mess in the castle, should we alert you of it?"

"Of course, I am in charge of you after all!" she snapped. The woman up front launched her hand in the air again.

"Yes, Ms. Fernfeather?" Ms. Woodround sighed.

The older girl smirked and pointed directly at Ms. Woodround.

"Ms. Woodround, there is a mess right there!"

People in the crowd began to giggle. Ms. Woodround practically had steam coming from her ears.

"Shut up, all of you!" She vigorously stomped her foot on the ground to regain our attention. She stomped her heels so hard that one of the heels broke. Ms. Woodround's papers were released from her grasp, and she stumbled to regain her balance.

Everyone in the group burst out laughing, I snorted trying to keep a laugh in. The man who made fun of Ms. Woodround was in tears; he was laughing so hard.

"Ah-hem!"

Ms. Woodround had stood back up and the crowd silenced.

"Group one, Edward Vilenter, Jeremy Greendale, and Sasha Fernfeather. Group two, Charles Brockfur, Liam Rocklen, and Bethany Brooks. And group three, James Smithon, Rosa Burgende, and Clarity Sunpink. Finally, group four, Madeline Tremer, Greg

Holland, and Tom Ray. Now, time to assign the work. Group one, you will sweep every room in the servant's hall. Group two, you will shake out the curtains in the servant's rooms and in the west wing halls. Group three, you will wash the windows in the servant rooms. I will not tolerate any shenanigans this year from any of you! That is why you're going to wake up early every morning and report to the servants' hall where I will have the work board posted at exactly five o'clock in the morning. If anyone is late, the whole group skips breakfast. This is the year of punishment for all of you who think it's funny to make fun of your superior. Dismissed!" she said, limping back to the servant's quarters.

I would have felt bad for the woman because she was just humiliated, but these rules seemed pretty harsh. I don't remember the last time I was up that early.

The crowd dispersed. Everyone headed toward the servants' hall to get their equipment. The only people left other than Charles and I was a teenage girl, who looked around the same age as us. She was short and thin with long dark brown hair and hazel eyes. Our eyes met, and she smiled.

"You guys must be Liam and Charles. Hi, I'm Bethany! I guess we are in the same group! Is this your first time working as a servant? I mean, I have never seen you around here," she said, walking over to shake our hands. She straightened out her white apron and fixed her brown dress. Bethany had a big smile and a cheerful attitude. Her friendliness was comforting after hearing Ms. Woodrounds threats. I was glad we were not stuck with someone else.

"Yeah it's our first time. Is she always that mean?" Charles asked.

"Yeah, she is pretty cranky. I would not be as risky as the rest are and try to make her mad. Where are you guys from?" she asked.

"Well, I am Liam. I am from Brendsworth. There are really no villages, so it's just Brendsworth, Brendsworth," I said chucking. She giggled.

"That cool. What about you, Charles?"

"I am from a farming village in Jarvally. Rockhold? You guys are probably not familiar with it."

"Sorry, I'm not. Well, I live right here in Trisanburg City."

"Really? I thought that only wealthy people could afford to live in the city?"

"My mom makes enough, and I contribute by working here. But, yeah, there are a lot of wealthy kids. Most of them are brats. You see I go to school with mostly all the rich kids in Trisanburg City. You probably have heard of Mrs. Opal's Preparatory School for Girls and Isaiah White's School for Young Boys?"

"Oh, yeah! All of the rich kids in Jarvally get sent there."

"I know a lot of girls in my school in Brendsworth who want to go there," I added.

"Yeah, a lot of rich kids from the regions pay to go there. Only a couple of the non-rich kids from Trisanburg City get in, but we have to take a test to qualify," Bethany admitted.

"That seems dumb. Well, not for the owners of the school. They get all that money from the rich kids," Charles added.

"I mean I wish it was not set up that way. The girls who go there do nothing but backstab their friends and gossip. We hardly do any school work."

Abruptly, a group of three older kids walked in with brooms. I recognized the girl who was making fun of Ms. Woodround from earlier.

"Hey, Jeremy, Sasha, look," one of the older boys said, pointing at us.

"Some new servants."

"Just a word of advice, the faster you get the work done, the more time you get to explore the castle or just hang out," the older girl advised.

After they walked away, Charles quickly took their advice. He hurried towards the servants' hall eager to get the work done and so we could have some free time. Bethany and I shared a look and I shrugged. When we got there, Charles was already grabbing the curtains from the rooms. Thankfully, they were not big curtains because the windows were small, so we could hold all of them in our arms. We took the curtains from the servants' room and shook them hard outside near the stables.

"Well, looks like we got all the work done, so see you guys tomorrow, I guess..." Bethany said, sounding less cheerful.

"Bethany, why don't you come back to our room with us? You know, so Charles and I can get to know you since we are going to be working together all summer," I offered, smiling.

"Sounds tempting," she laughed walking with us.

"Okay let's go! We're going! Let's do it!" Charles said, struggling to get us to walk faster. He had much longer legs than us and could walk almost as fast as I can run. I began to walk slowly on purpose just to mess with Charles.

"Come on, Liam!" he said, getting frustrated. Bethany then joined in walking as slow as she could.

"Oh my lord! Come on, already! Oh, this reminds me of when my brother and I used to mess with the Patrick kids. The Patrick family lived close to our farm, and they were so annoying! Every time I was with them, they would not shut up! Anyways, my brother and I would get in their way and walk slow just like you are right now. So don't think I don't know what you are doing!" Charles said, talking non-stop.

"Oh! If we get more time off like today, I can bring you guys to all of the best shops in Trisanburg City," Bethany offered, sitting down on the floor in our room.

"That would be awesome!" Charles said.

"Yeah, we should. What do you guys like to do for fun?" I asked.

"Well, I have work here, which I would not call fun, and I do horseback riding and painting, so I keep busy," Bethany said.

"Wait, you horseback ride? That's so cool! I used to ride horses when I was younger. What about you, Charles?" I asked.

"Read, I guess, climb trees and lift hay barrels. You know, got to get those muscles," He flexed his arm.

Bethany rolled her eyes.

"What about you?" She asked.

"Well, I recently have been practicing with a sword. Oh, and I also like to read."

"Wow, you have your own sword? Can you use it?" Bethany asked, becoming interested.

"Yeah, I am pretty good at it, I guess," I bragged.

"Do you have it with you? Can we see it?" Charles asked eagerly.

"Yeah! I can even teach you guys some moves."

I could not believe I had just found two awesome new friends! This summer might be not as bad as I thought. Now, I could hardly remember what I was so worried about from earlier.

Chapter 9

The next morning, I was not as excited to working as I had been yesterday. Uncle William opened the curtains to reveal it was still dark out. I dreaded getting up. Instinctively, I let out a long groan in response to the sunlight that shined through the window. My feet flopped onto the floor and I practically slept walked to the servants' hall. Charles was already in there waiting for me. He was standing with three other people. They were the same three that gave us advice yesterday. The trio seemed like they were a little older than us and they must already be acquainted with Charles based on their smiles and laughter.

"Hey, Liam! These are some of the other servants who work here at the castle. This is Edward, Sasha, and Jeremy," he waved me over.

"Looks like someone just got outta bed," Sasha laughed.

As soon as the words exited her mouth, Ms. Woodround stomped into the servants' hall.

"Good morning, inferiors! Looks like you all made it on time. However, punishment is still required. For some reason, someone thought it would be funny to change the assignments that were written on my board!"

She held it up revealing her name written in every slot for every single job. I let out a laugh. The room erupted with giggles.

"This is insubordination! My name does not belong in a single slot on this board! If I catch whoever did this, you will be in for a world of hurt!" she threatened, her face wrinkled up like a raisin.

My body was tense and my legs shook in fear. I could not even comprehend what Ms. Woodround might do to punish the culprits. The trio of Edward, Sasha, and Jeremy all held back their giggles, snorting quietly. It was clear who was responsible for the prank.

I looked through the crowd for Bethany. She was on the other side of the room. She noticed me looking at her. I smiled and gave her a wave. She waved back and then went back to listening to Ms. Woodround. I quickly tried to go back to listening to Ms. Woodround, but I had already missed the important information.

"So, get on it! Chop, chop! Shoo! And, remember, today, I'm going around to inspect your work! If it is not satisfactory, I will make you do it again!" Ms. Woodround said, waving us off on our way.

Charles filled me in on our assignment. Our group was assigned to wash the windows in the dining hall. We gathered the equipment and a ladder to reach the top of the tall windows. The dining hall was a large, long room with a table just as large and long stretching from one end of the room to the next. The room was elegant and matched the same theme of the throne room. There were four tall windows along the sides of the dining hall, ready for us to clean.

I soaked my rag with the clean water and climbed up the ladder to the top of the window. Bethany and Charles got to work, cleaning the bottom half. I accidently dripped some water onto Bethany's head. She put her hands on her hips.

"Really?" She said.

"Whoops, sorry!"

Time passed and we made our way toward the second to last window. We made sure to wash every inch of the glass.

"So, what is the plan for today after we get this work done?" Bethany asked, kicking conversation into action.

"I was planning on checking out the castle grounds. How about you, Charles?" I said, wiping in large circles.

"I would be down for exploring the castle. So, what do you think about the other servants? I think that Edward, Jeremy, and Sasha seem pretty cool. Not to mention they are pretty funny. You know, I heard that they have pranked Ms. Woodround twenty times in the last three years! We should play a prank on her one of these days!" Charles suggested.

"That sounds like fun! We can't get caught though because I can't loose this job," I said.

"I don't know, guys. I have worked here for four years now and have never gotten into any trouble. I don't plan on ruining my perfect record," Bethany said.

"If they can do it, we can too! We won't get caught, Bethany."

"Okay, let's say we do it. What prank would we play? I have never done anything like that," Bethany admitted.

"I don't know. I have never pulled a prank, either," I confessed.

"Well, if I was to pull a prank, I would take Ms. Woodround's desk and put in outside in the stables. Now, that is a funny prank!" Charles said.

I laughed just thinking about it. Then, my ears caught the faint sound of heels on the stone floor. Oh no...Ms. Woodround came bounding into the room.

"Ah, my favorite group of peasants, with young Mr. Rocklen. Let's see how your work is going."

I picked up a faint evil tone in her voice.

"Ugh, disgusting, dirty! I should be able to see my face in this glass! You will continue working," she ordered.

I looked at the window and then back at her. Excuse me? I looked into the window and saw my reflection. What is she talking about? This window is perfectly clean! I was so angry. I scrubbed the window even harder.

Ms. Woodround walked away with an evil grin on her face.

"What the heck was she talking about? It's already clean! Why do we have to do more work?" Charles asked.

"This 'lady' is just trying to torture us!" I said.

"More like torture you! For some reason, she hates you…and your Uncle William. I can't think of a reason why. I mean I never noticed any problems while working here." Bethany said.

"Well, she is crazy, and she clearly needs better spectacles if she can't see her face in this glass," I said.

We finished our work by noon and went to the servants' hall for our next job. Ms. Woodround had not changed the board, so we assumed we were done for the day.

We headed to the castle gardens for a walk before lunch. The gardens were right outside the ballroom, but the curtains were closed, so we could not see inside.

The garden was said to be the most impressive part of the castle, aside from the stained glass window in the throne room. A stone path led us on a walk through many breathtaking plants and flowers. I hoped we might be able to see the Queen outside in the garden where it was said that she spends most of her time.

"My mom has a garden, but it's not as amazing as this one. She would teach me all the types of flowers she had planted. Oh, that flower is a rose, and the one that has the bees all around it is a hyacinth; aren't they so pretty with their purple petals?" Bethany went on and on about flowers and how she and her mom would plant them together during the spring when she was young. I was impressed by how many flowers she could rattle off the top of her head. As we walked, Bethany would point out each and every flower and explain what type they were.

"Once, my mom and I were planting lilies, and a fly came, and she accidentally inhaled it! I screamed at her to spit it out, but she couldn't because she was choking!" Bethany said.

"Wait, what? She choked on a fly? I can't even think about that without wanting to throw up," I said gagging.

"What happened next?" Charles said.

"Well, I started to pat her on the back, and eventually, she coughed the fly out," Bethany explained.

"Eww," Charles said.

"The dead fly landed right on her lap. It was so gross."

"That's disgusting," I laughed.

Bethany's stories made me smile. The more I thought about her and her mom, the more I began to think about my parents. My heart ached. This was the first time that I would be away from them. I began to recall memories of my parents and me playing tag in the house. I was so young and didn't take the time to appreciate the good times we used to have. I wished I could turn back the clock and be a little kid again with no troubles whatsoever. Bethany started to talk to me, pulling me out of the clouds and back into reality.

"Liam?" she said, snapping her fingers in front of my face.

"Oh, yeah, what?" I said.

"I asked what your favorite food is."

"Oh, umm…chicken. No, instead, maybe muffins no, baked chicken is right," I said, trying to regain my focus.

"So, Charles, you like watermelon, and I like potatoes with cheese, and Liam likes baked chicken," Bethany said.

"Oh, getting fancy are we? Cheese and potatoes! Well then, I change mine to butterscotch bread pudding if we are being fancy. I would love to see you 'peasants' top that," Charles said in a posh sounding voice with a little disdain like Ms. Woodround's.

"In that case, mine is now lemon pudding," I said.

We walked until we reached the end of the garden. At that point, it was time to go back. When we got back to the servants' hall, Ms. Woodround finally updated the posted jobs. Under our names read, "Clean the floors in the servants' room". I sighed, and we began to clean again.

When we finally finished, it was time for dinner. Oatmeal was served today. Sadly, we didn't notice anyone in the servant's hall that we knew. Finding a seat might be a lot harder than it seems.

"Oh look, Jeremy just walked in to get his dinner. Why don't we sit with him?" Charles suggested.

I nodded, and Bethany just gave her classic smile.

"So, how is life as a servant these days? Ms. Woodround driving you crazy?" Jeremy said, sitting down.

Charles shrugged.

"Not to the point of totally flipping out. Hopefully, it stays that way."

"Is she really that rude all the time?" I asked.

"Yeah. All day, every day," Jeremy said.

"Is there any reason for it?" I asked.

"I actually don't know. Blah! This oatmeal is so bland! I hate it! Why do they serve us oatmeal for dinner?" Jeremy asked with disgust.

"They don't really care much for flavor in the kitchen," I added.

"You guys ever had salmon with a nice butter sauce? That's what King Bartholomew is eating tonight! Queen Emily had the cooks make a pudding! A whole pudding! What I would do for just a bowl of it!" Jeremy said, drooling over the thought.

"I am beginning to think that these protestors are right these days! I mean, what they have the cooks make is very lavish. It is so expensive to get the ingredients and takes so much time! Like, rare and expensive ingredients every night must be using up the kingdom's money or something. I know he is the King and all, but come on, he can't even follow his great grandfather's own words!" Bethany whispered.

"I can agree with that, but not the protestors! The protesters are insane!" Jeremy said.

"Wait, hold on a second, what protestors?" Charles asked.

"Yeah, and what's this about his great grandfather's word?" I asked.

"Oh, that's simple, King Harry made a promise that every Drandor would not take over too much of the King's power and not use up money for excessive amounts of unnecessary things such as fancy meals, clothes, and furniture. This was not only a way to conserve money, but also to help ensure that the Drandor line would not end or leave the throne," Jeremy explained.

"Drandor? As in the last names of the royal family, right?" Charles asked.

"Yeah," I answered.

"That's smart. What about these protests? Are they actually happening? Why have I never heard of this?" I said, confused.

"Makes sense. The royal committee tries their hardest not to let that information spread, so the rest of the Outer Kingdom doesn't join in. There is a group of people that protest the fact that the king is doing everything his great grandfather said not to do. They gather together and protest sometimes during fancy events the King holds. They don't like the royals' lavish lifestyle," Bethany said so quietly that you could barely tell if any words were coming out of her mouth.

"What do they do when they protest?" I asked.

"Usually, they bring pitchforks and yell loudly. It's extremely scary for us servants, though," Bethany shuddered.

"I can't remember what happened the last time they protested. I believe it was during the Winter Ball, back in January," Jeremy added.

"I'm a bit nervous for the Prince's Birthday Ball in a few weeks. I hope they don't get violent," Bethany said.

"Wait, Prince George's Birthday Ball is in a few weeks?" I asked with excitement.

Everyone who's anyone is at the Prince's Birthday Ball. All of the kids and adults in the Outer Kingdom envy anyone who goes to the

Prince's Birthday Ball. The only people in Brendsworth who have ever gone were the Lord and Lady of Brendsworth.

Still, I could barely process the new information about the protesting. I could only help but wonder, what other secrets about the Outer Kingdom are being kept from me?

Chapter 10

A week had passed since my first day as a servant. I feel less like a rookie now that I have some experience working here. Bethany helped teach Charles and I all the tricks to working at the royal palace. However, Charles and I are still not used to waking up so early.

"Are we even getting paid enough for this?" I groaned, rolling out of bed.

"Only five silver coins a day? So, no!" Charles cried.

We arrived at servants' hall early and read the chores for the day. Ms. Woodround gave our group the best job out of all four groups. We had the honor of cleaning up King Bartholomew's room and sweeping the dining hall. I was so excited. We could have a chance at meeting the King or even the Queen today!

Bethany tied her hair back into a neat bun.

"Do I look presentable? I have only ever seen the King from a distance so I want to make a good impression if we actually meet him in person. Oh, this is so exciting!" Bethany said, clapping her hands and bouncing up and down.

"Yeah, you look formal enough. I mean I know it's cool and all to clean in the high priority areas, but in reality she just gave us a ton of work!" Charles pointed out.

"Come on, Charles, it's still cool! Even if we don't see the king, we can see what living rich is like," I said.

"That's true. After all my years of working here, this will be the first time I get to clean a royal family members room," Bethany said with a smile.

"Let's go get the cleaning equipment," I suggested.

We climbed a circular staircase leading up to the second floor. The whole castle was built up of a variety of large stones that were all different shapes and sizes. The breathtaking architecture of the castle demonstrated the power and wealth the royal family had. Windows lined the stairs we walked up, showing off the beautiful city. We reached the top of the stairs to find ourselves standing in a short hallway. A long red carpet stretched across the hall, ending with a wall displaying an intricate tapestry of horses running through a field. Windows lined the wall to the right, while doors lined the wall to left. Bethany cautiously walked down the hall, trying to remember which room belonged to King Bartholomew.

"I think it's this one," she pointed to the third door.

At first, I was hesitant to open the door, but once I did, I was surprised at what I found. Right when you first walk in, you gaze upon a huge bed with a green canopy and a frame made of gold. I walked around the bed admiring it.

"Is that gold?" I asked myself out loud, in shock.

Maybe, the mobs were right? The Kings bedroom is extremely lavish and expensive-looking.

"I guess you where right Bethany. This defiantly looks like a king's room to me," I said in awe.

"Aww," Bethany said from behind me.

She stood behind Charles who was petting an old Great Dane. The dog sat on a large green pillow in the corner of the room. Above his bed was a gold plaque that read 'Reginald'.

"Hi Reginald! Guys, I literally love dogs so much! I never knew he had a dog," Charles admitted, petting Reginald.

"Hello, Reginald," I said, patting his head.

"I would consider myself as more of a cat person, but he is still so cute," Bethany said.

"Personally, I also like cats better," I confessed.

"Ugh, you cat people make me sick. Don't look at them, Reginald," Charles said, hugging the dog.

"Okay, guys, we should get to work," Bethany said, grabbing the broom.

"I call shaking out the rugs! I want to finish my part quickly, so I can sit with Reginald," Charles patted Reginald on the head and hurried off with the rugs.

"I will dust I guess."

I took the opportunity to explore the room more. I dusted the silver frame of a tiny painting of King Bartholomew and the shelf upon which it sat. I found two more small paintings to dust. The first was of Reginald, and the second was of Queen Emily. In the painting, Queen Emily had her brown hair in a coiled braid on each side of her head. She wore an elegant blood red dress that was lined with gold. If you could not tell by now how rich they were, you could take a look at the amount of jewelry she was wearing. In the painting she showed off her big fat diamond ring by elegantly placing her hands on her lap. The painting must have been made when she was younger because now she has more wrinkles and grey hair.

I continued cleaning and dusted a large bureau that had candles and golden trinkets displayed upon it. I accidentally dropped a gold quill behind the bureau.

"Great! Just perfect," I mumbled angrily.

I pushed the bureau out of the way and was shocked at what I found. There was a large hole in the wall filled to the top with gold and money. I looked around and made sure that Bethany was not looking. She was too busy sweeping in a corner.

What I just discovered could get me thrown in jail or worse... KILLED!

King Bartholomew has been hoarding tax money and gold in a hole inside his room! This is all supposed to be in the Outer Kingdom bank where it will be spent on the people and villages of the Outer Kingdom. The mob was right! He is a thief! I suddenly lost all the respect and love that I once had for King Bartholomew. Our king is a thief! Why would he need all this anyways?! He literally has a gold bed-frame!

"Liam, what is that...?" Bethany said with a worried tone in her voice.

I whipped my head around. Oh, no! Bethany saw the gold. Just then, Charles came in after shaking the rugs out.

"Guys, I finished the ru-" he dropped the rugs on the floor.

"Liam..." Bethany said, still cautious.

"OH MY LORD! Liam, what is that?" He said loudly. Bethany shushed him.

"Liam, what did you do!?" Bethany whispered urgently.

"I swear I just moved this and then there it was! It looks like the King has been stealing from the Outer Kingdom and hoarding the tax money here," I said, disgusted by what I discovered.

"Okay, so I would rather not be executed so…let's just never EVER tell anyone about this!" Charles said, becoming paranoid. I didn't blame him for feeling that way; I was nervous too.

"Agreed," I said.

"Yeah, this is ridiculous, though! Why would the King be so…so ugh! GREEDY!" Bethany said angrily.

"This is terrible. I mean, what kind of a king does something like- I HEAR FOOTSTEPS!" Charles whispered loudly.

My heart raced. We had to cover up what I found. We put everything back where we found it at lightning speed.

"Be calm, guys, and very quiet," Bethany ordered.

If it's Uncle William coming, we will be in a world of trouble. If it's Ms. Woodround, we will be in even more trouble. If it's King Bartholomew, let's say we will not have to worry about eating a disgusting meal tonight or eating in general!

I grabbed the dusting rag, and Bethany ran over to the broom. Charles leapt head first into the rugs. A simple ewerer walked by us carrying a bucket of hot water. He must be bringing hot water for Queen Emily to bath in.

I let out a sigh. Bethany was using the broom to hold herself up, and Charles popped up from under the rugs.

"That was a close one," she said.

"Yeah. I agree entirely! You guys, we can't tell anyone about this. Got it? If anyone asks please do not reveal I was the idiot who found it," I pleaded.

They nodded.

"Of course we would not rat you out," Bethany said.

In the end, Charles was right. It was more work than it was worth seeing King Bartholomew's room. I still wished I had never seen it.

We walked downstairs to the dining hall and grabbed the equipment for our second job. The rest of the afternoon was spent sweeping the large dining room.

"Yes! Finally! WE FINISHED!" Charles cheered.

All of a sudden, the sounds of heels approached the dining hall. Ms. Woodround burst into the room. Finally, it was my chance to show her she had no reason to hate me because we did such a good job cleaning.

"Ah, young Mr. Rocklen. Is there any reason why none of you are sweeping?" she said.

"Well, Ms. Woodround, we just finished. We were just about to go empty this dust bucket," Bethany said, gesturing to the bucket in front of her.

"Hmm...I don't believe you are finished yet," Ms. Woodround said. Her words were like an arrow to my chest. In a split second, she walked over and did the worst thing imaginable. I watched in horror as she tipped over the dust bucket with her heel. The dirt spilled all over the floor. She smiled.

"Happy sweeping!"

We were all in shock. This woman was insane! Why would she create more work for us!? And not to mention, make the castle look dirty by doing so! We angrily cleaned up the mess she made and then headed to dump the dust bucket before she could come back and tip it over again.

Throughout the rest of the week, we were cautiously on edge after the incident in the King's bedroom. I was waiting for someone to point a finger at us and say 'That's them! They are the ones snooping in the King's bedroom! Arrest them! Execute them!' I shuddered at the thought.

Not to mention, Ms. Woodround was also torturing us constantly. When Charles was shaking out the rugs near the stables, Ms. Woodround came to inspect him. She made him shake out a single rug for twenty minutes straight. When Charles was finished, she ended up causing him to drop the rug in the dirt making him start all over again. This, however, was not the worst of it. We had been polishing the dinner plates when Ms. Woodround came in and "accidentally" spilled the polish all over the floor. Bethany had to buy new polish and not to mention, we had to clean up the stained floor.

However, out of the three of us, she treated me the worst. She made sure I did every job twice- whether it was 'accidentally" tipping over the bucket of dust, dropping food on rugs that I just cleaned, or tracking dirt all over the freshly mopped floors for me to clean up.

What made this most aggravating was her reaction. Every single time she creates a mess for us, she smiles and says, 'Whoops, clumsy me!'

"Charles, I don't know if I can take her any longer," I said, plopping down on my bed face first.

"Liam, you don't even want to know what she did to Bethany today," Charles said, sitting down on his bed.

"What? What did that dark witch do this time?" I asked, preparing myself to hear the normal evil action of Ms. Woodround.

"Well, Ms. Woodround called Bethany into her office for an inspection. She said that Bethany's aproned needed to be cleaned and then had Bethany update her moms contact information. So, Bethany took off her apron and began to fill out the paper. While she was doing that, Ms. Woodround 'accidentally' spilt ink on Bethany's brown dress. Bethany said she just responded with her usual 'clumsy me'. Right now, Bethany is trying to clean it off," he replied.

"Wow, if that isn't one of Ms. Woodround's dirty schemes, I don't know what is!" I said angrily.

"Bethany suspects Ms. Woodround only does this to us because were friends with you. And it's kinda obvious she doesn't like you because you are Mr. Rocklen's nephew. It's stupid. I know, but there is no changing that ladies mind about you. Hopefully, Ms. Woodround will eventually tire herself out with the torture and go bother someone else," Charles said, beginning to read out of "Sir Frederick's Adventures".

"Hey, have you ever met an elf?" he asked.

"No, why? Is that the chapter your on?" I asked.

"Yeah, it says here their race is going extinct. Soon, it will just be centaurs, humans, witches, mermaids, trolls, and fairies," Charles said.

"Is that supposed to sound like not that much?" I asked with a chuckle.

"Yeah. But, it's sad to see so many magical creatures going extinct. I mean what I would do to bring back wizards. I would love to have that magical power," he said.

"Yeah me too."

"Oh, it says here that elf's can be identified by pointed ears and white hair."

"Pretty interesting," I commented.

"I wonder what I would look like with pointed ears? I bet I would look like a donkey," Charles asked with a chuckle, attempting to cheer me up.

Sadly, I couldn't take Ms. Woodround's bullying off my mind. Maybe she was just evil?

Chapter 11

Today is two days away from Prince George's birthday party. The castle was bustling with noise and life. Ms. Woodround had us creating decorations and preparing for the party for the past few days. We had to hang up new drapes and shake out the tapestries. The other groups were carrying chairs into the throne and ballroom. Today, all the groups were scurrying around, shining the thrones and sconces. Bethany and I were ordered to shine the floors. Almost every worker in the castle has been busy trying to get this place ready for the Prince's party.

"As organizer for this birthday party, I must have it perfect! Mr. Brockfur, that is on an angle! Ms. Sunpink, you are not shining that enough. Oh, for goodness sake, Mr. Vilenter, stop sitting down in that chair!"

Edward glared at her and sat up. Clarity started to shine the throne at such a fast pace you could barely see her hands. Charles mumbled to himself and his eyebrow sunk into an angry expression.

"This is getting a bit excessive," Bethany whispered to me.

"How many days have we been cleaning for this party? Five?" I asked.

"Sadly, I mean I would like to not clean the same thing every day!" She whispered.

"Oh, come on! Stop tilting!" Charles whispered at the sconce he was putting up.

"Just don't make a fuss! We want to get out quickly!" Bethany reminded me.

Ms. Woodround had promised us the day off if we finished early. Finally, she would allow us to leave the castle and go explore the town. We had been waiting ever since I got here for the chance to go.

It was almost noon, and our work was nearing an end. However, Ms. Woodround was doing her best to make us do the work over and over again. None of us listened though; we pushed through it.

One of King Bartholomew's advisors strolled through the throne room giving us judgmental looks. He inspected our work, walking around slowly with his hands behind his back. Ms. Woodround noticed him.

"Keep going Ms. Brooks! Mr. Rocklen is that the best you can do?!" She ordered, eyeing the advisor.

I rolled my eyes. Bethany and I have been shining the same floor for hours. It cannot possibly get any shinier.

"Excuse me, Ms. Woodround I presume?" He said approaching her.

"Yes, sir. How can I assist you?" She said with a curtsy.

"Are these your servants?" He asked, taking off his monocle and beginning to clean it with a handkerchief.

"Oh, why yes, they are."

"Okay, Ms. Woodround, tell me, how long have these servants been cleaning this room?"

"Oh, all morning sir," she said with a prideful smile.

"Now tell me, Ms. Woodround, why are we having these servants work all morning in the same spot? It appears the room is not getting any cleaner than it is already," he sternly said.

"Well, I-"

"So, by having them clean all morning are you telling me that you are incapable of instructing your staff to keep this room clean regularly? And you are telling me you are pleased with the fact they are in the way of the other workers here? And you are fine wasting the kingdom's time and resources by having them use all of the polish on a single throne?"

"You see, sir-"

"Because if that is what you are saying, things are not looking good for you, Ms. Woodround. You know a lot of women and men in this kingdom would die for your job. Don't think we can't find you a replacement, I assure you it will be easy," the advisor said placing his monocle back on his face.

Everyone's jaws dropped to the floor. The whole room was silent as we watched Ms. Woodround being torched at a stake by the King's advisor. She was speechless. Justice had been served.

"I suggest you start taking better care of your staff, before you loose it. Ahem. Listen here, you are all finished for today. Clear yourselves of this area so the decorators can prepare for the party. Thank you and good day," He placed his hands behind his back and strolled away.

I almost felt like clapping as he exited the room. Everyone's face had a smile on it except Ms. Woodround.

"You heard the man. Stop disrupting the workers and leave!" Ms. Woodround ordered. She fled the room, her face bright red from embarrassment.

"YES, WE ARE DONE!" Sasha shouted.

"YES!" I high-fived Bethany.

"Who was that guy? He might be my hero!" Charles asked Bethany.

"That was King Bartholomew's main financial advisor. His name is Ian Green III. His family has worked for the royal family for generations," Bethany informed us.

"Wow, I already love that guy," I said.

"That was a whole bunch of cold hard facts he just said," Charles nodded in respect.

"So, ready to go to the market?" Bethany asked.

"Yeah! Let's go right now," I said.

We made our way out of the castle and began our decent into the city.

"I have two gold and three bronze coins. I don't really need anything though," Charles said.

"I have three gold and two silver," I said holding my coin pouch tightly in my hands.

The city was bustling with people. Regular shoppers rushed from store to store while tourists moseyed around, looking through the windows. Bethany led us past houses and apartments to the shops.

"Guys, let's go in here! I love this place."

Bethany skipped into a toyshop called 'Linkler's Toys.' As soon as I walked into the shop, the smell of wood and the sound of loud children overcame me. I looked around; there were shelves covered with toys and a counter next to the door. Bethany led us to the back of the store. A sign read "Magical Items". Children ran around and grabbed toys off the shelf to buy.

"Guys, I used to come to this shop almost every day. My mom would give me a couple of loose bronze coins she would find and let me go buy a toy from here. Oh, and Mr. Linker is the nicest old man ever! Plus, the stuff in this shop is great. I mean this is some high quality toys. Look here, it says invisible ink. That would be good to prank Ms. Woodround," Bethany suggested.

"Ha, look, here is a cup that water never comes out of!" Charles picked up the wooden cup.

"That's such a great idea! We can use that to prank Ms. Woodround," I said.

"Oh my gosh, yes! That will be perfect!" Bethany said.

Bethany took the cup and brought it to the counter.

"Hey Mr. Linkler!" She said loud enough for the old man to hear.

"Ah, hello Bethany! Looks like you brought some friends with you. I am Mr. Linkler!" He smiled at us.

"Hello," Charles and I said in unison.

"So, looks like you got some fairy magic products here. Those always cost more than the normal toys here. But, for you, my most popular customer, I here will give you half price," he offered.

"Oh, no. That won't be necessary."

"No, no. Here, just give me the two gold coins and be on your way," he insisted.

"Thank you, sir," Bethany smiled while paying the man.

"Now, you folks here better have a wonderful day!" He said.

Bethany continued to show us around Trisanburg City. We gazed into a candle makers shop, watching him practice the art of candle making. Charles pointed to the bakery and drooled over the sweet smell of cakes. Bethany walked by a dress shop and stopped us to look in through the shop windows.

"Guys, we have to go in," she said with a twinkle in her eye.

"Umm…I don't want to buy a dress anytime soon," Charles said.

"Ugh, it's for me, silly. Remember when Ms. Woodround spilled polish on this dress? I need a new one," Bethany said, going in.

"Are you going?" I asked Charles.

He shook his head. I walked into the shop and instantly took in the scent of flowers. The smell was very similar to the smell of the meadow next to my house. Bethany walked towards the back, looking through dresses and fabrics.

"Oh, you came in. Good," she said, waving me over.

"That looks like a cool color," I said, pointing at the one she was holding, trying to connect with Bethany.

"I don't think that green is my color. What do you think of this pink one?" She held up a long dress that had a big bow on the front and bows all over the sleeves.

Sometimes, being a good friend means trying to connect with them and value their interests, so I was trying hard to adhere to Bethany's interests. However, I don't know much about dresses.

"That looks so weird," I said, laughing and then realizing I might have hurt her feelings.

"Oh…sorry," I said.

She started to laugh and agreed it did look ridiculous. We looked at three more dresses. Each one was even funnier looking than the last one. Then, we came across a big ball gown on display.

Even though I don't care much about dresses, I could not help but be in awe of this one. The dress was a dark pink color that popped out, screaming, "look at me". It had puffed sleeves and a heart-shaped top. The bottom of the gown was big and puffed out with layers of white cloth underneath. A rose crown was placed next to the mannequin with a pair of white and red shoes. I looked at Bethany. I saw the same excitement in her eyes that I had when I first saw my sword.

"Oh wow…this dress is made for a princess!" she said, still staring at it.

"That must be at least fifty gold coins at best," I said, trying to pull her mind back into reality.

"Yeah, you're right…" she sighed.

I acted quickly and looked for a new dress.

"Hey, what about this one?" I held out a plain red dress with short sleeves.

In an attempt to cheer her up, I made an effort to make this dress sound as good as the last one. She smiled and held the dress up.

"See how nice the seam is on it! It is a real beauty! Look at how strong this fabric is, oh so soft," I joked.

"Thank you, Liam, you're so nice. Red is my favorite color, so I love it even more," she said, giggling.

"Really? Red and green are my favorite colors," I said with enthusiasm.

Bethany bought the red dress and we walked back outside.

"Well, that couldn't have taken longer," Charles complained.

"Let's go back and get dinner," I suggested.

"Yeah, I have been sitting out here listening to my stomach growl," Charles complained.

We got back to our room and got ready for dinner. I looked over at Uncle Williams neatly made bed and frowned. Unfortunately, I had not seen Uncle William much in the past few days because he had gotten so caught up in setting up for the Prince's Birthday Ball.

As we entered the servants' hall, the cook brought out a bowl of chicken soup made from leftover chicken. Chopped potatoes and carrots accompanied the meat.

"I heard that because of the protests, the King's reputation has been hurting, so they can't afford to throw out leftovers," Edward said, shoving a spoon into his mouth.

Charles had become good friends with Jeremy, Sasha, and Edward over the past few weeks during their breaks. Now, he invites them to sit with us. Thanks to Charles's more outgoing personality, Bethany and I have also become friends with them. Sasha is a year older than Jeremy and Edward, who are nineteen. From spending time with them, we have learned a lot from their life experiences and received some helpful advice. However, calling them wise roles models might not always be accurate, seeing as they all share a hobby of pranking Ms. Woodround.

"Did I ever tell you the first prank I ever played on Ms. Woodround?" Jeremy said with excitement.

"I?" Sasha said, putting her hands on her hips.

"Sorry, I mean, we," he said correcting himself.

"I don't recall," I lied, still knowing that he told us over five times.

"It was around our first day; that was about three years ago. Anyways, she had told us the groups, and we were in the same group. So, we had been cleaning all day, and she insulted Edward, so Sasha suggested that we should play a prank on her. Sasha had one in mind," he said talking fast.

"Wow, you tell the story so well," Sasha said sarcastically.

Edward leaned over and kissed her cheek. I learned that they have been dating for two years, which is one year after they all first met. Edward is very tall and pale, with stylish black hair, while Sasha is tall with caramel colored skin and charcoal black wavy hair that falls past her shoulders. Her green eyes vividly remind me of spring and green grass while Edwards were a cold icy blue color.

"Anyways, we decided to put a bucket of water over the servants' room door. Get this, though, it was during dinner!" He started laughing. Jeremy laughed so hard he could barely finish his story. Tears started to come out of his eyes.

"Okay...okay, I'm good. Anyways, we knew right when she would be coming in and when the door opened, BAM! Right on her head! She yelled and screamed at the whole room trying to find the culprits, but she never knew it was us!" he bragged.

"Yeah, we have only been caught three times. Pretty impressive," Edward said.

"I remember when that happened. Everyone in the castle talked about it. I never got to see it though because I was younger back then and only worked in the day time," Bethany commented.

"The first was the best prank," Sasha bragged.

"Ehh…I don't know if it's the best, but it's pretty okay," Charles said.

"What? Oh, do you think you can do better?"

"Why, yes, I think we three can come up with a prank that is better than that," Charles challenged.

"Three?" Bethany questioned.

"Yeah! Just you wait guys!" Charles said crossing his arms.

"Pfft, I would like to see you try," Jeremy challenged.

We finished up our soup and left the servants' hall. Later, when we got to our room, I made a promise to myself that I would find more time to read, so I took the time to get a chapter in.

'Sir Frederick walked into the woods and discovered a large cave. That cave had a small light glimmering inside. 'Looks like there is a torch in there- I know for a fact there is only one creature that lights torches in caves besides humans.' Sir Frederick snuck into the cave with his sword in hand. Hero's Note: always have a weapon at hand when going into a possibly dangerous situation. Inside the cave was a troll eating a deer carcass. The cave reeked of dead animals. A collection of random junk was scattered on the floor. Trolls are known to be messy and idiotic. However, their amazing strength has an advantage over any human. Never try to take one on alone. Most trolls are ten to fifteen feet tall, but some can get to a height of nearly twenty feet tall. Only a skilled fighter, like myself, can take down a troll at that height. The troll that stood steps away from Sir Frederick was average sized.'

My eyelids began to fall, and the book fell out of my hand. I fell into a deep sleep.

The next morning was the day before the Prince's Birthday Ball. It was more hectic than ever in the castle. Ms. Woodround had given our group the job of cleaning the ballroom, which was very exciting. The ballroom is one of the sights in the castle people rarely see. It is only ever open if there is an event as important as this one going on.

On our walk to the ballroom, people were running around and putting up fancy sconces and decorating the halls with flowers. The hallway we stood in is called the Main Hall, and it is located next to the Throne Room. Edward told me that the Main Hall is the most prestigious hallway in the entire castle. Empty suits of armor lined the hallway along with tapestries and sconces. The dining hall and ballroom are located in this hallway, which makes it the only hall that guests will pass through.

We pushed open the big, wooden doors to reveal a pitch-black dark room. Before we left, Ms. Woodround instructed that we close the doors behind us as soon as we enter the room. She went on about how no one could see the room before the party. We followed her instructions, not wanting to risk causing a reason for her to hate us even more.

"I am starting to suspect that Ms. Woodround was lying when she instructed we have to close the doors behind so no one sees the ballroom early," Bethany said slowly closing the doors behind her.

"It's so dark in here, I can't see a thing," I said almost tripping over myself.

"Can we just open the doors again, Ms. Woodround was obviously just being a jerk," Charles said, getting fed up.

We stumbled around blindly in the dark. I felt the side of a smooth wall and walked around the room feeling the wall.

"Yeah Bethany, just open the doors. It is really dark in here," I said, feeling like an idiot.

"Umm, I can't find the door," Bethany sheepishly said.

"Let's try and find a curtain then," I suggested.

"This is so dumb. I mean how can it be this dark in here," Charles continued to complain.

"Hats off to who ever designed these curtains thought. They really let no light in," Bethany pointed out.

There must be a curtain here somewhere, I thought. Suddenly, I felt something soft in my way. Please be a curtain. I slid the fabric to my left, shining light into the pitch-black room.

"Found it!" I called out, opening the rest of the curtain, which caused the room to light up. My eyes stung from the sudden change.

The light revealed Bethany in the middle of the room and Charles on the exact opposite side of the room that I was on. We waited until our eyes adjusted to finish opening the rest of the tall, red curtains that covered five tall windows. Each of the windows stretched from the bottom of the floor to the top of the ceiling. They lined the wall, revealing the Queen's Garden outside. The garden stretched across the length of the room, providing a perfect view of the flowers. Two of the windows were actually glass doors that led straight out to a large stone circle shaped patio. I could imagine people dancing from inside the ballroom out to the stone path during the ball.

"Oh, wow, it's amazing! Look, you can see the outside gardens!" Bethany pointed out the window to where bees flew from flower to flower.

I made my way to the middle of the ballroom. My boots created a tapping noise when they hit the large creamy white colored tiles on the floor. The walls were a light blue color, which caused the gold sconces on the walls to pop out like ships on the ocean.

I watched as Charles walked around with his head up, staring at the ceiling. I look up as well to see what he is looking at. The ceiling had a beautiful mosaic of gold flowers and vines leading into a golden Trisanburg Elk in the center. My mouth dropped. It was amazing. I had never seen such intricate art in my life. There are not many artists in Brendsworth.

"The inside is just as amazing as the outside!" Charles said to Bethany.

"I wish we could go to the ball as guests. I would love to dance to the elegant music in this ballroom," Bethany said sighing. I walked over and took her hands and began to dance. She was surprised at first but then started to laugh.

"Liam!" She giggled.

"And now for the elegant music!" Charles laughed and soon began whistling a tune. I smiled at Bethany and spun her around the room.

"I believe that your next dance partner is umm…Prince Mort of the far lands of the West," I announced, spinning her over to Charles.

"Who me? Oh, okay. Ahem. Madam," Charles played along.

He took her hand and began a more formal waltz than what I did. I took over the music and hummed a tune from the Winter Festival.

"Okay, okay. Thanks guys, but, we have to get to work," Bethany laughed.

The fun had to end eventually, so we got to work sweeping the dust and dirt. I watched as Bethany would twirl and dance with the broom every so often. Charles helped me open the large glass doors so we could sweep the dust out of the ballroom. I stepped outside in the June heat and felt my energy being sucked out of my body.

"Why is it so hot?" I complained.

"Yeah, it's only June. It should not be this hot out," Charles agreed.

"Guys, you have to agree the heat is so much better than the cold," Bethany said from inside.

"Nope. I can just put on more clothes when it gets cold. It's not like I can take off my skin when it's hot out," Charles argued.

"Eww, that's a little weird," I said walking back inside.

We finished sweeping, but still had to scrub and polish the tiles. I closed the doors and got back to work.

We are going to be the last people to clean this floor before the ball, so it must be spotless. I carefully and precisely scrubbed each individual tile.

We scrubbed the floor peacefully until I caught the faint earth-shattering noise of heels clicking on the floor. My heart jumped out of my chest. Ms. Woodround had been torturing me so much lately that I feel terrified when I even hear the sound of heels on the floor. I shuddered and braced myself. Bethany reacted like a deer and froze. Charles looked like he had just seen a ghost.

"Ah, if it isn't young Mr. Rocklen. This floor needs to shine for the royal family and guests! And I don't see any shining!" She walked over to our water bucket and tipped it over.

I watched in agony as the dirty water spread across the tiles I had just cleaned. Ms. Woodround walked over to the windows and gazed over the garden. She took a deep loud breath.

"Ahhh, what a beautiful day! Isn't it, Mr. Brockfur?" She walked over to Charles. He stubbornly didn't answer her.

"Isn't it?" she said, placing her heel right on his hand.

Bethany gasped. I squeezed the sponge in my hand so tight, all the water drained out of it. Charles kept his head down and refused to make eye contact.

"Hmm?" She waited for his reply.

"Yes," Charles said, without moving his teeth.

She smiled wickedly. We were no longer dealing with a sane women-this lady is a psychopath!

"Well, looks like you have a lot more work to do, get to it," Ms. Woodround left the room laughing manically.

As soon as she left, Bethany rushed over to Charles.

"Oh, my gosh! Are you okay!?"

"Yeah, I'm fine," Charles brushed her away.

"You should have punched her for that," I said.

"She is so evil! Why...why would she do such a thing!? There is no way she is getting away with this! We have to do something!" Bethany said, holding up his hand for me to see. A large indented circle was in the back of his hand.

"It's fine, guys," he said, pulling his hand back.

"We have to get back at her!" Bethany insisted.

"Bethany, I thought you said you didn't want to pull a prank on her?" I asked.

"We have to do it after what she just did to Charles!" Bethany said. Charles smiled.

"But, doesn't it seem like a bad day to do it? It's the day before the Prince's Birthday Ball," I asked cautiously.

"Ugh, Liam! Ms. Woodround should have thought of that before she stepped on our friends hand!" Bethany complained.

"I think Bethany is right. She won't even suspect us since it's always Edward and them all pulling pranks. Besides, she can't even get them or us in trouble if she doesn't have evidence we did it. And Sasha says she is almost always to angry to even go an accuse anyone." Charles said perking up.

"She has to pay! Isn't it you she has tortured the most?" Bethany convinced me.

"All right, I guess…" I said.

We began to concoct a plan while we cleaned up the mess Ms. Woodround made. After carefully considering all possible outcomes, we figured out the perfect plan. Bethany would start the plan off by heading into Ms. Woodround's room.

"So, I say 'Ms. Woodround, I overheard the other workers talking, and they said they will break open the extra pillows right before dinner and scatter the feathers all over the throne room you worked so hard to clean, so they could make a statement about the food.' Is that right?" Bethany confirmed, smiling.

"Good, just emphasize the 'you'. While you're in there, me and Liam are going to be in the dining hall getting her meal ready," Charles said, smiling deviously.

My job was to steal hot sauce from the kitchen. I was up for the challenge.

Overall, the plan was quite impressive. Ms. Woodround gets to have strawberry jam in her oatmeal anytime we have it. Obviously, this upsets all of the workers because no one else gets any flavor in their oatmeal. So, this is the perfect way to punish her for hurting Charles and for getting special treatment when she doesn't even work as hard as the rest of us.

"Let's get this plan into action," Charles said picking up the cleaning equipment.

"Let's do it!" I say, exiting the room and following Bethany down the hall to the servant's quarters. I gave her a thumbs-up and mouthed the words 'good luck' as she entered Ms. Woodrounds room. I could faintly hear through the wall Ms. Woodround talking.

"Ugh, Ms. Brooks what do you want?" Ms. Woodround said as she entered.

I opened the door to the kitchen and quickly remembered my lines and task. I enter and was overwhelmed by the smells of spices and the sounds of pots and pans. The kitchen was filled with skullies cleaning and cooks scrambling around trying to get the royal family's meal served. I walked quickly to the cabinets in the back. No one seemed to notice that I was even there! I maneuvered my way around the busy workers. They were all rushing around and shouting back and forth. I even noticed Roman, cooking what looked like a sauce for the meal.

Thankfully, he didn't even give me a sideways glance. This didn't surprise me.

I ducked under a cook who was holding a hot pan. Thankfully, I reached the shelves without getting in anyone's way. Quickly, I scanned for hot sauce.

Right now, Bethany should be rushing with Ms. Woodround to the throne room to catch the hooligans and stop the plot that we made up. That means Charles has filled the magical cup with water and placed it at Ms. Woodrounds personal table. I grabbed a glass bottle that was filled with ground up chili peppers in liquid form. I smirked and headed out of the cook's storeroom.

"Eh, boy! Take this to the King's table!" a cook said to me.

I froze. Darn it. The cook thinks I am a server. There is no way I am going to get out of this. I have to play the part.

I took the plate of small cooked chicken breasts surrounded by cabbage leaves and cherry tomatoes. I slipped the hot sauce in my pocket without anyone noticing.

Five other men and women formed a line in front of me. We walked in a straight line into the throne room. In perfect unison, we walked down the main hallway. At the end of the hall was the dining room. Everything looked similar to the last time I cleaned in here except, this time, the enormous chandelier was lite, spreading light across the entire room. I followed the line. My stomach turned. I'm not a part of the kitchen staff! I have no idea what to do and where to go. The line dispersed and went to each of the dinner guests they were supposed to serve.

That is when I realized this would be my chance to see the royal family up close! I could not believe it. Byron will be so jealous! Heck- the whole region will be jealous!

The man in front of me moved toward the Prince, giving me a clear view of the King and Queen. My mouth dropped open, and I could not believe I was looking at the royal family. Queen Emily had aged since her portrait, but she still had on more jewelry than I could count. I admired how polite and proper she was.

King Bartholomew sat proudly in his big chair. He wore a big crown on his big baldhead that indicated his royalty. Along with that, he wore red shirt with a gold and leopard print cape. I could tell King Bartholomew has expensive taste.

As I got closer to him I noticed his meal fit his big appetite. He had a big stomach, but his gold belt kept it all in…sort of. I carefully placed the food in front of him; he didn't even give me a sideways glance. I moved to each of the royal family members and gave them their food. I have never been more nervous in my life. If I mess up, all hell will break loose.

There were three other people at the table that I had never seen before. Two adults, who appeared to be noble, sat at the table along with a beautiful girl in an expensive dress. She had flawless brown skin with beautiful black hair piled high upon her head.

Why are they having dinner with the royal family? The other servers quickly got back in line. I rushed to catch them. We all stood up straight and waited by the exit.

"So, Lady Jules, Lord Russel, how is Cordelia's singing going?" Queen Emily asked.

"Oh, her singing is the prettiest in all the land!" Lady Jules exclaimed.

"I am confident my daughter sings the best out of everyone in the Outer Kingdom! In fact, last week she sang for one of the neighboring Lord's," Lord Russell bragged.

I knew exactly who these people were. Jeremiah had told me that the Prince was interested Cordelia. Or it was the other way around.

Suddenly, the servers headed back to the kitchen, and I felt my nerves float away. I had finished my fake job without messing up. Now, time to get the hot sauce to Charles.

As we walked back through the throne room, I saw Ms. Woodround and Bethany waiting there.

"Any minute now…" she said to Ms. Woodround while looking around the room.

Her eyes practically popped out of her head when she saw me with the servers. I hurried out before Ms. Woodround noticed me too. I was running out of time to get this done.

"Ms. Brooks, I am starting to think the servants were trying to trick you!" Ms. Woodround said, laughing like a donkey.

"Yeah, you must be right. Silly me! I must be heading in to dinner! Here I go!" Bethany said loud enough, so I could hear.

Quickly, I broke apart from the line, disposed of the serving plate, and grabbed the sauce out of my pocket. When I reached the servants' hall, Charles was waiting at the table. He let out a sigh of relief at the sight of me. Now was the hard part. I had to get the hot sauce in her bowl without anyone seeing me.

Quietly, I opened the bottle and then casually pretended to trip. I pretended to use the table for balance. While getting up I tipped the sauce into her oatmeal. Thankfully, the color blended with the strawberries. Our plan was going perfect. I sat down at the table with Charles and the others.

"Wow, Liam, you're such a klutz," Sasha laughed.

"What took you so long?" Charles whispered trying not to look suspicious.

"I got caught up in the kitchen, but that doesn't matter now; here comes Bethany," I pointed to the door.

"Hey guys, she is right behind me!" she tells the table.

Surprisingly, Uncle William was eating with us today, and I could not wait to see the look on his face when I tell him it was me who played the prank! I imagined him laughing so hard at the scene of Ms. Woodround struggling for water.

The door to the servants' hall opened abruptly. She looked very hungry. I felt a slight bit of regret.

"Ugh, it's her," Jeremy said.

Ms. Woodround sat down at her table, neatly placed a napkin on her lap, and picked up her spoon. Ms. Woodround then carelessly mixed her oatmeal; the plan is going perfectly. I grew more and more anxious by the second. Ms. Woodround carefully lifted her spoon high enough for everyone to see that she gets special treatment. Then, she shoved the spoon into her mouth.

We braced ourselves for what was about to happen. Bethany covered her mouth to keep in a laugh. I pulled my lips into my mouth while Charles' mouth was wide open in suspense.

"You good, Charles?" Jeremy asked.

All of a sudden, Ms. Woodround pushed the table and bench away and stood up. She began jumping up and down fanning her mouth with her hand. Everyone in the room turned their attention to the odd scene. Conversations began stopping. I hadn't expected her to have such a low spice tolerance.

"HOT, HOT, VERY HOT!" She yelled over and over again. The room erupted with laughter and an occasional question of "what is going on?"

"Wait for it!" Charles whispered.

Ms. Woodround deserves every bit of this. She scrambled back to her table and knocked over her bowl of oatmeal. Like a dog to its bowl of food, she recklessly reached for the cup of water and attempted to drink out of it.

"What is this? Watah, Watah, AHH!"

Ms. Woodround was clearly in distress. She shook the cup upside-down, but the water still stayed in the cup. I began laughing so hard my sides hurt.

"WATAH!" Ms. Woodround yelled at people.

She ran over to another table and searched for a glass of soothing cold water. The people at the table "accidentally" knock their glasses over when she ordered them to give her their drink. Ms. Woodround grabbed the closest bowl of oatmeal and shoved her face in it. She began drinking up the flavorless oatmeal like a pig eating slop. When she pulled her face away from the bowl, her hair, face, and dress were all covered in oatmeal.

The room was still filled with laughter. I actually felt good for making everyone else laugh at Ms. Woodround, which I know is kind of wrong. I wished that Ms. Woodround was a nicer person but maybe after this she will change.

Ms. Woodround stormed out of the room in anger and embarrassment. I pulled the hot sauce out of my pocket. It was almost empty.

"Anyone like hot sauce on their oatmeal?" I ask the table. Bethany laughed and retrieved the magical cup without anyone noticing.

"You three!" Uncle William said with a serious tone. He doesn't look pleased.

"Nice job! That was a great show!" Edward said, giving us high-fives.

"Looks like she got a taste of her own medicine. Too bad her medicine is so spicy," Charles laughed.

"I'm impressed. Looks like you do have a couple of tricks up your sleeve, Charles," Jeremy said.

"Bethany, Charles, Liam, that was not a very nice thing to do to her. I know she is cranky but –"

"Mr. Rocklen, she deserves it! Today she stepped on Charles' hand with those darn heels of hers!" Bethany said defending us.

"What?" He was shocked. Charles showed everyone the mark in his hand. It was faint but still noticeable.

"I will have a very serious talk with her later. Her actions will not be tolerated here. But that was still the wrong way to go about dealing with it," Uncle William stood up.

"Very clever prank, though" he said, leaving the room with a slight smile. I smiled back, but he was still right. Now, she might just come back at us harder than ever. Hopefully that won't happen. For now, I am just going to soak in the laughter that we brought to these workers in need of justice.

Chapter 12

The next morning, we headed into the servants' room. Excitement echoed in the halls. Everyone was anxious and excited for the big event to start. Ms. Woodround glared at all of us as we entered, as usual, and grabbed her sheet of paper. Everyone was waiting in anticipation for her to tell us the plan for today.

"Alright, now that everyone is here, today is the Prince's big Birthday Ball! You will need to work quickly in the morning. I want to see everyone in the servants' hall at noon for further instructions. If anyone gets done early, you have to stay in your room. I want no one to leave this castle today! I have very high expectations! Here are the jobs: Mr. Vilenter, Ms. Fernfeather, and Mr. Greendale, you are going to start by washing the windows and shaking out the drapes in the ballroom; Ms. Sunpink, Mr. Smithon, and Ms. Burgende, you are going to wash the tables that were carried into the ballroom last night; Mrs. Tremer, Mr. Holland, and Mr. Ray, polish the thrones again; and Ms. Brooks, Mr. Brockfur, and Mr. Rocklen, you will dust the Prince's study as a little birthday gift from the servants, and by that, I mean, I will tell him it's a gift from me," Ms. Woodround said, walking away with an evil grin. Everyone dispersed.

"Well, this is exciting! I have never seen the Prince's study. Maybe we can see the Prince! He is so handsome," Bethany dreamed.

"That would be cool. I bet he has a bunch of cool stuff that only rich people can have," Charles added.

We walked into the Prince's study. Charles pushed open the wooden doors. Bethany and I looked at each other with our mouths open in disbelief. The walls were covered entirely in bookshelves stacked with millions of books on them. A table with books and parchments sat in the middle of the room. The only other furniture was a red couch in the back corner of the room.

"Holy cow…" Charles said getting a look at everything in the room.

"Someone likes to read," I said.

"Yeah, you're totally right," replied Charles.

We quickly got to work dusting every book and shelf. I didn't know that Prince George was this well read. I had just assumed he spent all his time fighting with the knights or flirting with girls.

"Oh, yeah I totally forgot! I actually saw the Prince and the Queen and King last night," I remembered.

"Wait, what? When!?" Charles said excitedly.

"I mean he lives here so it's not hard to find him," Bethany joked.

"So, what was he like!?" Charles asked ignoring her.

"Well, he is very tall and thin. I bet he trains a lot with the Royal Knights. And he has brown wavy hair. I mean he is like what you think any normal prince is like but, I didn't think he was this much into books," I admitted.

"You can't judge a book by its cover. Get it? You know, because we are dusting books," Bethany said, waiting for us to laugh.

We ignored her and continued to clean.

"Geez, tough crowd." Bethany continued to dust.

"Well, he sure does have a lot of them," Charles said gesturing to the shelves of work left for us.

As we finished dusting, I noticed the Prince's desk was cluttered with papers and books. I stepped off the ladder that I had been standing on and began to organize his desk. I am sure he won't mind if I help organize his things. As I was moving papers, I noticed he had lots of letters from around the Outer Kingdom. Then, I came upon something strange that I had never seen before. I picked it up to further examine it.

"What in the Outer Kingdom...?" I was confused at what I was looking at.

It was a drawing of some type of creature. It had four individual snakes growing out of the single snake body. I had never heard of something like this. Maybe it was just a doodle?

In addition to the weird picture, the monster had a large stinger on the end of its tail like that of a scorpion. Under the illustration was the name of the beast.

"Fearhine," Bethany said from directly behind me. I jumped.

"Whoa, don't scare me like that!"

Bethany and Charles must have noticed me examining the paper. I can't blame them for being curious.

"What is that?" Charles asked.

"I am not sure. It's called a Fearhine, I guess. Weird. I have never heard of a monster like that and there sure as hell is nothing on it in 'Sir Frederick's Adventures'," I said.

I looked through the papers on his desk for anything else about it.

"Have you guys ever heard of this thing before?" I asked. They shook their heads.

"It's probably just a sketch," Bethany said.

"That is what I thought at first but, I have a feeling Prince George doesn't have time to doodle," I inspected the room for more clues.

"We obviously found something we were not supposed to find," Charles said.

"I say we just leave it and forget we ever saw it," Bethany said, gathering the cleaning equipment.

"It is as simple as that," she continued.

I was just too curious to let this go.

"But, we could have stumbled upon something incredible," I pleaded.

"Liam, it's just none of your business. I mean, we are just servants, we are not, like, princes or knights," Charles said.

I put the picture back on the desk, and we left the room. As we walked down the hall, we greeted three of our fellow servants.

Rosa, Clarity, and James waved to us from across the throne room. We dodged through staff members setting up for the Prince's ball. I had never really talked to them more than a hello before, but Bethany was really close with the girls.

Rosa adjusted her rounded glasses that sat high up on her nose. Rosa's black curly hair was tied up in a ponytail and wore a pink short sleeve dress that matched her bright and cheerful personality. Small dimples appeared in her dark brown skin when she cracked a smile. Clarity, on the other hand, has short straight red hair and pale skin dotted with freckles. She wore a grey dress with the same type of apron as Rosa, Bethany, and Sasha on top of it. Bethany says she is very opinionated and typically focuses all her energy on her work as a servant. You could say that Rosa and Clarity are basically polar opposites. James on the other hand is the youngest servant at age twelve. I felt bad that he had no one his age to talk to but Clarity and Rosa seem to get along with him seeing as they are only two years older than him.

"What are you guys up to?" Bethany asked.

"Well, we were just about to go up to the tower," Rosa said.

"We don't want to have to wait all day in the servants' hall," James admitted.

"Wanna come?" Rosa asked with excitement hopping on Clarity's shoulders.

"Are we allowed to go?" I asked.

"Ha! Of course! It's not like we are gonna get in trouble!" Rosa said, punching my arm.

"Ow…all right," I said, grabbing my arm.

"Let's go, then!" Rosa said with much enthusiasm. Clarity crossed her arms.

"I think we could spend our time more wisely by getting some more work done," Clarity stopped us.

"Come on! Let us have this one moment of no work!" Rosa complained, leaning on Clarity's shoulder.

"Please!?" James asked.

"What work is there left to do?" Charles asked.

"Yeah, Ms. Woodround doesn't have anything planned until noon," Bethany added.

"Ugh! Fine, but if we get in trouble you guys are taking the blame," Clarity gave in.

"Yes!" Bethany cheered with Rosa.

"Come on!" Rosa shouted.

"Those are some cool boots!" I said, pointing at James's black leather boots.

I still felt bad that James didn't have any guy friends his age to hang out with. I decided to make an attempt to be like Charles and make new friends. Besides, maybe James needs an older male role model to look up to. He looked down at his boots and smiled.

"They are nicer than mine!" I said, smiling and pointing at my dusty brown boots.

"Thanks! They are brand new," he smiled.

Rosa skipped ahead moving at a fast pace. I was almost out of breath from walking up all these stairs.

"Come on, guys!" she said, turning around and waving us forward.

"Not all of us have long legs!" Bethany said, running up to her.

"Almost there, guys!" I heard Rosa shout.

Clarity dragged her feet up the stairs. Unfortunately, Charles and I got stuck behind her so, we ran up the stairs to catch up to them.

"Look, a door," James pointed.

We reached the top just in time for them to open it. We entered a room with nothing in it but a desk and a large window. Everyone ran over to the window, but I moved over to the desk out of curiosity. Why would the royal family have a random desk up here?

"Wow. We are really high up!" Bethany said.

"I have a fear of heights! I knew coming up here was a bad idea," Clarity said, grabbing onto James's arm. He struggled to pull her off.

"You are like so much older than me! Why are you being the sacred one? It should be the other way around!" James said, still struggling.

Rosa ran right over and put her face so close to the glass it was almost being pressed against it.

"Wow! You can see everything!" She said, adjusting her glasses.

I looked over the desk. It was very dusty, and every drawer was empty. That is, except the bottom drawer, which had an inkwell and a quill. Someone had definitely been up here lately because the inkwell wasn't dried up. I became more curious and began to feel around the drawer. The top of my hand brushed against something that was lodged in the top of the drawer. The more I felt it, the more it felt like a book. Clever. Whoever put this here did not want anyone to find it. However, I can't look at this with everyone here. Stealthily, I closed the drawer and promised myself I would come back later to uncover the secrets of the book.

I joined them by the window. Rosa was right; the view was amazing. I could see all the people in the town and further out toward the gates on the Tri Border.

"What a view!" Charles said in awe.

"That's for sure!" I agreed.

"I would love to have a room up here," James said.

"Oh my gosh, yes! Me too!" Rosa said.

"Guys, we should head back down, we have been up here for long enough," Clarity advised, slowly inching away from the window.

"Ugh, fine…" James said.

"Party pooper," Charles mumbled.

"Bye window!" Rosa shouted as we closed the door.

We all headed back down the stairs and got back just in time for Ms. Woodround's meeting. Everyone was waiting at the tables for Ms. Woodround to instruct us.

"I can't wait to see all of the people in their fancy clothes tonight!" I heard Sasha say.

Everyone around me was talking about the Prince's Birthday Ball. I just as excited as everyone else, but I still could not get my mind off the desk drawer book and the drawing of the Fearhine.

"Alright, tonight is the Prince's Birthday Ball!" Ms. Woodround said.

People cheered and clapped.

"We will have all staff on duty serving and greeting people at the ball tonight. I have personally paid for you all to have matching uniforms for tonight and every other ball!"

Everyone clapped with excitement.

"Well, I personally took money out of your salary for it," Ms. Woodround smiled wickedly. The clapping stopped and was replaced by angry remarks and insults.

"AHEM! Now, you servants will only be working when the servers and greeters are taking their breaks. So, you will all be eating a late lunch and an early dinner right now," she said, gesturing to the bowl of spinach in the corner.

"This is ridiculous!" I whispered to Bethany.

"If that is all the food we get to eat then, I am going to starve," she held her growling stomach.

"Go and get your uniforms on! The guests will be arriving in two hours."

Bethany looked at the list.

Only Charles, Edward, Tom, and Greg would be greeters. Everyone else, including me, would have to serve the guests in the ballroom. We got back to our rooms.

The uniforms were actually not that bad looking. They were plain, white pants with a button up collar shirt.

"I'm not gonna sit here for two hours in that. Instead, let's go hang out with Sasha, Jeremy, and Edward before our shift starts," Charles suggested.

Two hours seemed like it would be more than enough time to go inspect the book in the drawer.

"Actually, I'll go there later; I think I am going to go to the bathroom," I said, leaving.

"Okay, suit yourself," he headed to Edward and Jeremy's room.

I made my way up to the tower, trying to blend in with the last minute decoration staff. Carefully, I opened up the bottom drawer and stuck my hand on the top. Then, I pulled the book out from where it was wedged. Quickly, I flipped through the pages. They seemed slightly worn but were defiantly not older than a couple of years. Inside one of the pages was the same picture we found earlier of the Fearhine. I had a gut feeling this belonged to the Prince. I guess we really had found something we were not supposed to see. However, I had to find out more about what this creature was. I began to read to myself.

"The Fearhine was first spotted in Jarvally this spring. It destroyed a house and killed the family that lived inside it. Three are dead. The second time it was spotted was by my followers in Arone. It was found in the woods devouring a deer. Its recent sightings have been in the lower regions of Jarvally. Three villages have said to have spotted it in the forests, and ten known people have been killed in the woods by the Fearhine. One person is missing. The King has not shared this threat with the rest of the Outer Kingdom, and when he was told, King Bartholomew put it aside and focused on the King's Day preparations, which is three months away. The focus of the castle is shifting."

I could not believe the words that I read. This could not be true! That was no made up beast, it was real and killing people! Lower Jarvally is not far from where I live! How did I not hear about this?! I felt scared for my parents back home. They have no idea the Fearhine exists. At any moment, we could be the Fearhine's next victims. I quickly placed the book back and cautiously rushed down to Charles. When I reached Edward and Jeremy's room, they were all laughing at a story Charles was telling. I kept myself from shaking in fear of what I had uncovered. I am beginning to realize the Outer Kingdom is not as safe as I thought it was.

Chapter 13

"Guys, come over to the window! I see some carriages pulling up!" Bethany said, pulling us into her room.

Charles and I entered Bethany's room to find James, Rosa, and Clarity all sitting near the window. I looked through the glass, which had a perfect view of the cul de sac in front of the castle. A large silver and blue carriage pulled up, and three little boys came bounding out. Their mother gracefully followed, holding up her large blue gown to exit the carriage. I laughed, watching her yell at them to stop running.

"Oh, this is the best part of any ball! The hard work is defiantly worth it! " Clarity said with a smile.

Rosa jumped up next to Bethany and pointed at the three little boys.

"Look! They are triplets and wearing the same clothes! That's so funny! I can just picture how hard it is to tell them apart!" She laughed hysterically in the back of the room.

Bethany rolled her eyes with a smile. Edward, Jeremy, and Sasha walked in.

"Oh, are we watching the early arrivals? They are so funny! Remember last year that one guy that fell?" Sasha said to Edward.

"Yeah, and the other woman who tripped!" he laughed

"Early arrivals? Aren't they just regular guests?" I asked.

"Well, not really, they are just the rich families that come early. The kids don't stay awake that long, so they have to always leave early. But almost all of them are funny to watch," Jeremy explained.

"Look at her outfit, it looks so funny," James giggled and a woman wearing a yellow gown covered in stuffed birds.

"It's not appropriate to make fun of the upper class," Clarity crossed her arms.

"Ugh, fun killer," James mumbled.

We watched as a tall man managed to get himself stuck in his own carriage.

"I feel like we are watching something from a fantasy book. The people here are like from another world," I comment.

"I can agree with that. Like who wears a ball gown that can take up a whole carriage," Bethany points at a woman being pulled out of her carriage because her dress was stuffed inside. Everyone in the room laughed, except for Clarity.

"Look, look, look, here comes the Lord and Lady of eastern Dorgan! They are my favorite to watch," Jeremy points.

"What, did they bring the entire village with them?" I ask.

"Funny, but no. That is actually their whole family," Sasha points.

We watch as the large family pours out of their three carriages. I could only imagine how full the ballroom will be tonight. Just that family alone could take up a quarter of the dance floor. I couldn't help but wonder if the lord and lady of Brendsworth will be here tonight.

About one hour went by, and the sky began to darken. A knight walked around the courtyard lighting torches, so the guests could see. Soon, you could hear the loud voices from the ballroom.

Ms. Woodround called all the servants into the servants' hall. We rushed inside. All the boys had their white uniforms on, and the girls had on white blouses with yellow skirts.

"Okay, everyone, you have about two hours on the floor while the servers take their breaks," she said.

The group quickly dispersed. I rushed over with the others to the platters of food. My palms began to sweat.

I grabbed the platter with cheese. Bethany and I followed the group to the end of the hall. We watched a large man and his small wife walk down the hall into the ballroom. As we entered the ballroom our breaths were taken away. Bethany's face lit up like a chandelier.

People in fancy gowns were dancing gracefully across the dance floor. Men and women with expensive dresses, suits, and jewelry walked by us without even noticing we were there. Music echoed throughout the entire room.

"Look at her! She is so pretty!" Sasha said, pointing to a woman with long black hair and a big pink puffy dress. White pearls hung from her ears, neck, and wrists. She looked amazing. The man that escorted her had brown facial hair and a fancy black suit on. Nothing close to this ever happened in Brendsworth. The Princes Birthday Ball makes our Winter Festival look like a kids birthday party.

Sasha walked off toward a corner in the ballroom and began serving the champagne she had on her tray.

I looked up and noticed the big golden chandelier hanging from the ceiling. Tables full of desserts lined one of the walls. I could not take my eyes off of the puddings and cakes. I turned back to the dance floor. The ballroom dancers were beautiful! They floated gracefully across the floor with little effort. I swayed to the regal ballroom music. The violins and flutes created a beautiful symphony of sound.

I walked around, holding the plate up near my head. It was hard work trying to hold it. No wonder the servers need a two hour break.

"Young man, come here," a regal man called me over. He was an old man and had two older women standing next to him.

"My, you don't look like a servant at all. What a proper young man he is," the man said to the two women next to him.

He grabbed a cube of cheese and stuck it in his mouth. One of the women gasped.

"Mr. Rowley! Don't talk to the servants! We are high class people and he is beneath us!" the woman wearing a grey dress said, hiding her mouth behind her fan.

"Oh, pish-posh, Dresilda. This young boy is a person just like you and me. There is no reason why I can't compliment him. Now, may I ask you a question?" he said, looking at me.

"Yes, sir," I said hastily.

"What is it like working here in the palace?"

"Very nice, sir," I replied quickly. I don't want to risk getting fired so, I keep my words short and simple.

"I would expect no less. It was very nice talking to you. You're doing a very good job here," he took another piece of cheese and walked away.

The two women rushed after him. I walked on, serving the guests in the room.

"Hey Liam, did that man over there with the two ladies just come over and talk to you?" Sasha whispered next to me.

"Yeah, why?" I replied.

"Wow, that was one of the richest men in the Outer Kingdom," Sasha revealed.

"Really?" I asked in awe. I could not believe I just talked to a man that was probably richer than everyone in Brendsworth.

I continued serving the guests. People would grab cheese from my plate as I walked by. I noticed one woman took five pieces off the plate. She had wine in one hand and tons of cheese in the other. I listened to her tell a story about how she managed to get stuck in a regal woman's bathroom for twelve hours. So far, she was coolest person I had met at the ball.

The food soon vanished from my platter. I headed back to the servants' hall to restock. When I got there, I found Bethany in the servants' hall alone. She was sneaking a spinach puff into her mouth and hadn't seen that I was in the doorway.

"If I were you, I would have gone for the crab cakes," I said, smirking.

She jumped and put her hand over her mouth. If I had been Ms. Woodround, she would have been fired on the spot for taking the guests' food.

"Liam!" She said in shock. I laughed.

"Don't worry. I won't tell," I said, putting the empty tray down.

"You almost gave me a heart attack," she said, laughing.

"You have really got to be more stealthy," I said.

"Pfft, I knew you were there," she said sarcastically.

"I don't blame you for taking food. That dinner/lunch was not at all filling."

"Yeah."

"What do you think?" I asked.

"About the ball? It's beautiful! The people have such expensive clothes! I saw this one dress that had pink lace on the bottom. Not to mention the shoes! And there was also one that was yellow, and it had a big bow on it made of silk! And…oh, it's just all so amazing! I'm sorry. I'm probably boring you to death listening to me talk about dresses and such," she frowned.

"No, it's fine, I like that you're excited about something," I admitted.

"I know that it's kind of typical for girls to like dresses and clothes, but it's more than that for me; it's an art!" she said, smiling.

"No I can understand. I feel that way about some things too," I said thinking about my sword.

"One day, maybe, I can learn more about your passions, but for now, we should probably get back to serving," Bethany said, picking up a tray full of wine.

"You are right. We don't want to get in trouble with Ms. Woodround. She is still mad from the prank that we pulled yesterday," I laughed.

We walked down the hallway back to the ballroom. I continued to serve the rich guests. Suddenly, the music stopped. Trumpets erupted, and a small man yelled out a name I could not hear. Everyone was whispering excitedly about what he announced. Prince George gracefully strolled into the ballroom. People had formed a circle around him, trying to get his attention. I was surprised by how he ignored the attention and fame. Now, no one was on the dance floor except Prince George. Dancing music began and the same girl from the dinner last night ran out and took his arm.

The Prince and Cordelia began a beautiful waltz. Her fluffy pink dress swung around as Prince George swayed about the room. Everyone watched in awe. Prince George was certainly not a stereotypical prince from my storybooks as a kid. He was strong, humble, and honorable. From what I could see, he was not even that interested in being at his own birthday party. Not to mention, Prince George is keeping some secrets that I need to uncover.

I looked over to the King and Queen; they were sitting on their thrones. I couldn't see that same things I saw in the Prince in King Bartholomew. He sat eating a turkey leg and sipping wine without a care for anything but his food. Besides, I could never see the king as honorable after what I uncovered in his room.

The song ended, and the next one began. I watched as girl after girl ran out to try and dance with the Prince. Cordelia could only keep him to herself for a while until a girl in a very wide blue dress bumped her out of the way and took her place. Then, a tall girl in a green dress ran out and took that girl's place. Every minute, a girl would rush in and take the other girl's spot with Prince George. It was funny watching the girls fight to dance with him. I wish I were the Prince right about now.

Suddenly, I noticed a group of beautiful girls come over to my plate. Sadly, this was no time to be flirting with girls; I had a job to do.

"He is so dreamy!" said a girl in a long orange dress.

"I can't wait for our wedding day!" a girl who looked exactly like the other girl said. I assumed they were identical twins.

"You mean, my wedding day, right, Zane?" a girl with short brown hair hissed.

"Well, Kali, I was the one who danced with him!" Zane said angrily.

"Only because you took my spot! And if anyone is going to be Prince George's wife, it's me! Not you, and not Tomiko!" Kali said, stamping her blue heal on the ground.

"He wouldn't choose you in a million years! He would choose me because I'm the pretty one here!" Tomiko said, pulling at the straps on her straight yellow dress and flipping her long straight black hair. Then she flashed a cute smile. Zane flashed back a look of disgust and stuck out her tongue.

"Oh, so that's how it is!" Kali said, glaring at Tomiko. Tomiko took a piece of cheese off my platter.

"Tomiko, if you are so confident in your beauty, why don't you go ask the Prince who he thinks is the prettiest?" Kali challenged.

"No way! You go talk to him!" Tomiko said.

"No! You go! If you talk the talk you gotta walk the walk," Zane said.

The girls walked away, bickering. Charles would be falling all over these pretty rich girls, but I don't see anything but spoiled brats.

The night seemed to stretch on for hours. I noticed Sasha and Bethany also watching as two workers came and opened the glass doors to the outside. The garden courtyard was lit by three torches, which were unnecessary because the thousands of fireflies that flew around outside were enough to brighten the garden. It was stunning outside with the flowers, the fireflies, and the fancy people dancing. I wished Bethany could have been a guest instead of a servant. She deserves it. So do all the servants. Working for Ms. Woodround is a job all on its own.

I walked over to the dessert table to find my next distraction. That was not hard at all. My eyes fell onto the four-tiered strawberry cake. My mouth watered at the sight of the white icing and strawberries placed neatly on each tier of the cake. I looked away to resist taking a slice. My eyes were then drawn back to gaze at the chocolate and rice puddings. Oh, how badly I wanted to eat the desserts. A tall man grabbed a spoonful of the tropical fruit salad. I held myself back from taking some. The last time I ate a good dessert was back home with my mom. She makes the best cinnamon buns and muffins. I have yet to find someone that can create a chocolate chip muffin better than my moms. Another man came over for a slice of the four-tiered strawberry cake. I walked away from the table to resist temptation.

The music of the orchestra took my mind off the treats. Its soothing sound made my body sway back and forth to the beat. I was finally able to relax.

Chapter 14

The main serving crew appeared at the doorway. They all took our places as they walked around with white wine and bite-sized desserts. As Sasha, Bethany, and I walked back to the room, Charles and Edward were walking toward us from the main doors in the throne room.

"Did you see that one guy? Man, did he have an awesome carriage! That thing must have been like two hundred gold coins! I can't believe how much he tipped you!" Charles said, excited.

"Oh, and that one lady who gave you a silver coin! She was so pretty!" Edward said excitedly. Sasha crossed her arms.

"Well, well, well, if it isn't "lazy" and "lazier". You two seem like you had such a horrible time out front," she said sarcastically.

"Oh, my gosh, Sasha! You would not believe the tips we got from these people!" Charles said.

"Wait, you got tips?!" I asked.

"Wait, you guys didn't?" Edward asked surprised.

"Oh my lord! All you guys did was stand and greet the people and open a carriage door!" Sasha complained.

"Oh…sorry guys," Charles apologized.

"I bet if you were out there they would tip you a hundred gold coins," Edward said to Sasha trying to butter her up.

"My arms hurt so bad from carrying those plates," Bethany grumbled, rubbing her wrists.

"Tell me about it" I agreed.

We all headed back to Bethany's room to relax. Edward and Bethany stood by the window with me watching the guests arrive and leave. Everyone else was being entertained by a story Charles was telling. As we were watching, Bethany noticed something odd in the distance.

"Liam, Edward, what…what is that?" She pointed to what looked like tons of lights coming up the hill.

"I can't really tell," I said pressing my face against the glass.

Then, it became clear what it was as the lights came closer.

"Holy-!" Edward shrieked.

A large mob was coming straight toward the castle. They had pitchforks and stakes along with tons of torches. The mob was chanting and yelling angrily. I rubbed my eyes, doubting if it was real.

"Oh my gosh, it's a mob!" Bethany said frantically.

Jeremy and Rosa ran up behind me to look.

"Oh, no! What do we do? We have to tell someone! Do something! We have gotta do something!" Rosa shouted flailing her arms around.

"Why me!?" Clarity yelled in fear, grabbing onto James's arm. He tried pulling her off.

"What is happening?" James innocently asked.

"We have to tell someone!" Jeremy shouted, running out into the halls.

It looked like someone had beaten him to it because the hall was now filled with people running back and forth. Shouting echoed through the servants' quarters.

One of the adult servants, Greg, burst into our room.

"A mob is marching toward the castle. I need everyone to return to their rooms immediately and stay put!" He ran back out into the hall.

"Charles, come on!" I said grabbing his arm.

Sasha grabbed Edward's hand and held him close to her.

"Stay safe!" he said, kissing her.

"Pfft, you're telling me!" She called back to him, trying to put on a smile.

"All my hard work and for this," Clarity continued to complain.

"James I will take you back to your room seeing as 'drama queen' over here won't do it," Rosa grabbed his hand.

We all hurried into the chaotic hallway.

"This is insane!" Charles shouted to me as we dodged people in the hall.

"Why is this happening?" I shouted over the noise.

As soon as we got into our room, we ran to the window. From what we could see the Royal Knights stood ground in front of the castle doors. Uncle William burst into the room and pulled me away from the window.

"You two need to get to bed. I don't want any of you near that window. Do you understand?" he demanded, closing the curtains.

I nodded. The entire castle was in chaos inside and out. People ran back and forth in the halls in panic. The glowing red torches lights flickered into our room through the curtain gaps. The mob chanted loud into the night until the knights finally drove back the furious mob. I held my pillow tight in fear. It was only then could I bring my eyes to close and fall into a deep sleep.

I woke up suddenly early in the morning. Everyone was still sound asleep. I stared out the window. It was hazy outside and hard to see through the glass. The courtyard looked surprisingly untouched after last night's events. I closed my eyes shut and gave an effort to go back to bed. However, once I wake up, I physically cannot go back to sleep. I opened my eyes, got up, and then tiptoed over to the window.

The Outer Kingdom seemed perfectly fine when I was living blissfully in Brendsworth. Now that I'm here, where news travels fast and it's hard to hide secrets, it seems like the Outer Kingdom is falling apart.

"Liam, what are you doing? Are you asleep or awake because if you were asleep that would totally be weird. I have a fear of sleepwalkers, you know," Charles whispered to me from his bed.

I hadn't realized that I had woken up Charles. Uncle William then opened his eyes, wondering what was happening.

"I'm awake," I whispered, laughing quietly.

"Liam, what are you doing out of bed this early?" Uncle William questioned.

"I was just…not tired," I said, looking back at the window away from them.

"Are you sure that nothing is wrong?" Charles asked.

Samuel was snoring away in the background. We kept quiet, so we wouldn't wake him up.

"Yeah, I'm sure…"

Suddenly, something shiny caught my eye. I studied the stables. A silver object was on the side of the stable that I had never seen there before. Normally, I wouldn't think much about something like this but, after last night, anything out of the ordinary could be dangerous. The more I looked at it, the more it became clear.

"Is that a knife?" I asked, walking out.

Uncle William held his arm out, half asleep, and pointed to my bed. Then he made a sleeping signal with his hands. I shook my head and continued out of the room. This seemed too important to ignore.

Charles jumped out of bed after me and fully woke Uncle William in the process. We raced down the hall and outside to the stables. I looked back and forth to make sure no one was watching me. If there is one thing Sir Frederick would want me to remember, it would be that in any suspicious situation, you need to constantly watch all around you, in case of a sneak attack. I could hear Uncle William's frantic whispering of my name behind me. I looked back to see them tip toeing toward me. I kept moving forward. I had to find out what I saw in the stables. They were not going to keep me from looking at it.

As I came up to the wooden walls of the stable, I could not believe what I saw. A knife was lodged in one of the stables wooden posts, holding up a note. I knew that something was off. I put my hand on the knife. It felt uncomfortable holding it, like the knife had been used for evil.

"Liam! What are you doing!?" Charles hissed.

"Liam, where did you find that?" Uncle William said, shocked.

I ignored him and pulled the knife out. The note fell, and I caught it before the dew-covered grass was able to get it wet. I then began to read the note out loud.

"It says, 'If you want to see Prince George again, you will come to the hill cave right outside of town. If you tell anyone, I will kill the

Prince as soon as the words come out of your mouth. Time is ticking.'" My mouth dropped.

Someone kidnapped Prince George, and no one knew! This is impossible!

"How did this happen? Did it happen recently? I don't remember seeing a note on the stables last night. How is it that no one knows about this? This cannot be real?" I hysterically questioned, beginning to freak out.

"How do we know this isn't some prank?" Charles asked.

"We should tell someone about it," Uncle William said.

"No! We can't tell anyone or else Prince George will die! Didn't you hear what I just said?!" I stressed.

"There is no one around. They won't know if we tell someone," Uncle William said.

"No! You don't know if there are people hiding somewhere watching us. You can't just jump to conclusions with this! I mean the Prince of the Outer Kingdom is KIDNAPPED! It could have happened during the mob or after the mob. I mean what if you tell someone and then he does get killed and it's all your fault!" Uncle William quickly shushed me.

Uncle William quietly stroked his mustache. You could tell he was trying to think. I paced back and forth with the knife and paper in my hand. This is not good at all.

"I am gonna go run upstairs and check the Prince's bedroom and his study. If he isn't there, we know it's real," Charles said, scurrying inside.

"Charles! Wait; do not-" Uncle William put his hand on his head. He was definitely stressed out. We waited for Charles to return.

"Guys, I can't find him!" Charles panicked as he ran back to us.

"Uncle William, we have to do something," I pleaded.

"Boys, this is what we are going to do. We will go show King Bartholomew this paper and not say a word. That way they won't kill Prince George because we didn't actually say anything. He doesn't get up for another three hours, mind you, but this is all we have. So, let's go inside and wait calmly," Uncle William instructed us, turning around and walking back to the door.

"Come on, Liam," Uncle William said.

"No," I said.

"What? You have to understand, Liam, this is bigger than us!" Uncle William said, walking toward me.

"I said no. The Prince will be long dead by the time King Bartholomew and his knights get to this cave place. We can get there in half the time. Uncle William, if we don't go now, we will be the reason why the prince would be dead," I pleaded.

Uncle William put his hand to his mustache and began stroking it again. This is the most daring thing I have ever suggested.

"Okay," he said.

"Okay?" I said, astounded.

"Okay, let's do it. Charles, can you handle that knife? You are going to need a weapon of some sorts. If not, we can let you have my sword. Liam, you had better know what you're doing because I'm following you with this."

My mouth dropped as I heard his words.

"Are you serious?" I asked.

He nodded his head, still dead serious.

"Okay, well, this is crazy. Okay, we should start by getting ready, I guess," I instructed.

We all ran inside and got dressed to go find the Prince. I quickly grabbed my sword. Charles began practicing throwing the knife before we got had to leave. He pulled his arm back and then threw it forward releasing the knife. It flew threw the air and hit the side of the stable.

"Liam, I don't know about this. We could be going up against a whole army," he pulled the knife out of the wood and walked toward the inside of the stables.

Charles had been aiming at the center of a coiled rope, hanging on the side of the wall. He threw the knife and hit right in the center of the rope. I was impressed.

"Wow, that was pretty good! You have a good aim!" I said.

"Thanks. I should. I spent hours during the harvest season with my older brother on my farm throwing apples from the trees into baskets on the ground," he said.

"I never did anything like that in Brendsworth."

"Liam, where exactly is this cave?" Uncle William asked.

"Hmm…why don't we go into town and ask where it is? I'm sure someone might be up this early," I suggested.

"How do we know the Prince is okay? What if he is already dead?" Charles asked.

"I've met him multiple times before, and he seems smart enough to stay alive," Uncle William comforted us.

We ran into the town. I could have never guessed in a million years that we would be doing this today. When we arrived in the market, almost all the shops are closed. It looked like a ghost town.

"Where is everyone?" Charles asked.

"Last night was the Prince's ball, so naturally, everyone stayed up late drinking," Uncle William answered.

"Okay, so no one is awake yet, but that's okay. We still need to get our information. Unlucky for us, I have no idea where to get answers," I confessed.

We look around for any signs of life. Suddenly, I began to hear a faint sound of soft whistling and a squeaky cart rolling toward the square. Could this possibly be the help I was looking for? I look behind me to reveal my sign of hope: an old man pushing a cart full of dolls made of cornhusks toward us. He parks his cart in front of the elk fountain and sets up his stand, waiting for any customer. I looked around. No one but Uncle William, Charles, and I are here. Why would anyone set up a cart to sell in an empty market? This is hopeless. Clearly, this man is strange. Charles strolls over to the old man, who is happily whistling to himself.

"Umm, Charles? Where are you going?" I walked over to Charles.

"Good morning, sir. Are you familiar with this area?" he asks the man politely.

The man stops whistling. Now that I was closer, I noticed the big wart on the strange old mans nose and the abnormally small ears on the sides of his head. As he began to speak, I noticed some of his teeth were missing.

"Young boy, are you interested in a corn husk doll? I have a buy one get one free deal for everyone who buys before the afternoon!"

"No thanks. Are you familiar with this area?" Charles asked again, being surprisingly patient. The old man looked back with a smile as if he didn't hear a word Charles said.

"You see, sir, we are looking-"

"Yes, I am very familiar with this cobblestone market square. See, here is the fountain, and this is the road, and this is my chart, and here is a cornhusk doll, and-"

"No, no, no, I mean the area of Trisanburg. We are looking for-" Charles says, cutting the rambling old man off.

"Eh, yes! I know it all! From the castle to the wall!" he said, giving a smile.

"Do you happen to know how to get to the uh, hill, uh, rock cave thing?" Charles asked.

"Oh yes! I know where many hills and rocks are! I am standing on a few rocks right now! Actually, rocks are quite delicious."

"Charles, this is a waste of time," I whisper.

"No! We need to know where the HILL CAVE is!" Charles pronounced his words very clearly.

"Oh! Oh, yes, I know where that is. Head down that road all the way out of the city. Then, the first thick bunch of trees you pass will be where the hill cave is. Corn husk doll?" He said holding a doll out in front of me.

I shake my head. He holds it out to Uncle William; he shakes his head and politely declines. Charles face-palmed himself and let out a long sigh.

"Then, why didn't you just say that in the first place," Charles mumbled, walking away.

"Umm, thanks, sir," I said walking away with Uncle William.

Quickly, we headed out of Trisanburg City. The air was beginning to warm up, and the sun was peaking out above the treetops. People would soon be up in the town.

"Hey Uncle William, if people in the town are getting up, then that means people in the castle are getting up, and that means that someone might notice Prince George is not in his bed. What is gonna happen when they see we are gone too?" I worry.

"Let's hope they won't assume the worst."

I began to pray for the sun to go back down and for it to be night again. We needed more time! Even just one hour of darkness would give us enough time to save Prince George. I had almost forgotten we had to face whoever kidnapped him. My nerves built up and my palms grew sweaty. I frantically wiped them on my pants to keep them dry. I have never actually fought with my sword. I also have never saved anyone, let alone Prince George, who is only the most important person in all of the Outer Kingdom! Besides his father, that is. I felt like butterflies were flying around in my stomach having a grand old time making me nauseous.

We continued walking down the path, and trees came into view. My heart raced, knowing we grew even closer to this mysterious kidnapper.

"What if we get there, and there is no kidnapping?" Uncle William asked.

"I hope not, but it would also be good because the Prince would not be in danger. And then we will be able to go back and pretend that we were on a morning walk or something. So then Prince will be safe at home. And the old man won't have to shove cornhusk dolls in our face again. Does that make sense?" Charles said rambling nervously.

"Sort of…" Uncle William answered with and uncertain tone.

We reached the woods, and Uncle William led us over rocks and fallen tree branches. Suddenly, we all stopped for some reason, and Uncle William lifted his right arm to signal silence. I could only hear the sounds of the birds and my heavy breathing. What was he listening for? A voice cried out "Help!" It was very quiet, but I had a feeling it belonged to the Prince. We all broke into a run.

"Run faster! We must help Prince George!" Uncle William cried as we ran to the spot we heard the voice coming from.

I was surprised at what I saw. A small dark cave sat in front of us. Thick moss grew over the top of it, making the cave appear to be under a hill.

"My guess is the Prince is in there. In that dark scary cave…" I quivered. Charles pulled out the knife.

"What are we waiting for?" Charles's voice was shaky, but he continued toward the cave.

I can do this. I can do this. I can do this.

We cautiously reached the entrance and raised our weapons. As we took a step into the cave, something dropped from the trees. I jumped back. My eyes bulged as I watched a giant man slowly stand up in front of us. He was tall and muscular, and a big black cloth covered his face. All you could see was his eyes. My sword wobbled in my hands, almost slipping from my grip.

The large man swung his sword back and forth, walking closer trying to intimidate us. It was working.

Uncle William steadied himself, and then jumped at the kidnapper. Without thinking I launched myself toward him. Uncle William's sword clashed against the kidnapper's sword. They hit back and forth. I ran up and blocked a swing from the kidnapper. I struggled to hold him back. I need to start doing more hay barrel lifts. Something whipped past my face and cut the kidnapper's arm. I looked to Charles who had just thrown his knife. The kidnapper turned his attention to Charles and ran at him. It was almost as if the ground shook every step he took. Uncle William chased after the kidnapper to stop him. Charles ducked as the kidnapper's sword swung passed him. I ran up to help.

"Charles, go in there and find the Prince!" I yelled.

The kidnapper took a swing at me, I ducked and then swung back. A gush of adrenaline and power rushed through my veins. I dodged and swung my sword as quickly as I could. Swing after swing, we backed the kidnapper right to the wall of the cave entrance.

"You have nowhere to go, vermin," Uncle William spat.

"GUYS!" Charles yelled. He came running out. Prince George was not with him.

"He isn't in here," he said breathing heavily.

The color drained from my face. Uncle William rammed the kidnapper into the wall, and I helped hold him down.

"Where is he? Who are you?" Uncle William ordered the man to speak.

"There is only one way to find out," I said, pulling off the black cloth.

The man had a short black beard and a yellow smile. None of us recognized him.

Suddenly, I heard a slow clap from behind me. I whipped my head around, and my mouth dropped.

"What the-" Uncle William said.

Prince George walked out from behind a tree, clapping with a smile on his face.

"Good show, gentlemen! Very good fighting skills." Prince George looked unharmed and still wearing his fancy princely suit. I was intrigued by the Prince's accent.

"You're okay?" I asked, confused.

"In this day and age, is anyone feeling anything but just okay? I mean, who feels amazing in this economy? Thank you again, Mohammed, you did a supah job."

The kidnapper shook us off him and walked over to the Prince, giving him a brief firm handshake.

"But, what?" Charles stuttered.

"Sir, what are you doing? Why did you pretend to be kidnapped? What is the meaning of this?" Uncle William dropped his sword.

"Well, aren't you quite the team! Mr. Rocklen, please excuse me for the fighting. I am more impressed than I thought I would be. Now, Mr. Rocklen, what are the names of these two gentlemen?" Prince George said, handing Mohammed a bag of coins.

"Liam Rocklen, sir," I said quickly.

"Oh, yes, of course! I've heard all about you from your Uncle over here."

"Charles Brockfur."

"Please, gentlemen, you must be tired. Come sit, and I shall explain everything," he said calmly.

"Your highness, I am just confused by this whole thing! I don't understand why?" Uncle William said angrily.

We followed him to a rock and took a seat.

"Be prepared, gentlemen. This will be a lot to take in." Prince George said.

"Okay, were listening." Uncle William crossed his arms.

"Once, there was a kingdom. The ruler in this kingdom was once great, but he is lost in a dark cave with no light at the end. As the king walks deeper into the cave, the kingdom sinks with it. It is up to the people who can see the light to save the kingdom and the king. Do you know what I mean, gentlemen?" he asked.

"Okay, I'm just going to be real with you right now. That just made this whole thing ten times more confusing," Charles said.

"What I am saying is the Kingdom is falling apart, and it is up to me and my followers to save it. I mean you witnessed the mobs last night. Someone has to fix this, and that's just the surface of the problems. I need more followers who can help me, and I can tell that you three are perfect candidates for the job," he said.

"What?" Charles asked in shock.

I tried to process this information. The kingdom is in trouble, and it is our job to save it? What could he be saying? This must be a dream.

"Hold on. Us?" I asked.

"Yeah. Us? We are just some random servants," Charles questioned.

"Your highness, why did you fight us, though? You could have just said this back at the castle," Uncle William asked.

"And why would you choose us?" I stressed.

"I cannot answer that until you answer this: will you join me in my fight?" The Prince continued to talk in riddles.

"I'm sorry, your royal highness, sir, but, I don't know if it's a royalty thing or you just are way more educated than us but, I have no idea what words are that are coming out of your mouth! Again, no offense sir, your highness, great Prince George, but, you sound like your speaking gibberish," Charles said, absolutely lost. Prince George sighed and looked to Uncle William.

"Mr. Rocklen, I have known you for a long time, and you are a hard worker and have always been true to the throne. Not to my father, but to the Outer Kingdom as a whole. I am sure these two boys are the same way. I need all of your help. Will you help the Outer Kingdom?" the Prince requested. I had no idea what was happening but I immediately wanted to say yes to his offer, but Uncle William opened his mouth first.

"Forgive us, but can we have a word in private?" Uncle William asked. Prince George nodded.

We got into a huddle, and Prince George walked away.

"He is crazy!" Charles whispered.

"Uncle William, I think he really means it. I think the kingdom is struggling and this is our chance to save it. I mean, why would he hire that guy if it weren't serious? I mean you saw the mob last night!" I said.

"I just don't know, Liam. What do you think Charles?" Uncle William asked.

"Well, I am saying yes just because I want to figure out what the heck is going on," Charles admitted honestly.

Uncle William sighed and smacked his hand on his four head.

"Are we really doing this? I swear, if we become crazy lunatics or get ourselves killed, I am gonna kill the both of you for this," Uncle William sighed.

"I can live with that, Mr. Rocklen," Charles gave a thumbs-up.

"Prince George, we will join your fight. Can you please explain what we can do and what is going on?" Uncle William said.

"Yes. You see there is an...umm-evil source who has done something to the king. I know they are trying to distract me and keep me from curing him. I am still unsure of any of this but, I know something is wrong. I needed someone to defeat the distraction for me," Prince George began.

"Okay, so far, seems only a little crazy," I mumbled.

"And back to your question of why I would choose you. I know you are good candidates for many reasons. Mr. Rocklen, you have always been a humble and honorable man. I have always considered promoting you to being one of my advisors when I become king. Not to mention, your nephew and Charles have taken an interest in the truth. I could not help but noticed you found my drawing when you cleaned my study and took a deep interest in it. And Liam had also found my notebook and read it. I don't see that as a bad thing. To me, I value your concern for the safety of the Outer Kingdom. I knew you would be perfect for this job because of this and your interest in the Fearhine," Prince George explained.

My face grew bright red. I was in shock.

"How... how did you find out?" I asked.

"I am very observant. I saw you coming down the stairs last night before my party. Also, the job board said you were working in my room when I noticed my drawing was out of place," Prince George said.

"What!? You boys are in so much trouble! Snooping around like that!" Uncle William yelled.

"What you found a diary and you didn't tell me?" Charles said.

"Gentlemen! Please, it's all fine now. I am not angry; in fact, I am very impressed. Now, I knew that I needed a person with skills to help me, and I just found three! Mr. Rocklen, don't think I don't listen to you telling the advisors about your trip to get your nephew. I heard about the imps you were able to fight off. That is impressive," Prince George said.

I had no idea how much Prince George knew about me. I didn't even think he knew I existed!

"Anyways, I needed to create a test. The morning after my party, I wrote the note and planted it in the wall with the knife. I knew you would notice it because I had placed a mirror above the stable to reflect the suns light into your room as soon as the sun came up. As I walked to the cave, I ran into a crazy old vendor man who I paid to tell you where to find the hill cave. I had also paid him to take his time, so I could have time to make it to the cave. I tested your mind and your strength all in one morning. Not to mention your ability to think for yourselves and not blindly alert my father or the Royal Knights. I need followers who are going to fight, not for my father but the Outer Kingdom. Now, all I need you to do is go and kill a beast for me," he finished.

All of our mouths were open, and I couldn't believe it was that big of a set up. We were just pawns playing his game.

"You can't be serious," Uncle William said.

"You expect me to believe that you somehow knew Liam would wake up early from the light and then see the knife, wake us up, and expect we won't go tell the King or his advisers about this! And on top of that, you somehow were able to make sure we would talk to that creepy old man and find our way here to this cave?" Charles questioned in disbelief.

The Prince looked back at him with no emotion.

"Yep," he said.

"Hmm…okay then, makes sense," Charles gave up and accepted the events that transpired this morning.

"What is the beast again?" Uncle William asked.

"The beast was created by a dark witch and is called the Fearhine," the Prince said.

"A what?" Uncle William asked, confused.

"The Fearhine has the body of a snake with four snakes growing out of it and a stinger on the end of its tail; if it is struck by that stinger, it results in a slow and painful death by poison. The dark witch wants to distract me from my mission, so she created this beast. The witch expects me to go hunt it down and stop looking for her, so that's why I must have you do it for me," he said.

"Excuse me? Us? Why not have that big Mohammad guy do it?" Charles asked.

I thought about our mission and could not believe it was real.

"I know it sounds crazy, but the beast has terrorized villages and killed many poor innocent people. This dark witch will be the end of all of the Outer Kingdom. You must help me!" he pleaded.

"Uncle William, we have to help!" I said.

"I don't know, Liam," he replied.

"Uncle William, if this monster is in the Outer Kingdom, it could make its way to Brendsworth and my parents! We can try and save them!" I stressed.

"The beast was spotted in lower Jarvally, not too far from Brendsworth. I will reward you with a hefty amount of gold if you succeed," the Prince informed us.

Uncle William sighed.

"Okay. Fine."

"No way!" I cheered.

This was my chance to make a difference and be a real knight! I could never have guessed this would have happened! It was like fate!

Prince George led us back through the forest to the main road. A short, fat man was waiting for us in his wagon. It seemed to be filled with our belongings.

"I have all your things and food in here. You will have to begin your trip today. This will not be an easy task," the Prince said.

"Today?" Charles said.

"But we won't be able to say goodbye to any of our friends," I thought of Bethany.

"Under no circumstances will you talk about this to anyone! It is top secret! The whole kingdom is relying on you killing the Fearhine," the Prince ordered.

Uncle William climbed up into the wagon that the prince provided. He sat up front and took the reins from the large man. Charles joined him.

"What about our jobs? Won't they notice our absence?" Uncle William asked.

"I have already taken care of that, Mr. Rocklen. As we speak, Ms. Woodround is reading your note of absence. I informed everyone you are on an urgent job search in every region for servants," Prince George said, fixing his tassels.

"Alright. Do you have supplies in here?" Uncle William asked.

"There is enough food for three days, maps, and travel supplies. I hope you will be able to reach and defeat the Fearhine within a week. Any more than that, and your excuse for your absence would be invalid."

"So, are we getting paid for this?" Charles asked.

"That's not what matters though, Charles, saving our home is what matters," I said, confused as to why he was not convinced to go by just being able to be a hero.

"And that is why you are the perfect people for the job. Just remember, don't trust anyone. Just like I have my followers, so does this dark witch. She is plaguing our kingdom and you must stop her. I would have loved to do kill the Fearhine myself but, like I said, I need to hunt her down."

"Alright. We won't let you down, your highness!" Uncle William said.

"I wish you good luck! This is the most important task you may ever be given," the Prince said.

Uncle William cracked the reins, and we were off. I knew at that moment that my life would change forever. Would it be for the better or the worse?

Chapter 15

The wagon bumped along the dirt road. I sat down and leaned over the wooden railing. The trees passed slowly by me. This was the biggest change in my life. I would have to face a monster that could possibly kill me, my uncle, and/or my friend. Or worse, we could fail, and then the Fearhine could kill everyone!

I looked back the way we came. The castle was still in view. All of the beautiful towers peaked over the horizon. Bethany popped into my head. She will never forgive Charles or me. I left her and never said goodbye. If I die, then I will never get to see her again. My heart felt heavy, and I felt regret. But, no, I have to do this! King Bartholomew, Prince George, and everyone in the Outer Kingdom all need me to defeat the Fearhine.

I grabbed my wooden dragon out of my bag and enchanted it. Scales flew up and down next to my leg. I held out my hand as a landing spot for him. He gently flew down. I smiled and began to pet him softly on the back. Scales rubbed his head against my fingers.

"Well, boys, our lives just escalated very quickly," Uncle William said, still shocked.

"I don't know if I will be able to fight some monster...I mean, I have never even fought a person before," Charles admitted.

"I still can't figure out why he picked us for the job..." Uncle William thought to himself.

"I guess we will have to practice fighting every day," I said. We sat in silence, all lost in our thoughts.

I decided to read "Sir Frederick's Adventures". I opened to a random page. The chapter title was "Mermen". I looked over at my comrades. Uncle William looked worried and Charles seemed scared. I had to take their minds of the Fearhine or at least change their attitudes.

"Hey guys, want to learn about mermen? It's very interesting. Oh, look at this, there is even an illustration. How interesting!" I jokingly said.

"Alright, fine, I'll listen," Charles said. He turned around, and I started to speak in a mysterious and scary voice. This would definitely cheer Charles up.

"Sir Frederick walked slowly toward the water, the ocean glistening in sunlight. In the distance, he saw a figure on the rocks near the rocky cliff. Could it be a mermaid? Sir Frederick prayed that it was not, due to him being in the southern mermaid territory. It was not a mermaid, but a merman. The merman had a long pointed piece of driftwood resting in his hands. Sir Frederick assumed it was to defend himself against the southern mermaids. His hair was brown and shaggy and his tail was a vibrate color of blue and silver."

I turned the book around to show the illustration. Charles nodded, and I turned the book back toward me.

"You could get all the ladies if you looked like that! Am I right, Mr. Rocklen?" Charles said jokingly. I let out a chuckle.

"Charles you can just call me Uncle William. I mean after all this, there is no reason to pretend we are all just coworkers."

"Yeah, no problem," Charles agreed.

"Okay then, back to the mermen."

"Like most mermen, this one had big muscles and enormous strength. Mermen have been around just as long as humans and mermaids. Unlike mermaids, territories and tribal groups do not separate the mermen. Instead, mermen live like sharks, secluded and alone. Most of them do not marry or fall in love with mermaids; most of them have a child with a mermaid and then go on their way. The mermaids hate merman and only view them as useful during the mating season.

Every year, some of the mermen meet the mermaids at a breeding ground. When they are done, they disperse far away from each other. This is why this merman is armed. At any moment, a group of mermaids could come and attack him. It is rare to find a mermen and mermaid living happily together.

In the ruling of King James Turner III, a witch named Cleopatra Marionette was ordered by King James's advisor to experiment with different species. However, the King's advisor, Charlie Hangur, was giving orders without King James permission. Soon, the authorities found out about his treason. However, when he was caught, Cleopatra had already completed his first order. Charlie Hangur was punished and executed along with Cleopatra for creating a monster that could plague the sea. Cleopatra had created a new species called Death Callers, a merman hybrid. Before Cleopatra's death she fled with her creation to the ocean. She carried the three Death Callers she created in a sack toward a cliff that overlooked the ocean. Hangur was forced to tell the king where Cleopatra was and what he ordered her to do. King James had no intention on killing Cleopatra, but he sent his guards to retrieve the beasts she created. The guards caught up with her and found her at the edge of the cliff. Cleopatra saw the guards and without thinking threw herself and the three Death Callers over the cliff. The four fell into the water.

When the sac hit the ocean, the Death Callers swam out into the dark seas. They looked like normal mermen, but are really mad killers. Cleopatra climbed onto nearby rocks. The guards called down, telling her they would come help her up. The Death Callers saw her on the rock and started to sing to her. She was caught in a trance and unwillingly fell into the water where she was attacked by her own creation. King James's knights shot arrows into the water to try and kill the monsters, but they had all escaped. A bleeding Cleopatra washed up on the rocks and was sentenced to death for creating the Death Callers and releasing them. There were five more reported deaths before these murderous monsters were hunted down. Sirens, although a myth, were a form of reality within the form of Death Callers.

The question you may be asking is, how can I tell if it is a Death Caller or a merman? As explained on page 57, Death Callers can be identified by their large fin on their back, which mermaids and mermen do not have. Also, they have a second set of razor sharp teeth hidden to deceive women with their beauty.

King James and his father Baren Turner searched for the three Death Callers immediately after their release into the wild. They found all three before they mated with any mermaids. The two were able to kill the beasts. Sadly, in the act, they were bitten and bled to death in the oceans. However, the crew managed to gather this information about the fins and hidden teeth. Sir Frederick walked away from the merman and continued down the beach toward his next adventure."

I looked up at them, and Charles was not laughing anymore. His face was serious.

"That witch basically ended the Turner dynasty. That's some pretty scary stuff," Uncle William said.

"I can't believe that happened. You know, I had a great uncle who was a fisherman, and he doesn't believe in Death Callers," Charles said.

"Well they are not alive anymore so no need to worry about them," I said.

"Yeah," Charles agreed.

"Hey, look at this, a section on popular weapons used by mermen. It looks like they use sharp pieces of driftwood and tridents. Hey, Charles, here is a weapon for you, a seaweed net," I said, laughing. I closed the book and saw that the sky had already dimmed. The day had gone by so fast.

"Uncle William, I think we should pull over and set up camp. I mean, we still need time to practice our fighting skills," I suggested.

He pulled the wagon into a clearing. Uncle William told Charles to go find wood for a fire. I was ordered to make a space for us to sleep on the wagon. Uncle William was preparing a fish that was packed for us by Prince George. We built the fire as soon as Charles came back. The temperature was dropping. Even though it is summer, some nights get very cold, and I had to sleep with lots of clothes on to keep warm in the palace. I prefer heat over the cold any day. Uncle William placed the fish in a pan that he had fixed to balance on sticks over the fire. I watched as the wood cracked and burned under the intense heat of the flame.

Charles and I began to practice sparring. Uncle William watched us for a while, but then, he took his sword and joined in. We all taught each other different techniques and moves. Uncle William also found a log for us to lift up and down to make our muscles stronger. Maybe we will have a small chance of beating the Fearhine.

We sat down by the fire, ready to enjoy our meal.

"Hey, Uncle William?" I asked.

"Yeah?"

"Do you really think we are gonna have a chance at beating the Fearhine? I mean we aren't Royal Knights or anything," I asked.

"I think we have just as good of a chance as any of those Royal Knights," he answered with a smile.

"I don't know about that one," Charles mumbled.

"Did you boys know that it is faster to travel by boat than by carriage?" Uncle William said, changing the conversation.

"That's interesting. We should have done that instead of a wagon, but it is probably much harder to steer a boat. I have never steered a boat before so, I wouldn't know," Charles said, tossing twigs into the fire. Then, he gave a fist bump from out of nowhere. What is he doing? Every time I looked over at him, he is breaking up small twigs and throwing them into the flame. Was he playing a game? After further examination, I figured out what game he came up with. If he made it into a hole, which is three big branches leaning up next to each other, his face lit up, and he did a fist bump or a quiet "yes!" I secretly started to play his game. He noticed me and began a small competition in secret.

"What are you two boys doing with those sticks? You are acting like crazy people. The fire has enough wood in it," Uncle William laughed, confused. I explained to him what we were both doing.

"That sounds like a brilliant game! We should make a tournament of it!" Uncle William cheered.

We began many rounds of the tournament. After the thirteenth round, Uncle William suggested we should make the game more interesting.

"Okay, for three points, you have to make it in while sitting on the horse. And for that, I'm going to make this interesting- person with the most points by the time the fish is cooked wins the biggest piece of the fish!" Uncle William said, mounting the horse.

"I will take that bet because it seems I am in first, you are in second, and Liam is in last. So, I will enjoy my fish," Charles said, waiting to mount the horse.

Uncle William took his shot. He missed by just a hair. Charles cheered, and Uncle William shouted out in agony. I took my shot and missed, but I knew that I wouldn't have won anyways.

"I don't even have to make this one in because I already won!" he said with a chipper tone in his voice. Charles took the shot and made it. We all cried out in joy.

"I can't believe you made it!" I yelled.

Charles patted the horse and hopped down.

"I would like to thank all of my fans, I'm looking at you Mr. Horse," Charles joked.

Uncle William pulled the fish out of the fire. He cut it into three pieces and gave the biggest piece to Charles.

"This fish is so much better than the food we have been eating in the castle. I wonder what is happening there right now. Do you think anyone noticed were gone, I would have noticed," Charles wondered.

"Anyone noticed? The real question is who didn't notice we were gone! Ugh, this means that Ms. Woodround has my job. Poor Bethany. She will be very upset that you guys are not there. Bethany will have to do all of your work for you," Uncle William explained, biting into his piece of fish.

"Wow, way to make us feel better, Uncle William. Bethany is going to be so mad at us. We actually left her all alone with all of our work. She is going to kill us," I stressed out. Suddenly, I pictured us coming back to find her grave. Carved into the mossy stone would say "Bethany died from overworking and spending too much time with Ms. Woodround". I shuddered at the thought. How could I do that to my friend?

"Aww...I am going to miss so many good pranks. Edward and Sasha were planning on putting fake spiders in Ms. Woodround's bed! That would have been so much fun!" Charles said, disappointed.

I rolled my eyes. All I could think about was how furious Bethany will be when we come back. *If* we come back, that is.

"Okay then, it's getting late, and I think we should be heading to bed," Uncle William said, putting out the fire.

We laid down side by side in the wagon and slowly fell asleep.

The next day was one of the most uneventful days of my life. Hours and hours went by, and the scenery stayed the same. The cart smoothly moved down the never-ending road. The sun beat down on us, making the whole ride ten times worse.

"Well boys, it will be a really long ride through northern Jarvally because it is all hot meadows. We should change courses and head through the woods of Pineswood. Right now we can still change direction because were not too far into Jarvally, but we should turn and go into the woods soon," Uncle William suggested as we slowly suffered through the hot meadow.

"Let's do it, then," Charles said.

It only took us a half hour to make it to the shady wood trails through Pineswood. It felt so good to be relived of the boiling heat from the sun.

"We would originally be heading straight through Jarvally but this new plan would be better. Besides, northern Pineswood is more interesting to look at. Not to mention, now the horse will not be as hot. Let's see; we can play a game or sing a song. What do you want to do, Liam?" Uncle William asked.

I stared at him with tired eyes. All I wanted to do was sleep. The sun had drained almost all my energy.

"Alright then, I will whistle a song to myself," Uncle William started to whistle. The tune was happy and lulled me into a deep sleep.

"Hey, Liam! Wake up! You have to listen to this story about your dad," Charles said, poking my leg with a stick he found.

I opened my eyes and tried to not complain about the fact that I was being poked with a stick. I must have been asleep for a long time because now the sky was turning into dusk.

"Okay, I am listening," I said rubbing my eyes.

"Alright then. When me and your father were young boys, about seven, we encountered a unicorn," he said, hiding a giggle.

"Oh, come on, stop joking around. There are no such things as unicorns. They are make-believe," I said.

"Oh, but it was real. The horse had a horn, and when it walked, flowers came up behind it," Uncle William said trying to convince me.

"Yeah, sure it did," I said, rolling my eyes.

"No, I'm serious," he said, quietly laughing.

"Ha, ha, ha, you're hilarious," I said sarcastically.

"Charles believes me. He was there, and he was riding the unicorn," he said making Charles laugh.

"Wow, real mature, waking me up to tell me a fake story," I said.

"Oh, you think that's the reason? I was just messing with you. You need to-" Uncle William started.

"Hey look at that! An inn," Charles said, pointing to a sign next to a big house.

In the middle of the woods sat a beautiful inn. A garden of roses surrounded the house, and a big crescent shaped driveway wrapped around a big oak tree in front of the house. A sign on the side of the road read "Rosemary Inn".

"Mr. Rocklen, we should stay there. It would be an upgrade from the ground and the wagon," Charles suggested in a convincing tone.

"Charles, for the fifth time, you can just call me Uncle William! Lord, you sound like the tax collectors when you say that!" Uncle William laughed.

"Uncle William, you saw how tired I was today. We need sleep comfortably if we want to face the Fearhine. And it's getting dark anyways. Please, Uncle William," I begged.

"Please..." Charles pleaded.

"Fine," he said, pulling the wagon into the driveway.

We all hopped out of the wagon. I grabbed my satchel and walked up to the door. Uncle William gave it a knock. No one answered, but you could hear voices inside. We all looked at each other. Uncle William knocked again. A short bald man with black facial hair opened the door. However, his most prominent feature was the big smile on his face. The scent of the warm cozy house brushed over me.

"Hello, welcome to the Rosemary Inn! You look like weary travelers in need of a place to stay! Come in, come in," he said in a cheerful tone.

I looked at Charles, and he smiled back. Uncle William followed the man inside. The inside of the house gave me a warm feeling. There was a woodstove blazing with fresh kindling and a pot of water over it. A doorway leading to a kitchen was on my left, and a table with chairs and a vase full of roses was on my right. For some reason it reminded me of the kitchen in the castle. It was probably because of the warm fire and the subtle smell of food cooking.

"Gwen, please come here. We have guests," the man called up a staircase in the back of the room.

"Can I offer you gentlemen a drink?" asked a woman who was walking into the room.

Her brown curly hair was up messily placed in a bun. The woman held up a pitcher of water, so it was visible to us.

"Yes, please, Mrs. Rosemary, I presume?" Uncle William said.

"You presume correctly!" she said, giving us a big smile.

"Gwen dear, show our guests to their room!" Mrs. Rosemary said, without moving her mouth from her smile.

I looked to Charles. By his expression, I could tell that he thought the smiling was weird. I agreed. It is nice that the Rosemary's are happy but I think they could go without smiling so much.

A girl who looked to be about eighteen years old walked us upstairs. Her short curly black hair, light brown skin, and cute small nose made her almost identical to Mrs. Rosemary. Like both of her parents, Gwen smiled a lot.

We entered a big room. It had two beds and looked a lot like the downstairs part of the house.

Gwen lit a candle and placed it on the bureau. She gave a curtsy and then left. When I saw her leave, her smile disappeared and was replaced by a worried expression.

"That was weird," I mumbled to myself.

"They seem very friendly!" Uncle William said as he unpacked his things.

"Yeah, but, did anyone get a weird feeling about them? It seems weird the way they smile all the time," Charles asked.

"I don't know, they seem like lovely people," Uncle William said.

"I agree, they do seem nice, but something is kind of odd about that excessive smiling," I said.

"I don't know about that but, I think we should unpack and then head down for dinner," Uncle William suggested.

Uncle William took a seat down at the table. Charles and I followed. Mrs. Rosemary came in with a plate of cut-up ham and a loaf of bread.

"Ah, so glad you came down. I just pulled a ham out of the oven, and we have some bread. Are you hungry? It's very good," Mrs. Rosemary said, temptingly.

"Thank you," I said.

"Looks good," Charles got his fork ready to dive into the ham.

"Yes, very good indeed. Thank you," Uncle William said, taking some bread and shoving it into his mouth.

The ham was very good, but the bread was a little stale. After I finished, Uncle William and Charles were still eating their food.

While I waited for them, I looked around the room. Mrs. Rosemary was standing still, smiling, next to the kitchen door. Gwen was sitting on the stairs watching us. She saw me looking at her and rushed back up the stairs. Something here was strange, but maybe Uncle William was right. The Rosemary's might just be attempting to make us comfortable. If they are, it is doing the opposite effect.

We thanked the Rosemary's again for the meal and hospitality, and then, we went to bed.

"So, who gets the beds, and who gets the floor?" Uncle William asked.

"Obviously I get the bed. I'm the better fighter so..." I bragged with a smile.

"What!? First of all, I get the bed. Second, I am the better fighter. Third, why are we deciding this by who can fight better?!" Charles questioned.

"Boys! Either way, I get a bed. So, there is only one way to do this. I will pick a number, and you will guess it," Uncle William said.

"Okay, three," I picked my number. Hopefully it's right. I don't want to be on the hard floor all night like back in the wagon.

"Seven," Charles answered.

"The number I picked was two. Liam, you get the bed," Uncle William revealed, climbing into his bed.

"Yes!" I cheered.

"Boo!" Charles said angrily marching over to his bag and pulling out a blanket. I got into my bed and blew out my candle.

"Goodnight!" Uncle William said, blowing out his candle.

I closed my eyes and fell asleep.

Chapter 16

Suddenly, I woke to the sound of Charles shouting and making noises. The room was pitch black, and I couldn't see what was happening. It looked like there were two shadows wrestling with each other in the dark. I listened for Uncle William. Oh my lord. I can't believe he is still sleeping!

"Liam! Help an intruder! Mr. Rocklen!" he yelled.

I sprung into action and woke Uncle William up. It was so dark that I had to reach my hands out awkwardly to find anything. I felt his shoulder and frantically shook him up and down.

"Wha- what's happening? What- Charles?" Uncle William jumped out of bed once he figured out what was happening.

We rushed over to Charles and managed to pin down the intruder.

"Liam, go light the candles!" Uncle William ordered.

I found the candle and rushed to light it. Who could have possibly broken in? Why would anyone want to break into an inn that only had three guests?

I nervously fumbled around with the lit candle and I ran it over to reveal the culprit.

"I caught him stealing your bag!" Charles said, holding it up.

I walked over, and the light revealed who it was. A wave of shock rushed over me.

"Mr. Rosemary!" we all shrieked, gasping. Uncle William practically had steam coming out of his ears.

"WHAT IS THE MEANING OF THIS?" he yelled.

We let go of Mr. Rosemary and stood up. He stayed on the floor, cowering.

"Please, sir, don't hurt me!" he begged, curling up like a helpless child.

"Boys, gather your things, and let's go down stairs and have a talk with the Rosemarys. Get up!" He grabbed Mr. Rosemary's arm and pulled him up.

I packed my satchel as quickly as I could. Charles did the same. It was still dark out when I looked through the windows as we walked down the stairs, holding Mr. Rosemary like a prisoner. I wondered why he would want to rob me? Mr. Rosemary walked with his head down like a dog that had gotten into the left over dinner.

Mrs. Rosemary was waiting with Gwen in the common room. When they saw that Mr. Rosemary was caught, their faces turned white as ghosts. Mrs. Rosemary gasped and put her hand to her mouth.

"Now, explain yourself, you crook! We paid you for the stay! What else could you want from us?" Uncle William shouted.

Charles and I stood next to the stairs away from my raging Uncle. I know very well not to get on Dads or Uncle Williams bad side. Strangely, Gwen had a straight face and walked backward slowly to the fire. Uncle William was yelling at the Rosemary's now.

"I want an explanation!" Uncle William yelled.

"T...times are hard and…" Mr. Rosemary said, shaking like a leaf.

"What kind of explanation is that?" Uncle William shouted.

"I-," Mr. Rosemary continued.

"What type of operation are you running here?!" Uncle William questioned.

I thought back to Sir Frederick's advice that he gives young heroes like me. I remembered the first chapter saying that being a hero was about surroundings. I took a deep breath and closed my eyes. I opened them and looked around the room. Charles was standing next to me with his mouth open. Uncle William was interrogating the Rosemary's for an explanation. The Rosemary's were standing next to each other, shaking in their boots. Gwen was standing near the fire with her head down and mouth closed tight.

I wanted to find out a way to fix this or to help, but nothing came to mind. I stood watching. Minutes of arguing passed, and we still had no new information. This interrogation was basically useless. I looked over at Gwen. I had to take a second look since strangely, she was no longer standing. I walked over to her, crouched by the dying embers of the fire.

"Psst, Liam, where are you going?" Charles hissed.

Gwen was hunched over the fireplace, pulling ashes out of the fire and onto the floor. Is she insane? Why would she be creating a bigger mess for her to clean up? Then, she flattened the ashes out evenly across the floor. Charles came over and gave me a questioning look when he saw what she was doing.

Gwen looked over her shoulder and waved us down. Charles and I crouched next to Gwen. She looked at Charles and then at me. Her eyes looked like the eyes of a sad dog. Oddly, she began to write in the ashes. Charles looked at me, and we knew that something was not right with the Rosemary family. Gwen finished writing.

"Help me?" I said out loud.

My head hurt. Why is she asking for help? Gwen lightly ran her hand over the words, erasing them.

"What does she mean? Gwen, what do you mean?" I asked.

I knew she could hear me, but she didn't seem like she was listening to the words I was saying. Gwen seemed nervous and scared. She leaned back over the ashes and started to write again. Charles shrugged.

We all huddled over the ashes. None of the adults seemed to notice since the loud sounds of arguing continued in the background. If I were them I would defiantly notice a bunch of teenagers huddling over a floor covered in ashes!

"T...R...O...L...L, troll! What is that supposed to mean, Charles?" I asked out loud.

"I have no idea. Gwen, what are you trying to say? Stop with this mysterious writing stuff and just tell us. I mean that's why humans invented talking so we could like actually understand what the heck people are saying," Charles said, getting annoyed. Gwen quickly wrote another word.

"Brother?" I asked.

"So, your brother is a troll, and he needs help? I don't know how your brother could be a troll, but okay then. Maybe she is trying to say that her brother is mean and acts like a troll?" Charles asked.

Gwen's "hints" were just making me even more confused. I looked at Gwen's face. She was frustrated. We obviously don't understand what she is trying to say, why doesn't she just tell us?!

"I don't think that's right. Maybe her brother knows a troll who needs help. What if the troll asked her brother to help the troll? Or something like that," I wonder.

Gwen made a grunting noise and smacked her hand on her forehead. She aggressively pointed at the words.

"Oh! I got it, the troll is trapped in a well, and her brother went to save the troll and needs help pulling the troll out!" Charles guessed.

"That's ridiculous. Obviously, the troll offered to help her brother, but they ended up getting caught in a hole and need help getting out," I argued.

"That's even more ridiculous! That was the craziest thing I have ever heard! The troll is maybe a metaphor for something?" Charles argued.

Gwen was getting angry, and the noise level in the room was not helping.

"You people are hiding something, and if you don't spit it out, I'm calling the authorities! I know a lot of Royal Knights that would help me out!" Uncle William threatened.

"That is ridiculous!" Charles said to me.

"I think the troll needs help, and the brother went to help him, and he needs our help," I guessed again.

"No, the brother was asking us to help, and the troll was already helping him," Charles said.

"MY BROTHER WAS TAKEN BY A TROLL, AND WE NEED YOUR HELP GETTING HIM BACK!" Gwen yelled at the top of her lungs.

Mrs. Rosemary screamed bloody murder and fainted. Mr. Rosemary yelled in agony. Gwen put her hand over her mouth. I had no idea what just happened. This family is psychotic!

"GWEN, WHAT HAVE YOU DONE!?" Mr. Rosemary wailed.

"My sweet baby boy! Oh, Octavius!" Mrs. Rosemary said crying.

"I'm sorry! We can't keep living in silence, Mother! Father, these men have weapons, and they can save Octavius! I saw those two had swords!" Gwen cried.

"Gwen, you can't possibly believe these men would want to help us!" Mr. Rosemary said.

"Hold on! Hold on! Everyone stop talking!" Uncle William yelled.

The room went silent, and all eyes were on him.

"Now, everyone calm down and explain what is going on here," Uncle William ordered.

"It was about a month ago. Octavius and I were outside, playing a game together. Mother and Father were inside. Then, all of a sudden, you could hear big thumps coming from the woods. The ground started to shake like someone was slamming a big rock into the ground over and over again. Then, a troll appeared from out of the trees. I grabbed my brother and waited for the troll to strike, but it stood and just looked at us," Gwen explained.

The story was overwhelming, and I could not have imagined what I would have done if that happened to me.

"The troll was about thirteen feet tall. Its skin was grey with a hint of green. It wore an animal skin and had a big long branch in its hand," Gwen described.

I remembered reading about trolls in "Sir Frederick's Adventures". The troll she described was an average one, but is still very big compared to a human.

"The troll told us to get all of our valuable goods and bring them to him. We did as he told. Then, he told us to steal the valuables that the customers brought. Stuff like metals, gold, silver. We told him we would never, and then, he took him. He took Octavius! He said that if we didn't steal from travelers and give him the loot he would...he...he would kill Octavius!" Gwen shoved her head into her hands.

"Why didn't you go ask for help?" I asked.

"Well, the troll has super hearing and vision, so as we speak, he can hear us, and our son is probably dead!" Mrs. Rosemary cried.

"What! Super hearing? You guys don't know much about trolls do you?" I said shocked.

They shook their heads.

"But that's what the troll told us!" Mr. Rosemary defending himself.

"The troll tricked you! They don't have super hearing or vision!" I said, dumbfounded. Why would they believe that?!

"Well, then, what are we waiting for? Let's go get your son back!" Uncle William said, pulling out his sword.

"You will actually help us?" Mr. Rosemary asked.

"Uncle William, wait! We can't go charging in there without a plan!" I stopped him.

They all looked at me. I thought quickly about what to say.

"Well then, Liam, you seem to know a lot about trolls. You should be the one to lead us into battle!" Uncle William suggested.

My eyes popped out of my head. Me?! Suddenly I realized, I was being given yet another quest to be a hero! Maybe I really am meant to be a knight!

"Seriously?" I asked with excitement.

He nodded. I pulled out my sword and crouched down next to the ashes. Using the side of my blade, I smoothed out the ashes and began to draw a map of the inn and the road.

"Gather round, everyone!" I announced. They all came over and circled around me. This was the most amazing thing to ever happen to me. I was actually leading them into battle! Never have I felt more alive.

"Okay, first I'm going to need some more information on the troll. Where is he located?" I ordered.

"I know where he is! He is not far from here. He lives in a cave in the woods!" Gwen said, pointing to the corner of the ashes.

I drew a cave and some trees. I remembered everything "Sir Frederick's Adventures" had taught me about fighting a troll. Using the information, I concocted a plan. When they heard my plan, they all nodded in approval.

"Let's go save my son!" Mr. Rosemary cheered.

Mrs. Rosemary came out of the kitchen with what I told her to get. Mr. Rosemary armed himself with a pitch fork and gave Gwen a shovel. We all exited the house. I think that we brought hope back into the Rosemary's lives. I saw a fire in them that was not there before.

It was dark out, and the only thing that lit our path was the light from the moon. I took a deep breath of the crisp summer night air.

"Now, I need everyone to watch where they step," Uncle William said.

"We can't bring any torches, if we do the troll will see us coming. They may not have super hearing, but they are still very alert creatures," I instructed.

"Yeah, having the element of surprise is key!" Charles added.

"We just need to quiet down as we get closer," I continued.

Gwen led us to the back of the house and through the woods. The only sound you could hear besides our heavy breathing was the repetitive sound of crickets. My stomach turned as we walked deeper into the woods. I felt my sword begin to slip in my hand from how much I was sweating. I rubbed my hands quickly on my pants. I had to get rid of my nerves if I wanted to save Octavius. If I can defeat this troll, then maybe the Fearhine will be a walk in the market.

We drew closer to the troll's lair, and the top of a dark cave could be seen through the trees. I clenched my fists and puffed out my chest. I can do this. I can do this. I have learned so much from Sir Frederick, so there is no reason why I should not be able to "beat the beast," as Sir Frederick says.

We reached the outside of an enormous cave. Quickly, we all hid behind the trees. We didn't want to risk being seen since the cave is too dark to see if anyone is watching from inside. I nervously looked at everyone and gave a nod. That was the signal to start my plan.

Mrs. Rosemary scurried through the bushes to a large bush right next to the cave. I waited for her signal that indicated the area was safe. She threw her thumb up in the air. Everyone rushed out from behind the trees and to the cave entrance. I ran up to the others, who were waiting for me to lead them into the darkness. I held my sword tight and stepped into the cave. This was it. Time to prove I am a hero. They followed behind me in a straight line. I shook my hands out in the air since they continued to sweat.

I looked up to find the top of the cave was covered in sharp stalactites. They looked sharp enough to puncture a man and kill him in seconds. I shuddered at the thought. That would be an awful way to die.

The cave slowly began to light up, and we were no longer walking blindly through the darkness. The light grew brighter until you could see a big circular room formed at the end of the cave. I stealthily walked along the walls. We had finally reached the entrance to the troll's room. The room was bigger than a house and about a hundred torches lined the walls. You could vividly see a big pile of metal and gold objects in the middle of the cave. I suspected the pile was all of the items the Rosemary's had stolen for the troll.

A boy that looked about ten or twelve years old lay unconscious next to the pile. He had cuts on his face and arms, and dried blood covered his body. The boy had short, curly black hair and looked exactly like his parents. We had found Octavius.

Gwen gasped and quickly held her mouth. Uncle William held his finger to his mouth to signal silence. A big shadow came out from where my blind spot was. We had found the troll.

My teeth started chattering, and my body shook. The troll shadow stretched long across the cave. My hands shook as I held up the signal and gave a thumbs-up. Uncle William and Charles snuck up next to me. I counted to three.

"One…" I whispered.

The troll came out from the blind spot, and the ground shook a little when he walked.

"Two…"

The troll's hideous face came into view. Just like Gwen said he wore an animal skin around his waist that came up over his shoulder like a toga. I looked in fear at the enormous club that he dragged lazily behind him.

"Three…" I said.

My legs began moving before I could think about it. Charles and Uncle William were running with me to the troll. It caught sight of us and made a confused face.

I ran faster than the others, so I reached the troll first. Looking directly at the troll, I could only see his waist. In order to see his head, I had to look up. This was not going to be easy.

I winded my arm back and threw the sword forward as hard as I could into his legs. I pulled my sword away. It was colored in a black liquid. The troll howled in pain. At the same time, Charles threw a kitchen knife at the troll's shoulder and missed. I ran backward as Uncle William came up and cut the troll in a similar spot.

We all ran backward away from Octavius to take the troll's attention off his prisoner. I could see Mr. Rosemary out of the corner of my eye. He ran out and picked up Octavius by the shoulders. Gwen came behind her father and took Octavius by the feet. Now all we had to do was give them time to get out. After that comes the hard part - getting *ourselves* out.

All of a sudden, a club swung right past my face. I looked back at the troll. He was closing in on us and swinging at Uncle William.

"Hang on, Uncle William!" I shouted, running up and jabbing my sword into the troll's foot.

The troll turned to me and swung his club down on me.

"Liam!" Uncle William yelled.

I quickly jumped out of the way. My heart beat faster than a hummingbird's wings could move. That was way too close of a call. I shook my head and focused again.

I dodged the troll's club and swung at him when I got the chance. The troll howled in pain when Charles threw a knife right in the troll's chest. The troll swung furiously at us. His hand came at me at full speed knocking me backwards into the cave wall. My back and chest burned as the wind got knocked out of me.

I looked over at Charles and Uncle William being smacked around and swung at by the troll's club. The troll threw Uncle William into Charles, and they fell onto the floor. I struggled to stand up and help.

The troll turned its attention back to Octavius and discovered his prisoner was being taken away. Gwen noticed and ran for her shovel. I could see in her eyes that all of her anger was about to be let out on the troll. I would feel the same way if my brother was taken away and I was forced to keep it a secret.

Gwen sprinted at the troll and leaped up to the troll's chest. With great force, she swung the shovel into the troll. The blow looked like it could have knocked a man out. However, trolls have much thicker skin and bones than humans. The troll yelled, holding his head. Gwen landed next to the troll's leg and quickly rolled out of the way as the troll stepped backwards. In that moment, I knew that it was the perfect time to escape.

I saw the exit and yelled, "LET'S GO!" Charles grabbed Uncle William, and they started sprinting toward the exit. Gwen ran back over to Octavius. The troll followed her back to her brother.

"LOOK OUT!" Charles yelled.

The troll swung his foot at Mr. Rosemary and Octavius. Both were knocked to the ground. Gwen gasped and ran over to the wall. She pulled a torch off and threw in right at the troll's head. The fire hit the troll in the nose and eye. It screamed out in agony. I copied what she did and threw one right at its back. It was working! Gwen threw one last torch right at its chest, catching the troll's animal skin toga on fire.

The troll screamed and stumbled about the cave, trying to put out the fire. We made a run for the exit. The troll hopped up and down, putting the fire out. The entire cave shook like in an earthquake.

My legs moved faster as soon as I caught sight of the exit. Bats escaped with us toward the forest that was outside. The cave shook violently. I looked back in fear. The troll was bounding toward us. He smashed his body and club up against the walls, still trying to put out the fire on his back. The cave shook, and I tripped over my foot. Before I fell over, I regained my balance and started to run again. The troll swung his club, and the cave shook more.

Screams and shouts from my comrades echoed in the unstable cave. I could not make out what they were saying but it was obvious they were panicking.

Stalactites fell left and right. We all dodged them quickly. My heart beat faster and faster. Practically everything around me was either shaking or crumbling onto me. Still, my legs pushed me forward.

"Hurry! RUN!" Mrs. Rosemary screamed from outside the cave.

We were almost there. Suddenly, the troll tripped over himself and knocked into the cave. As the troll hit the ground, the cave entrance quickly began to collapse. Rocks were falling all around us, and my heart pounded.

Just as Gwen, Charles, and I exited the cave, a stalagmite was falling right above Charles. In a second, the stalactites fell over him. As if time slowed down around me, my heroic instincts kicked in and I shoved him out of the way. I fell down as I pushed him, and felt a sharp pain in my leg. I howled out in pain. Fear took over me as I tried but could not get up. Gwen turned around and dragged me out of the way of the falling rocks. My head became dizzy. All I could see was Gwen picking one of my arms up and Charles picking up the other. I felt the soft grass brush up against my legs as they carried me into the clearing in front of the cave. I looked over at the cave entrance, it was covered in rocks, and the troll was trapped. My head fell back and I gazed up at the beautiful night sky. Mrs. Rosemary ran out from the bushes and over to me. Her husband and son followed. Soon, everyone was surrounding me. I tried to speak but no actual words came out of my mouth.

"LIAM!" Uncle William yelled, tears in his eyes.

I could tell people were talking to me, but the words were hard to hear. I could only hear my name being shouted. Everything was going fuzzy. All I was able to make out was Mrs. Rosemary grabbing a towel and placing it around a small stalactite that was in my leg. Blood dripped down, staining the grass. Uncle William and Mr. Rosemary knelt down next to my leg and grabbed onto the rock. My eyes bulged out of my head. The sight of a large rock impaled in my leg immediately woke me up from my daze.

"What is going on?!" I screamed in shock.

They pulled up as hard as they could on the rock. I screamed at the top of my lungs. The rock yanked up. Mrs. Rosemary and Gwen quickly poured liquids in the wound. Blood gushed all over my pants and the grass. My leg stung like a million bee stings. Suddenly, my eyes went black, and they closed.

Chapter 17

Suddenly, I woke up in the Rosemary Inn bedroom. My leg was numb. It felt as if I had no leg at all. Sunlight shined through the window and into my eyes. I peered out it at the beautiful day forming outside. My head ached. What happened last night? How did I get in here?

"Uncle William?! Charles?!" I called for them.

Gwen came rushing in with a tray full of eggs and three pieces of bacon. She placed it on my lap. I looked at her, and she gestured to eat. The tray warmed the only leg I had feeling in. I dug into the meal. I don't know if it was that I was just really hungry or the eggs actually tasted good but they were the best I had ever had.

"Thank you," I said.

"So, you are probably really confused, Liam. A rock fell into your leg. You are a very lucky guy. The rock missed your bone by an inch. My mother and I had treated it as well as we could. We did pour water on the wound to clean it as best as we could but it didn't do much. We also gave you some medicine to reduce the pain. It's not very effective though. I mean I wish we had better medicine here but we did wrap it up with a bandage. That was a very brave thing you did for my brother. He was not hurt very badly. I am so grateful for your help," Gwen said, tearing up.

"No problem. So, how is he? Your brother?" I asked.

"He is a little scratched up. The troll had beaten him only once when he tried to escape. But, he could not stop thanking your friend and uncle. I am so grateful though. I still, can't believe you guys offered to help after everything we did. Am I talking too much? Sorry. It's just that I have not talked in like forever. I just want to talk and talk, and I can't stop," Gwen giggled.

I smiled at her and ate my bacon.

"Well, I will leave you to it. We will be right down stairs if you need anything." She left and gave me a curtsy.

I felt so important with the breakfast in bed. This might be the weirdest thing to ever happen to me. Not to mention the most painful.

I finished my meal and placed the tray down next to me. Taking a deep breath, I turned my body and tried standing. I was shocked. I was standing, but it felt weird. I had expected pain, but I felt nothing in my leg. Still, it might not be a good idea to put pressure on my injury. I walked with the tray to the stairs as if I had a peg leg. When, I reached the top of the staircase, I could hear voices coming from downstairs. Carefully, I sat down on the step and then scooted down the stairs. Everyone was huddled around the table. Uncle William noticed me as soon as I approached the last few steps.

"Liam! Are you crazy?! Why would you go down the stairs with your leg like that? Charles, come give me a hand," Uncle William ordered, rushing over to me.

Charles ran up and grabbed my arm. Uncle William grabbed the other, and they picked me up. We walked over to a chair, and they sat me down. All eyes were on me.

"Liam, you are a lifesaver! I can't thank you enough for saving me! I mean I could have died!" Charles thanked me.

"Thank you for coming to save me!" Octavius said, shaking my hand.

"You did a great job, Liam!" Uncle William said.

"Thank you! Thank you ever so much for saving my sweet baby boy!" Mrs. Rosemary said giving me a tight hug.

Everyone was swarming around me. I was so overwhelmed I could hardly keep up with who was talking to me. I could not believe it. I was a hero!

I thought back to when I was younger. Like every other kid in Brendsworth, I wanted to be a knight when I grew up. I would run around with Byron trying to help anyone we saw. However, my efforts were never worthy enough of the title. My whole life I have only had one dream, and even if at some points I did not acknowledge it, all I wanted to be was a hero. Now, I am one.

"You really did a good job, Liam. Now, Mrs. Rosemary, give us the report," Uncle William asked.

"So, Liam, your leg is not fully healed or even cleaned. If you don't go get this leg cleaned, we could be talking infection and, possibly, death. I know that it's a dark thing to be saying after all the good things you did but these are the facts. You have to go to the Ocean Bay Market. It is about a three-hour ride south. There, you can get the medical help you need. I am giving you seven gold coins to pay for some food and medicine. I wish I could do more to thank you," she said. Uncle William accepted the money.

"I wish we could give more, I feel horrible about trying to steal from such kind and honorable people," Mr. Rosemary said.

"Thank you. All of last night is water under the bridge. You just wanted to save Octavius over here," Uncle William smiled.

"I've heard of Ocean Bay Market. It's one of the best places in the Outer Kingdom to get magical goods and potions. A ton of witches shop there. I have not met a witch that hasn't been!" Charles shared.

"Thank you, again. You boys better be heading out if you want to get to the market before it gets really busy," Mr. Rosemary said.

"Thanks again!" Octavius shook our hands.

"Make sure you keep your bandage on, Liam," Mrs. Rosemary advised.

"Yeah, that would be horrible if it got infected. But, thank you, I know we have said it a lot but, I am so happy my brother is safe." Gwen reached over and gave her brother a hug.

"Thank you for the food. Hope you guys have a nice day," I said, waving goodbye.

"Believe me, I will be spending my day trying to recover all the stole items from that horrible cave," Mr. Rosemary said waving back.

Charles and Uncle William picked me up, and we hobbled over to the wagon. My leg still felt numb. The Rosemary's now had a real reason to smile. They waved us off, and we continued on our real mission.

"Okay, boys, we are going to take a three hour detour to the Ocean Bay Market for Liam's medicine," Uncle William said.

"I just hope that our detour won't result in something bad, like, regarding the Fearhine," Charles said.

The leaves rustled in a soothing way. I spent the time I had playing with Scales. The cute dragon came to life and playfully jumped around the wagon. It was nice to sit back and relax.

As time passed, the medicine's effects weakened. I felt a sharp pain in my calf. It felt like someone was biting at my leg.

"Hey, Uncle William. My leg is hurting really badly," I alerted him.

"We are almost there. Can you be strong and last twenty more minutes?" Uncle William asked.

"Ugh…sure," I said, gripping the edge of the wagon.

I squeezed it tighter and tighter as the pain got worse. I felt as if I would rip the wood right off the wagon if I squeezed it any harder. Soon, my leg began to feel like it had felt last night. I gripped the wood and stared up at the trees. Then, I tried to calm myself by breathing slower.

The trees began to thin, and we drove into an opening. There were thousands of carts parked in a large grassy field. Tons of tents and vendors sat in the opening. The Ocean Bay Market sat on a cliff that looked out over the ocean. I gazed at the never-ending calming blue water. A cool and relaxing breeze blew through my hair. It took my mind off my leg for a few seconds until the pain returned. Uncle William parked the wagon, and then helped me out. I limped down to the market section. There were so many people shouting and advertising their goods. It was obviously much bigger than the Brendsworth market. A man held out a roll of cheese in my face and yelled at me to buy it. I avoided eye contact with all the merchants as I limped through the crowd. My leg felt as if it was on fire. Uncle William and Charles looked left and right for a booth with medicine.

There were mainly booths selling exotic products for witches to make potions with, along with many informational books and potion recipes.

We walked on and on for what felt like forever. Finally, we saw a booth that appeared somewhat promising. A tall man with fancy blue hair sat in a booth that was filled with potions. We walked up to him.

"Welcome to Marty's Medicine Booth! We sell homemade medicine made by me. Oh…what's wrong with him over there?" Marty said, pointing to me.

I had seen many strange-looking vendors like Marty before back in Brendsworth. He had his blue hair twisted and curled at the top of his head like frosting on a cupcake. In addition, he wore a blue and white tuxedo along with a necklace around his neck that had a funny-looking glass squirrel on it.

"His leg was impaled by a rock. It happened last night up in northern Pineswood. We need a healing potion for him," Uncle William said.

Marty turned around and carefully plucked a bottle of medicine off the shelf and placed it on the counter. The liquid inside the square bottle was dirty and brown.

"Here is my leg and arm-healing potion. It is made from the finest ingredients. All the ingredients are found and grow right here in Pineswood. The leg should heal three weeks after drinking," Marty said.

"What? Three weeks? That's too long! Liam will be long dead before then!" Uncle William slammed his fist on the table.

"What kind of medicine is that? Witches' potions can make it work in less than an hour!" Charles said.

"Well, I'm sorry sir. I'm not a witch. Three week is the time it will take," Marty said calmly.

Uncle William turned around, and we continued walking through the market. Charles pointed to a booth to my right.

"How about that one?" Charles suggested.

"I guess we can try," Uncle William said, walking over.

The booth was made of branches and sticks that the vendor probably found on the ground. A blue star patterned cloth was draped over the top of it in a messy fashion. A small woman stood inside the booth, which was barely holding together. Like the booth, the woman looked as if she had just walked out of the forest. She had a large nose and shoulder length grey curly hair filled with sticks and leaves. Dirt-covered brown and green robes were draped over her shoulders. I noticed how she had to stand on a small stool in order to look over the top of the counter.

"Welcome to the Posture Pianist! Oh, no, that's not it. What was it called…oh! The Positive Potions! My potions are positivity perfect," she said with a toothy smile.

I looked at my Uncle William. Are they serious? This lady has lost her marbles. Even if she owned a potion that could heal my leg, I bet she could not even remember where she keeps it!

"We are looking for a potion that can heal my nephew's leg," Uncle William said.

She let out a cackle and jumped off the stool she stood on. The woman rummaged through her messy stand. She pushed bottles full of mysterious liquids aside until finding a round bottle full of green liquid.

"Ahh, there you are!"

In one swift jump, she hopped up onto her stool. The woman handed us the bottle, and she smiled a big toothy grin. I took it and examined the liquid.

"So, this should cure my leg as soon as I drink it?" I questioned.

"Don't believe me? Drink it right now, and you will see it works right away. If it doesn't, you get your money back," she said, offended by my question.

I looked at Uncle William. Cautiously, I popped opened the bottle. Quickly, I poured the liquid into my mouth. It tasted sour like unripe berries. I almost spit it right out. My eyes went black and blurred. I felt Uncle William and Charles let go of me. I opened my eyes, and suddenly, the whole world stopped. Everything was frozen. My leg buzzed, and I felt it healing.

Quickly, I looked around. It was amazing. A bird was frozen in the air. A man was trying to calm his crying child. The woman cackled. My eyes darted to the stand, and she was laughing. Unlike everything else, the woman was not frozen. I looked around once more. A figure in a black cloak next to an apple stand was also moving. In addition, a young girl was continuing her shopping. My head ached. Is this what being drunk is like?

I felt my bad leg was beginning to feel just like my good leg. The world slowly started to turn back to normal. Uncle William began to move again. The witch was laughing so hard now that she was on the ground. I felt my body shake, and everything was back to normal.

"Liam? Did it work?" Charles said.

I was amazed.

"What just happened?" I asked the witch.

 She just cackled. My leg feels like it had before I went into that dumb cave. I hit my leg with my hand to make sure it had worked. It was fully operational. How did that work so fast?

Uncle William paid the witch and bought one more bottle just in case. I didn't blame him for buying it because we were about to go up against the Fearhine in a few days. Just the thought of the beast made my stomach turn. Uncle William searched around the market for food to stock up on. Charles and I were allowed to go and pick out a pastry at a booth. I picked out a sweet blueberry danish, and Charles picked a cream cheese one.

We walked back to the cart to enjoy our treats. Uncle William showed up with a barrel of apples and a half-pound of dried meat. We all got settled in our seats, and we were on our way. While I was eating, I began to wonder what had just happened at that witch's stand. Why had the world stopped? More importantly, how did the world stop?

I opened my satchel and pulled out "Sir Frederick's Adventures". If I couldn't find the answers in this book, I didn't know how I would answer my questions. I opened up to the section on magic. Witches, wizards, spells… aha! Potions! I flipped through the long chapter.

I couldn't seem to find what I was looking for. I flipped through it once more. In the first few pages, I found something that might have my answer. I skimmed through the paragraph.

'When anyone takes a potion, the potion will act so quickly that for a few moments it will seem like the world is not moving to the person who took the potion because of it's effects on the brain. However, this is not the same effect for magical beings. Witches will still appear to be moving the same as before because of a side effect in our perceptions when we ingest magic. Like the effects of alcohol and other substances, potions can mess with our brains.'

I paused, taking in the information. That's bizarre. Does that mean the figure in the cloak and the girl I saw were witches too? Maybe that potion has more than one use in a situation.

Soon, my mind was drawn back to the Fearhine. I could not help but wonder what will happen when we find the beast. I don't think I am ready. Even though we had practiced early in the morning every day, I am questioning whether the three of us can defeat the Fearhine. This is no troll. It's a beast that has destroyed villages and killed many men and women who have tried to kill it. The large poisonous stinger haunted my mind. When we fought the troll, I was more nervous than I had ever been before. What am I gonna do when we go up against the most fearsome creature in the Outer Kingdom? Maybe Uncle William and I, with our swords, could hold it off for a small amount of time. That leaves Charles, who won't be much help with his one knife. With that we won't stand a chance! He needs to find a new weapon. However, even with a new weapon, would just the three of us fighting be able to kill the Fearhine?

232

"Uncle William, I think we should get Charles a new weapon," I piped up.

Charles picked up his head from where he was resting it on his hand. I could tell he liked the idea.

"That's an excellent idea, Liam. We are already a little too far to turn back to the Ocean Side Market, but in the next village we pass, we can stop in and buy him a new weapon. Until then, is there anything in that book of yours that shows the choices he has? I mean I already know a lot about weapons but, I just want to see what Sir whatever has to say," Uncle William asked trying to be inconspicuous.

"I would love to have a new weapon! This knife was not very helpful in that fight back there with the troll," Charles complained.

I opened the book and flipped quickly to the very beginning chapters on weapons.

"Okay, here we are. The first weapon is a sword. You could be like me and Uncle William," I said, looking at the image of a sword.

"I'm not very good with a sword. Besides, that means we all have the same thing, and that's boring," Charles said.

"Okay. What about a hammer? Actually, I think that would be too big and heavy for you or even Uncle William. What about a battle-axe? It says that only a few people have been able to master the use of them. It takes years of practice. What about it?" I asked.

"Battle axes sound cool. But, I don't think that I have the time to master using it," Charles said.

I turned the page. My eyes came across a better choice.

"Here is a good one-what about a spear? Oh! A trident would be cool! There is a story of a warrior who fought with a trident and fishing net. He would tangle up his enemy in the net and then pull them close, so he could stab them with the trident," I said.

I then wondered how I would be able to get out of that situation if I was captured in the net. I might try and cut my way out of the net...

"I don't think either of those are for me," Charles said, interrupting my thoughts.

"What about a bow and arrow?" I asked, flipping to the page with bows and throwing knifes.

"Huh, I don't know. Maybe a bow would be a good weapon. I mean, I could hide in the trees and shoot the Fearhine from above. The beast wouldn't see it coming," he said, becoming interested.

"That's would be a perfect weapon for the team," Uncle William said.

We waited in anticipation for the next village.

After a while, we finally reached a village. It was very small and hidden by the trees. The village was called Asti. It looked very similar to Brendsworth.

"Hey, we actually aren't that far from my parent's house," Charles realized.

We walked into the village blacksmith's shop in hopes that we could find a bow and arrow. An older woman was hunched over a table. She was trying to draw a type of weapon that I did not recognize. Uncle William knocked on the doorframe, and she turned around. She had grey hair pulled back into a ponytail and big glasses resting her face.

"Hello there. How can I help you?" she asked, brushing her hands off on her pants.

"We are looking for a bow and some arrows. A quiver of arrows would be nice, too," Charles said.

"I have a nice set of arrows in a leather quiver out back. Here, let me go get it. There are bows up on the wall." She pointed behind us.

On the wall with the door were six bows hanging on display. Uncle William picked one up and handed it to Charles. Charles examined it carefully. I held one out to him and he took it.

"This is a nice bow," he said.

He held it out in front of him and pretended to hold an arrow. The blacksmith walked back in.

"Good taste. That is a fine bow. I actually was given that from a tribe of centaurs. The inscription on the side is written in the ancient language of the centaurs; you know, the one they spoke before they switched to our language," she said.

I looked at the side of the bow, and carved in the wood was 'Raga corra horin ara darath.'

"What does it mean?" Charles asked.

"It means 'Strength and Heart of a Warrior,'" she said, wiping her hands on a rag.

"What is this going to cost us?" Uncle William asked.

"The bow along with the matching set of arrows and quill are seventy silver coins." She held out a brown leather quill filled with arrows. Charles took out his satchel.

"Charles, you don't have to pay with your own money. We have the money that you-know-who gave us. Also, we have some money left over from the Rosemary's," Uncle William said, getting the money out.

"No, it's okay. I want to pay with my own money," Charles said, smiling.

The blacksmith gave him the bow and thanked us for coming to her shop. Charles happily ran outside and found the perfect tree to try his new bow out on. Uncle William and I stood back and watched.

"Are you sure you don't need a lesson?" Uncle William asked, unsure that Charles was ready.

"No, I think I will just give it a try. I used to watch my grandma use one, and I think I understand part of it," he said.

Charles loaded an arrow and pulled back on the bow. He carefully aimed the arrow toward the tree. He let the arrow go, and it shot into the side of the tree.

"I did it! I shot the tree!" he exclaimed, jumping up and down.

"It's not exactly in the center, but that was an incredible first shot," Uncle William said.

"Whoa! How did you learn how to use a bow and arrow so fast?" I asked.

"I don't know! I guess I saw my grandma use it so many times that I picked up on it. I think she might have taught me when I was really little. I don't remember that much though," he admitted.

He ran to get the arrow and walked back loading it in the bow again. Charles prepared himself to take another shot. The arrow shot off the bow and cut threw the air. This time, he hit the center of the tree. I cheered, totally shocked by his skill.

"WHAT! Did you see that? I hit it again!" he cheered.

"You have like a natural talent for this!" I said.

"I am going to see how many more shots I can make."

"Hey, Charles, It will have to wait until we stop for the night. We need to get back onto the road," Uncle William said.

"Okay," he said.

We hopped into the wagon, and Uncle William cracked the reins.

"Wow, this is crazy!"

"Yeah, I guess everyone just has a hidden talent that they don't know about until they just stumble upon it," I said.

Thinking about it, I wondered what my special talent was. Do I even have one? I assume it is using a sword or something along those lines. Charles inspected his bow as we rode along the rocky path. I took Scales out of my bag again, and we played a game of catch using an acorn. I laughed as Scales ran around looking for the acorn I threw. Scales grew tired after about twenty minutes of playing. I turned him back into wood.

Charles sat in silence. My mind turned back to the Fearhine. My stomach turned. What if we don't beat the Fearhine? Prince George would not be able to find the dark witch he spoke of and he would be extremely disappointed in us. Maybe even furious! The Kingdom would fall because of us, and we would go down in history as failures. I can't let that happen to Uncle William or me. Everyone will be disappointed in us. Charles looked at me.

"Do you think Bethany is mad at us?" he wondered.

I was relieved by the distraction.

"Of course she is. We just up and left her alone. Not to mention all the work she will be doing for us," I said, frowning.

"Yeah, I forgot about that. I am sure that in the end she will forgive us," he said with a hopeful smile.

"Yeah, I am sure that saving the entire Outer Kingdom is a good enough excuse," I chuckled.

Still, I felt really upset and guilty about it. Charles stretched his legs out and fell asleep. I curled up into a ball in the corner. The sound of the wheels turning and the crunching of the leaves created a soothing sound. Yet still, I continued to worry about the approaching days.

Chapter 18

The sky began to darken, and the temperature dropped. My body shivered, missing the warm sunlight we experienced in the afternoon. I examined my leg again; it was still in good shape after I took the medicine. After just fixing my leg, having to sit in this cart the whole day feels like a punishment. I felt the sudden urge to run for miles and miles.

"Uncle William, we should stop and rest. I really need to get up and walk or something. Not to mention, the horse has to rest," I convinced him.

"Okay. I was just thinking the same thing."

Uncle William pulled the wagon over. We all made a spot for sleeping in the back of the wagon. Then, using kindling and branches, we started a small fire. The moon rose up into the sky leaving a trail of stars behind it. I sat down and ate the leftover fruits and vegetables from the market. I listened as the crickets sang loudly, filling the forest with noise. Charles let out a sigh, grabbed his bow, and began aiming an arrow at a tree.

"Charles is pretty good with that bow," Uncle William said to me.

"Yeah. I should probably practice with my sword. If I don't get any practice, I will never get better or good enough to fight off the Fearhine. I mean, everyone needs to practice at one point."

"Hey, do you mind if I borrow this here book of yours? I want to learn a little bit more just in case something happens during the fight,"

Uncle William said, holding up my copy of "Sir Frederick's Adventures".

"Yeah, sure. I will just be practicing over here."

I took my sword and walked up to one of the surrounding trees. I placed my feet firmly on the ground and took in a deep breath. It was time to focus. Quickly, I thought back to the book in my dad's room and the illustrations it demonstrated. I used the trees similar to the way I practiced at home. I preformed some warm-up exercises and then began to practice my stances.

Then, I closed my eyes and pictured the Fearhine. I stood ready to fight. Using the techniques the book showed me, I quickly stabbed at the tree. I visualized what the fight might be like. I pictured the beast's teeth, heads, and venomous stinger. Quickly, I dodged its attacks and imagined what it might do to fight back. I stood, breathing heavily and then focused once again, making a series of quick slashes, attacks, and dodges. Finally, I stopped to look at the tree. Deep cuts into the wood covered the trunk. My head dripped with sweat, and my heart beat as loud as a drum. I ran my fingers across the bark.

"Hey, Liam! Nice work with that sword," Charles said from above me.

I looked up to where the voice came from. In the trees, Charles sat with his bow in one hand, and the other hand was placed on the branch to help him keep his balance.

"How the heck did you get up there? What are you some type of squirrel? And, when did you even get up there?" I asked, looking up at Charles in the tree.

"What are you doing up there?" Uncle William noticed, looking up from the book

"I climbed, duh!" He laughed.

"We know that but, how? There are no ladders or branches for you to step on from down here," I wondered.

"Well, I spent my childhood climbing trees, so I got pretty good at it. And there are a ton of ways to get up here, you just have to think outside the box," Charles said, smiling.

I shook my head as he climbed down from his perch with ease. I could not imagine myself being able to climb that high. I would be way too scared of falling and breaking my neck.

"When I was little, I used to play in the apple trees we grew in the way back of the house. It was the one crop that we didn't sell for profit. I remember every Sunday in the fall we had to go pick the apples for my mom. We would race to the tops and then throw the apples down into buckets. Our aim was not that good when we first started so we missed almost every time. Our dad was so mad! Over time though, we got pretty good at aiming. Anyways, my mom would make apple cake or apple fritters with the apples. It was the best time of year," he said, smiling.

"I think my mom sold apple cake once in her bakery," I said.

"Apples are my favorite fruits," said Charles.

"I remember doing things like that as a child with my brother," Uncle William said.

"I never did that stuff," I admitted.

"That's too bad. I love it. It's like solving a puzzle but you and the tree are the pieces," Charles said.

"Actually, there is one tree in the market that I climb. It's not that tall or hard to climb but, I have a bird feeder on one of the branches that I like to fill," I remembered.

"I think there are bird feeders in the pink petal tree in Queen Emily's garden," Uncle William stroked his mustache.

"My mom and dad always kept bird feeders in the winter so the birds have a place to go," Charles said.

I couldn't help but think about my own parents. My heart ached to see them and tell them of the adventure I was having. I thought of my mom. She is probably working in the bakery right now. I pictured her taking the bread out of the stone oven. My dad would be coming home at night to enjoy dinner. I imagined their faces when I tell them about the Prince selecting us for this mission. They will be so proud. I hope to see that day.

More memories came back. I pictured my birthday. I was allowed to choose whatever I wanted for dinner. Of course, I always choose baked chicken with salt and pepper. Then, we would eat potatoes with it and sometimes green beans. I remembered biting into the succulent meat, grease dripping down my chin. The warm feeling and the amazing taste of the chicken was my favorite. Then, I would choose butterscotch bread pudding for dessert. Dad would take one of his books from his shelf and read it out loud. We would stay up late into the night, listening to the stories. My birthday is one of my favorite days of the year. I couldn't help but wonder if my sixteenth birthday would be my last. What if we don't win? What if I died!?

As is Charles read my mind, he started to speak about the very creature that haunted me. "So, are you nervous to fight the Fearhine?"

242

"A little. I mean it's not going to be easy," I lied about my fear.

I didn't want anyone to know I was terrified. Maybe if I lie, I will eventually believe that the Fearhine is nothing to be scared of. I wondered if Sir Frederick would be scared of the Fearhine?

"I mean, we are pretty good fighters. At least, Prince George thinks so," Charles said, sitting down on the opposite side of the fire. The wind changed, and the smoke started to blow in my direction. I jumped up quickly to avoid the smoke in my face. I sat next to Charles on the other side. I hate the smoke from fires. The smell of it never goes away.

"I guess…" I said without any confidence.

We waited in silence for the eggplant Uncle William was making to be cooked. I wished we had a sauce to put on it or maybe some salt, but I kept those thoughts silenced.

"Don't worry boys, we just have to have faith in ourselves," Uncle William said settling himself in the wagon.

His words echoed in my thoughts as I dozed off to sleep.

We woke early, before dawn. Summer was my favorite season, but as of now, it's my least favorite season. The days were becoming hotter, and I was becoming sweatier. Traveling began to feel worse than cleaning the ballroom at the palace.

"Uncle William, how many days left until we have to fight the Fearhine?" I asked as we got back on the road.

"Well, it should take only a few more days," he replied.

"How long is 'a few'?" I asked nervously.

"Anywhere from three to two," he answered.

"Oh, yikes," Charles whispered to himself.

My mouth dropped. Three days was barely any time at all. Suddenly, my throat got heavy, and I felt like throwing up. I lied down on my back and put my arms over my face. My whole body felt like it was made out of lead. I felt my stomach turn to tar. The image of the Fearhine stayed stuck in my head like molasses to a jar. I tried to shake the thought, but the name stayed, echoing in my brain. Would I be good enough to fight the Fearhine and win? I felt my mind play with the thoughts like a cat with a string.

Unexpectedly, Uncle William stopped the cart, and he hopped out. I looked at Charles, who was just as concerned with the dwindling days as I was. Uncle William tied the horse to a tree and pulled out his sword.

"What are you lazy lumps still sitting around for? Get up! Grab your bow and arrow. Liam, get your sword! Hurry up, boys," he said.

We acted immediately.

"What we are doing?" Charles asked as we bounded after Uncle William.

"What are we doing? Uncle William?" I shouted after him.

Uncle William kept walking deeper into the woods. He stopped and turned around quickly.

"Just stop asking questions and walk!" he hissed.

I looked at Charles, and he looked at me. We both bolted after him. Only the sound of crunching leaves and the morning doves echoed through the air. The sun was slowly making the journey up to the sky. We were deep into the woods when Uncle William finally stopped walking.

"Okay, this is far enough," he said.

244

"For what?" Charles asked.

I felt relieved, knowing we wouldn't have to walk anymore. Uncle William drew his sword and stood in a fighting position. It finally hit me what we were doing. I looked around at the clearing of trees we were in. Charles pulled out his bow and an arrow. My hands started to sweat as I got in a ready position. Uncle William cleared his throat.

"Alrighty boys; if we are going to beat the Fearhine, then we need to be prepared. Let's train! Liam, we are going to do a one-on-one fight, but first, Charles, I'm going to use this bark as a target. You have to hit it," he said, picking up a fallen piece of bark that was the size of my head. I looked up at the tall dying tree that the bark came from. It was one of the biggest trees I had ever seen.

"Let's start with you, Charles. Stay here. When I hold this up, you have to hit it. Got it?" he said, breaking into a run.

"Yeah…" Charles said with a shaky voice.

Uncle William ran so far away that I could barely see him. He held the bark up in the air high above his head. There was no way this was safe. Charles loaded his bow with an arrow and pulled back on the string, his hands shaking.

"Ready?" He asked.

"Ready! Fire away!" Uncle William shouted.

Charles released the arrow, and it shot through the air. It spun past the trees and hit the side of the bark. I jumped for joy and gave him a high five.

"Nice job!" Uncle William gave him a thumbs-up.

"Let's try again!" Charles called.

Uncle William held it up, and Charles loaded another arrow. Charles pulled back and released a second arrow. This one missed the bark. Charles frowned.

"It's okay, try again!" Uncle William shouted.

The second time, Charles was able to hit the bark right in the center. Uncle William rejoiced.

"Now that we have your aim down, we should work on how fast you can load and shoot. That ability will be crucial in the battle with the Fearhine. We have no idea how quick it is."

Uncle William ordered me to run over some more pieces of the bark. I quickly followed his orders. Uncle William dropped his sword and held the pile of bark in his arms. Promptly, Uncle William tossed the bark up in the air. Without hesitation, Charles loaded and shot an arrow so fast; I could have missed seeing it. As soon as Charles hit the target, Uncle William threw one up in another direction. I watched as he reloaded and shot the arrow right through the bark. For each one that Charles hit, Uncle William threw the next one up faster. It was crazy how quickly Charles was reloading his bow. Soon, Uncle William had me throwing bark up at the same time as him. Over and over, Charles hit them, only missing one or two.

Uncle William threw up the last piece of bark, and Charles missed it by just a hair. My mouth was open in awe. Charles had a big smile on his face.

"Charles, your performance was astonishing. You have only had your bow and arrow for a few days. How were you able to perform so well? Even though you missed the last one, you hit almost every single one before it. I am so proud of you!" Uncle William said.

"Next time, I am going to hit all of them!" Charles announced with determination.

"Okay, Liam, you are up!" Uncle William walked over to me and got into a fighting stance. I did the same.

"Alrighty, Liam, let's have a little duel," Uncle William said.

"Okay."

There was a pause after his words, and I waited for him to say "go" or "start". Suddenly, he jumped at me. I blocked his sword and quickly hopped to the side. I guess this is not going to be a formal duel.

Quickly, I jabbed at his side, and he scooted away. Okay, remember what Sir Frederick does. I looked around at my surroundings. There was a boulder not far from here. Uncle William continued to swing his sword at me. When he stopped to take a breath, I saw my chance and sprinted toward the rock. Uncle William came bounding after me.

What now? Do I use it as a shield? Then it hit me- Sir Frederick always said to get the high ground. I reached the bolder and scrambled to find a way over it. There was a small indent that I could put my foot in to give me leverage. I pushed myself up and used all of my strength to reach the top of the rock. Uncle William reached me just as I was up on the boulder. I scrambled to stand up as fast as I could. He attempted to cut my ankles, but I jumped before he did. Then, he tried again, and I jumped off the rock towards the ground just in time to get out of the way of his sword.

I rolled across the ground and then got back in my fighting stance. Then it hit me, this was my first ever fight with anyone without any help. I'm actually not that bad! I felt more confident than ever before. Uncle William ran over to me and jabbed his sword at me. I blocked it and then threw my weight at him, causing him to wobble backwards. In an instance, I gathered my strength and swept my leg under his feet, knocking him on his butt. I pointed my sword at him. He gasped and put his arms up in surrender. I had beaten him!

"Yes! Wow, I can't believe I won!" I exclaimed.

"Woohoo!" Charles cheered.

"Phew! I am getting was too old for this. Great work today, boys. I think we have a good shot at fighting the Fearhine. Now, let's find our way back to the cart," Uncle William said rubbing his backside.

"Dude! That jump with a tuck and roll was so cool!" Charles said.

"Are you kidding? Not as awesome as your shots back there!" I said.

"And that kick sweeping thing! Awesome! You have to teach me that!" Charles said.

"You have to show me how to move my arms as fast as you did back there, then. If I could swing my sword that fast no one would even see my blade hit them!"

We all walked back to the cart through the woods, raving about the amazing experience we shared. I spent the rest of the day sharpening my sword and practicing tuck and roll jumps with Charles. I wanted to make sure that nothing could go wrong. Maybe it's just me being paranoid or if it's me being safe. I just hoped that nothing wrong or unexpected happens. Hopefully, we don't run into the Fearhine anytime soon.

After a few minute more of practicing, we continued down the road. The wheels squeaked as we pushed forward toward the Fearhine.

"Uncle William, how much longer on the road?" I asked.

"I just checked the maps. We will be there tomorrow. I suggest you get some more practice in," he said to the both of us.

"Yikes... did not see that coming," Charles said.

"Yeah, this trip has gone by a lot faster than I thought it would," I said.

"Really? I feel like it has gone by slow, I mean just the other day you were impaled by a rock!" Uncle William said.

"Oh yeah, I totally forgot about that," Charles recalled.

"I don't think I will ever forget that," I shuttered.

"And not to mention we were being yelled at by Ms. Woodround not too long ago," Charles reminded me.

As the sun fell, I spent another night tossing and turning in the wagon. The Fearhine was becoming more real by each passing day.

The next morning, we woke early to the sound of Uncle William feeding the horse. I shot it a dirty look as it cried for more apples.

"There you go. Here are some yummy apples. Time to get up boys!" Uncle William smiled.

Charles covered his head with a bag. I rolled out of the wagon and onto the hard ground. I looked up at Uncle William. He gestured for me to be quite. Carefully, he placed an apple on top of the bag Charles place over his head. I held in a laugh. Then the horse walked over and excitedly ate the apple right over Charles.

"What the- Liam! Mr. Rocklen! What! Why would you guy- UGH! Now there is apple and spit in my hair! Come on! Really!?"

Charles jumped up and brushed the food off of him. The horse innocently continued to eat the apple.

"Good morning, Charles!" Uncle William laughed.

"Ha. Ha. Not funny," Charles said hopping down from the wagon.

"Liam, why don't you go and gather some sticks. We need to eat a big breakfast before we face the Fearhine," Uncle William requested.

I walked quickly out of camp and felt stress wash over me. Today, we face the Fearhine. Times up! I am in trouble now. As soon as I was far enough from camp, I began to talk out loud about the situation I had gotten myself into.

"Ugh! Now, look what you've done! Look what you got yourself into! You are going to die today! And the Fearhine is probably going to enjoy you for dinner, maybe even a pre-breakfast snack!" I worried, picking up sticks as I walked.

"This is just great! Just great…"

Suddenly, I heard a strange noise. Like a deer, I looked quickly back and forth for the source of the noise. Now is not the time to be paranoid. I shook the thought out of my head and continued complaining.

"I should just flee, but that would make me a coward, and that's not honorable. Oh, look, a big hill. That's steep -maybe I could hide behind this hill for the rest of my life! Yeah, that's great! Good idea! I can eat pinecones all the time! What about my clothes? I will just have to roam around like a crazy person with no clothes then. This is not what I had in mind for my life but it's better than being stabbed by a GIANT stinger!"

I heard the noise again and looked around.

"Hello? Anyone there?" I asked.

Maybe it is best if I walk in the other direction. Could this all be in my head?

I kept my eyes on the trees around me. The same noise came from behind me. I whipped myself around. I am not going to be snuck up on. I cautiously walked backwards away from the source of the noise.

Unexpectedly, I tripped over a rock. Without even processing what happened, I was suddenly tumbling down the hill that I once stood on, and in an instant, the sticks flew out of my hands. Leaves flew past me as I fell down the hill. I felt every part of my body being scraped and bruised. Something hard hit my head. The world looked blurry. I had finally rolled to a stop at the bottom of the hill.

Someone came bounding down the hill after me. I could only make out the blond hair and white skin.

"Charles?" I mumbled.

My eyes became completely blurry. I put my head back, and the world went black. I guess I get to hide behind the hill after all...

Chapter 19

My eyes opened, and I found myself in a strange campsite. Across from me were two large tents and a small fire. Bags filled with supplies were placed next to the log I leaned against. A loud neighing drew my attention to three horses tied to a tree. I looked for my rescuers but no one was here. I felt the back of my head; there was a big painful lump. The amount of injuries I am suffering from on this trip is beginning to make me even more nervous about fighting the Fearhine. And the number of hills I've fallen down in the span of two months is more than most people. Instantly, I remembered seeing the blond person that I thought was Charles. If it really was Charles, then why would he bring me here?

A man stepped out of one of the tents. He was tall with very long legs. On his head grew a perfectly trim goatee, handlebar mustache, and brown, short hair. The man wore a bycocket hat that looked similar to the type of hat that Robin Hood wore in my dad's childhood picture books at home. He noticed me and walked over.

"Good, good; you're up. That was a nasty fall you took there, young man. What were you doing so close to the edge of that steep hill?" he asked.

The man had a strong voice and an accent that was very common. He inspected my head, and then, he went back in the tent and came out with a towel. He pressed it to my head, and I felt the cold ice rush throughout my body.

"Thank you for saving me. Who are you?" I asked.

"Who I am? Of course; my name is Frederick Douglass Richard the Third, but everyone calls me Sir Frederick," he said.

My mouth dropped, and a memory of me in my classroom around Christmas time came back to me. One of my friends, Peter, had an autographed portrait of Sir Frederick. His father, who was an artist, had drawn the picture, and it was a striking image of the man who was now tending to my head. Peter's dad was a friend of someone who knows Sir Frederick but, even so, even seeing Sir Frederick is rare. I had felt so jealous then and wished to one day meet him. I could not believe that day had come.

"You're… you're Sir Frederick! No way! No freaking way! You're like my hero! I'm your biggest fan! I can't believe I am here in person with Sir Frederick! Hi I'm Liam Rocklen! This is amazing!" I yelled.

Excitement filled my body like an overflowing cup of water. The pain of my injury melted away. He smiled. I was having a fan-boy attack. I stood up quickly and started to walk toward the hill I fell down. I was so excited I couldn't even think.

"Hold on one second, let me go get my Uncle Charles and William - I mean Uncle William and Charles," I said quickly.

"Umm, young man, I don't think that is best. You are still injured."

I ignored him and I quickly ran up the hill. I could not even process what was happening- I was so excited. As I ran up, I could still see where I had fallen because the leaves were all flattened and moved around. Abruptly, someone started yelling my name.

"Liam! Where are you?!" the voice called.

It sounded like Uncle William. Charles yelled my name as well.

"Guys, I'm over here!" I shouted. Their heads appeared over the top of the hill.

"Liam, what the hell are you doing down there?" Uncle William said frantically.

"Just come here quick! I fell but… just come here!" I hurried them.

They ran down the hill. I was too busy running over to Sir Frederick to look back at them, but I had a feeling they were confused about what happened. We reached the camp, and Sir Frederick was still sitting where I left him.

"Oh, hello again! Hello, I am Sir Frederick," he said, reaching out to shake Uncle William's hand.

"As in the author? The author of the books you read, Liam? Oh, wow! How exciting! I am William Rocklen." Uncle William said, shaking his hand.

"What!? No way! It's Sir Frederick! Like in person!" Charles said.

He shook his hand with great enthusiasm. Sir Frederick smiled and looked at me.

"You guys must be big fans," he assumed.

"Are you kidding?! I'm probably your biggest fan! I have read your book over a million times!" I said.

"Well, you obviously know enough about me. Let's hear about you. First, are you okay? That was quite a fall. I think that you should sit down a little longer," he asked.

"Liam! What happened to your head?" Uncle William looked at the bump.

"Oh, I fell down the hill over there. It's okay; I'm fine," I said, squirming out from Uncle William's hands as he examined my head.

"Fredrick, who are these people?" a feminine voice asked from behind me.

I turned around to see a tall woman standing behind me. The women had straight black hair that was cut short. She had olive skin and a muscular build. I assumed she was hunting because she was carrying two dead squirrels by their tails.

"Oh, Roxanne, these are my new friends, who are also fans of my work," he said, gesturing to us.

"My? I think you mean ours," She grinned.

My heart beat faster when he said we were friends. Sir Frederick was both my hero and my role model, and now, he says we are friends! Roxanne placed the squirrels down. She turned and called back to the direction she came from in the woods.

"Just put them here, and I can teach you to skin them," she instructed.

A man came rushing out of the woods to catch up to Roxanne.

"Hey is that kid I fond okay?" He asked.

He looked like he was in his twenties, based on his tall, muscular build. He had a shield in his left hand and four more squirrels in the other. Strangely, he was almost identical to Charles.

"Chase? What the hell are you doing here with Sir Frederick?!" Charles stared at him in confusion.

"Oh my gosh…." Chase put down his stuff.

"Wait, what?" I asked.

"Charles?" Uncle William asked for clarification.

"Charles, what are you doing here?! You are supposed to be at home! How did you even get here!?" Chase started.

"What am I doing here?!" Charles asked, shocked.

"Well… I guess you are a little confused right now…but, why are you here? And who are these people?" Chase questioned.

"A little? I'm more than confused! You left two years ago to work with a traveling merchant! Now, you're *here*? And these are my friends who don't lie to me!" Charles said angrily.

"Yes, I know I said that but I-"

"Mom and Dad were so sad when you left. They thought you left to go work with a merchant, and here you are with my favorite author! Why did you lie to us?! I was so sad when you left! You didn't even write to us!" Charles said to him, tears forming in his eyes.

I had no idea what was happening. Charles never told me about this. Everyone appeared just as confused as I am.

"Charles, I am so sorry. I had to say that because no one could know that Sir Frederick was there. Let me start over. I had gotten a job with a merchant. I wasn't lying when I said that. But a few days before my departure, I met Sir Frederick. I hadn't known who Sir Frederick was at the time nor had I read the book; I only heard of him when you talked about him. He was studying a nest of baby falcons in a tree when I first saw him. I was very intrigued by his work. Roxanne had climbed all the way to the top and then back down when I first saw her," Chase said, smiling at the couple. They smiled back at Chase.

"Anyways, I was curious, so I asked them some questions, and they said they needed an extra hand to carry equipment, and Sir

Frederick did want an apprentice. So, I dropped the job with the merchant and went with them," Chase finished.

Charles had calmed down now, but his face had no expression. I wondered what he was thinking.

"I'm sorry, Charles. No one could know who Sir Frederick is or where he is. Do you understand why I had to lie? I swear I would have told you but-"

"I understand. I just wish I knew the truth," Charles sighed, cutting him off.

"Come on," Chase said offering Charles a hug.

Charles smiled and accepted his apology. I had never seen such a sensitive side of Charles.

"I have one question now that that's cleared up. Sir Frederick, I thought you traveled alone?" Charles asked.

I had been wondering the same thing.

"This is true, I don't work alone. You see, I am more of the brains of the operation. I write the books and study the creatures and history. However, I do help with the other jobs," Sir Frederick said, smiling.

"I do most of the fighting if we are troubled and the dirty work like going up close to a creature and hunting for our food," Roxanne said.

"Wait, really?" Uncle William questioned.

"Funny story- our honeymoon was spent studying mermaids. Wasn't that fun, Fredrick?"

"Very fun, honey. I loved writing that chapter. Anyways, Chase is, like he said, my apprentice," Sir Frederick said.

"Wow... I can't believe this is happening," Charles said.

"Okay, now let's get back to what the heck you guys are doing here? Charles? You're supposed to be in Trisanburg or at home with Mom and Dad!" Chase exclaimed.

I looked at Charles.

"We are going to defeat the Fearhine. You know the monster in the Outer Kingdom. The Prince himself told us to do it," Charles said.

I was in horror. He swore to Prince George he would not tell! Is he an idiot!? Steam practically poured out of my ears. How could he act so stupid?! He just let this precious information slip out without any thought!

"Really?" Sir Frederick questioned.

"What!?" Chase shouted, concerned.

I shot Charles a dirty look. He mouthed "what" and gave me a confused look. I slapped my forehead with my hand. He doesn't even know what he did wrong. I grabbed him by the sleeve and pulled him toward me.

"Excuse us one second," I said to Sir Frederick and his companions.

I waved Uncle William into a huddle.

"Charles, what the hell? I thought we weren't supposed to tell anyone! What happened to that? How do we know if we can trust them?!" I said.

"Oh, shoot. I completely forgot about that. Well, I'm sure it's not that bad. I mean, Chase is my brother, and it's Sir Frederick! He is probably the trust worthiest person in all of the Outer Kingdom. I'm sorry, I feel really bad about it, but I trust my brother more than anyone," Charles said.

"Well, let's discuss telling people about the Fearhine *before* we tell them next time," Uncle William clarified.

We broke out of the huddle. Sir Frederick had left and gone into his tent with Roxanne.

"Anything wrong?" Chase said to Charles.

"Nope. Nothing at all," Charles said.

Roxanne popped out of the tent.

"Hey Liam, Charles, William, come on in here." She waved us into the tent.

I walked in and was amazed by what I saw. The entire tent was filled with books. The only other item was a sleeping bag and a desk with a feather pen and ink. Sir Frederick was sitting at the desk writing in an empty book.

"Are all of these books you're writing?" I said, flipping through one of the books.

He nodded.

"Most of them are just copies of the first book, and the rest are just information that I record as we explore the Outer Kingdom. I would love to give you one, but I'm sure you already have one," he said.

"Wow, this is pretty cool. Liam here loves your work," Uncle William said.

"Yeah, I learned so much," I smiled.

"Well then you must know that I have only ever completed research. I only write these to educate the new generations on the Outer Kingdom," he said.

"Yeah, I know tons of kids who love what you do" I agreed.

"Charles here mentioned some beast. I am very fascinated by it. I know not what it is or even what it looks like," Sir Frederick started.

"Well, it's kind of not something you were supposed to know about…" Charles said.

"I have a proposal. You let Roxanne, Chase, and I join you on your quest. That way you get our help, and I get to learn about this creature," he said.

"I don't think we want to advertise the Fearhine like that. It is actually kind of a secret. Like a secret mission" Charles said.

"Yeah, I don't want you to put this beast in your books," Uncle William said.

"Guys, we could use the help. I mean who better than Sir Frederick to help!" I urged them to reconsider.

"Liam is right. We could use the help," Charles turned to Uncle William.

"Just make it private research," Uncle William said with a smile.

"We don't have any problem with that. Trust me, Sir Frederick has done research in secret many times before. This should be no problem for us," Roxanne said, leaning on her husband's shoulder.

"We shall start packing up right away! I am so excited to find a new creature!" Sir Frederick said in anticipation.

"I don't know if that's the attitude you should have about this…" Charles said.

"Hey, looks like you and I get to catch up a little longer," Chase said to Charles.

"If I'm not too busy getting my butt kicked by the Fearhine," he laughed.

We exited the tent, and I prepared myself to help pack up. Charles helped Chase pack the food into a large bag while Roxanne and Uncle William packed the items from the tent into other smaller bags. I offered to help Sir Frederick take down the large tents but he declined my offer. I was shocked as I watched Sir Frederick compress the tent poles down into four single rods. Then he rolled up the fabric and placed the poles and fabric into a bag. I had never seen such convenient traveling equipment. In less than a few minutes, the camp was all packed up into five bags.

"We normally travel lighter but, we had intended to stay here a bit longer before you came. Not that your being here is a bad thing. Things were getting a little too boring for Chase and I," Roxanne said with a smile.

"You can say that again. While, Sir Frederick is writing we have nothing to do but hunt," Chase complained.

"Alright then, let's get going! Your camp is up this hill, is it not?" Sir Frederick said throwing two bags on his back.

I smiled and followed my new team up the hill.

Chapter 20

We trudged up the steep hill and continued toward our wagon. Roxanne gestured for Chase to take the reigns of one of the two horses. Sir Frederick took the pack from Chase and carried the equipment on his back, along with the notebook and pencil he held in his hands. I couldn't believe the new additions we made to our group. Now that we have Sir Frederick and his crew helping us, we might have a chance against the Fearhine. They work so well as a team and obviously have fighting experience.

We got to the wagon and packed up both groups' bags and hitched up one of their horses to the wagon. If I thought there was no room in the wagon before, now I hardly had any room to sit down. Uncle William and Roxanne sat up front and guided the horses, while Chase rode alongside the wagon with their other horse. The rest of us sat cramped in the wagon along with all our belongings. I pulled my legs close to my chest so that Sir Frederick could have as much room as he needed.

"Well, it should not be a long ride from here to where ever the Fearhine is," Uncle William said, cracking the reigns.

"So it's a matter of searching then?" Roxanne asked.

"Yep."

"I think we won't have a problem doing that. Did you ever read about when Sir Frederick and I found a dragon baby in the woods of Arone. Very rare thing to find," Roxanne bragged.

"No, I believe I have not," Uncle William said.

"Well, it was around November..." Roxanne began to tell Uncle William.

I turned to Sir Frederick. I had so many questions for him, but I wasn't sure if he would mind me asking. However, if I wanted to have any chance as becoming a knight, I would have to learn from the best. Before I could say anything, Charles spoke up.

"Hey, Sir Frederick, have you ever killed a troll? We have," Charles bragged.

"You did what?!" Chase said, whipping his head around.

Sir Frederick also looked surprised by what Charles said.

"Yeah! You see, we met some people who needed our help saving their son from the troll. It is a bit of a long story but, Liam planned out the whole thing himself! It was pretty cool! We all got ready for battle and walked through the woods to this creepy cave. Then we went inside and found their son and the troll. Don't worry- it was a small one- the troll not the son. Anyways then, we actually held it off! I was throwing some kitchen knifes and Liam and Mr. Rocklen had their swords. Oh! And as we left, Liam even saved my life and got a stalagmite stuck in his leg! It was insane! I almost threw up when they pulled it out! Like I could have died if Liam didn't push me out of the way! But, we actually killed like a real troll!" Charles rambled on with excitement.

As Charles told the exciting tale, I began to wonder if I was going to tell my parents about all of this. They would certainly not act as calm as Sir Frederick did hearing the tale. They might actually kill me if the Fearhine doesn't beat them too it. This whole trip has been a rush of excitement for me, and even if my parents don't approve, I still wouldn't trade it for anything in the Outer Kingdom. Well, maybe I would get rid of the fact I was impaled by a rock or destroy the Fearhine.

"Blimey! A troll? That *is* something," Sir Frederick sat up on top of one of his bags.

"Yeah, it was one of the scariest things I have ever done. Thank goodness for potions! Am I right? If I didn't have that potion the witch gave me, I wouldn't be sitting here," I said.

"Yeah! Literally, if it wasn't for you, I wouldn't be here either!" Charles said.

Abruptly, Sir Frederick whipped out his notebook with great speed. His pen raced across the pages like a horse across a field into battle.

"Hey, Sir Frederick, what are you writing?" Chase asked.

"Drawing, actually. It's a bird. A Purple Spearhead, actually. They are very rare. I have only ever seen one once before. I just had to draw it," he said, turning the notebook around to show us.

The bird was small and chubby with a strange beak that was disproportionate to the rest of its body.

"I have never seen a bird like that," Charles commented.

"Why does it have such a big beak? Doesn't it fall over?" I asked.

"Surprisingly, no. The beak is used to dig deeper into the ground. Most birds can only eat what is on the surface, but this bird can go farther. I find this species to be very special to our world. There are so few of the Purple Spearhead's because of their rich and fatty meat," he explained.

"Why is that?" Charles asked.

264

"Well, it is a delicacy for many noble families. They have been hunted to almost extinction. It is very important to preserve the creatures of this world so that they don't leave it," Sir Frederick explained.

"It's so unfair that animals like the Purple Spearhead are endangered. You know what, I wish creatures like ogres went extinct instead. They hardly do anything good for the Outer Kingdom," Chase said.

"Now listen here. Just because in the past some ogres have done bad things, it does not mean all of them are bad. We can't judge all of them based on what ogres in the past did. People can change and not to mention, the ogres have children and families, too. As heroes our job is to protect the innocent and bring justice to the unrighteous. Always remember that," Sir Frederick said.

Chase turned red and quickly jotted down in his notebook what Sir Frederick had said.

"You see, Charles and Liam, we travel all over the Outer Kingdom to preserve the creatures, the people, and the culture of the Outer Kingdom- not just for the title of 'hero'. If humans were on this world to destroy it, then, so be it. But, as long as there is air in my chest, I will protect the Outer Kingdom," he said.

"That is a very noble way to live," Uncle William commented.

"Not to mention exciting!" Sir Frederick smiled.

Sir Frederick has shown himself to be a very wise man. I want to be just like him. Maybe one day I will inspire kids the way he inspires me.

"So, you boys say you like my book? Mind if I have a look at it? It's been a while since I have had time to read my work," Sir Frederick anxiously asked.

"Oh, I loved this adventure. Roxanne, dear, do you remember when we traveled into that cavern near the ocean?" He flipped through the book.

"How could I forget? I had the taste of ocean out in my mouth for weeks. Who ever said sea water is good for you was out of their mind," she said.

Immediately, I remembered what chapter he was talking about. It was not one of my favorites but it was still good.

"Sir Frederick, what adventure is that?" Chase asked.

"Oh, you don't know? Well, I can just tell you! Let see..."

My heart leaped. Now, Sir Frederick himself is going to tell me about his adventures! This day could not get any better!

"Well, me and my beautiful wife had been shopping in a coastal town when we met a sailor who told us about a nearby historic battle site where mermaids fought a ship full of pirates. Very nice destination spot is what he said, and he was right. Oh, and pirates and mermaids are natural enemies, by the way. That is very important because this is the battle that set them on that course."

"What about the mermen?" Uncle William interrupted.

"Come on! Don't interrupt him!" Charles complained.

"It's okay, he has a right to ask questions. Well, you see, unlike mermaids, mermen have no problem with pirates. That's just because there is no conflict with territories," Sir Frederick answered.

"Thank you, go on," Uncle William said.

"Anyways, we were heading down the beach, and across the way, there was a strange pull of the tide near the side of the cliff. I had said there might be a cave there disturbing the flow of the tides. Roxanne swam over and found that my theory was correct- there was a giant cave there. The clear blue water fell far into it, so we swam farther inside. There were small sand bars of land on the side of the cave walls, so just in case something went wrong we had land to stand on. And that land did play a key part in the battle," he explained using his hands to emphasize the story.

I listened in awe. I felt like I was right there with them in the cave. Chase sat sidesaddle on his horse to listen closer to the story.

"So, we traveled farther in, and the evidence piled up. It seemed there was defiantly a battle there. There were swords in some places in the sand and nets with tridents on the bottom of the crystal blue waters. We assumed that the swords belonged to the pirates, and nets and tridents are common weapons used by mermaids. We then noticed a couple of human skeletons covered slightly by the sand. A large trident was pierced through the rib cage of one. We were shocked by how long the artifacts were able to sit untouched."

"I really thought there would be nothing there to see. I mean I thought the ocean would have taken the artifacts away," Roxanne added.

"I thought that too! Anyways, we followed the site of the battle and recalled what the sailor had told us. The pirates had anchored on a sandbar not far from the cave and they speared the mermaids who were trying to fight them off their land. Then, the pirates jumped into the shallow waters with their swords. Left and right, mermaids were being killed."

"Not for long, of course," Roxanne butted in.

"As time went on, the tide began to rise. The pirates were drawn back into the cave and now the mermaids had the upper hand. The battle went on, and the water continued to rise. Soon, it was up to the pirates' ankles and the mermaids had cornered them into the small sand bars we stood on. The pirates in the cave were killed one by one, and the mermaids took their victory. The pirates that stayed on the ship tried to leave, but didn't get far because the mermaids had cut a hole into the hull of their ship. As the battle neared an end, the pirate ship sunk slowly down to the bottom on the ocean. From where the cave was we could see the shipwreck a couple miles off the shore. It was defiantly a historic and amazing sight," Sir Frederick said, finishing the tale.

"Not to mention, it was barely even a ship! It was like a skeleton of a ship!" Roxanne chuckled.

"It was, wasn't it?" He chuckled at his wife's attempt at a joke.

"Yeah, we found most of this out from stories in the town and evidence at the scene. We even stayed long enough to see the tides rise up. So, we got the full experience," Roxanne added.

"Wow! Did you get anything from your journey there?" Charles asked.

"A bump on the head; that's for sure! That cave was small," Roxanne chuckled.

"So do you often go to historic sights?" Uncle William asked Sir Frederick.

As Sir Frederick began to answer his question, I sat back and relaxed in the sun. The trees swayed silently in the wind, providing shade for us. The days seemed to be getting a lot warmer and a lot longer. Hopefully, now that we are traveling with Sir Frederick, he will help keep my mind off the heat. I looked up into the trees. Their leaves still had a vibrant green color, which meant that fall was months away.

"Charles, can you check the maps?" Uncle William asked.

"Yeah, uhh, I think we are getting close to somewhere around south western Jarvally," Charles said.

"That means we are getting close to where it was last seen," Uncle William responded.

I felt sick thinking about our purpose of traveling across the Outer Kingdom. The Fearhine was out there waiting for us. Well, not really but, I knew we were going to eventually cross paths.

Suddenly, a strange smell entered my nose. It was foul, and I had never smelt anything like it. A sudden memory came to mind of a lesson on hunting that my father gave me. My father had pulled back on the bowstring and released. I was so amazed when a duck dropped from the sky. I cheered and then ran to fetch it. I remember holding it far away from me because it reeked of the foul odor of death.

"That's an odd smell. It stinks of dead duck. Uncle William, what is that?" I asked, holding my shirt over my nose.

"Look, smoke!" Charles cried, pointing at the treetops.

Over the trees, you could see a huge cloud of smoke, slowly rising into the blue sky.

"I have a bad feeling about that..." Chase said, with a shaky voice.

Uncle William cracked the whip, and the horses trotted faster. I prepared myself for the worst. Soon, a village came into view- or what was left of one.

"Oh, lord, no. The Fearhine clearly came through here," Uncle William said, with a shaky voice.

The houses that remained in tack where filled with big gaping holes, while the rest were in ruins, just rubble really. Smoke filled the air, and debris and burnt wood covered the ground, kind of like charcoal after a fire. A sick feeling arose in my stomach as I noticed dead bodies hidden under the rubble. The blood had drained from everyone's faces. The sight was horrific and terrible. We stopped the cart.

"Look for survivors!" Sir Frederick said, leaping from the cart with ease.

We ran into the only houses that were almost standing. I followed Roxanne into one house. The inside was crammed with men, women, and children all covered in dirt and ash. You could see the children were frightened as they curled up behind the adults. Blankets and clothes were layered over the injured people.

"Help...we need water...f...f...food," a woman holding a young baby whimpered.

Her voice was so frail and fragile that you could mistake it for a helpless baby songbird that fell out of its nest. Roxanne acted quickly.

"FREDRICK! CHASE! We found survivors!" Roxanne yelled.

"Liam, run to the cart and get some food and water," she shouted frantically.

Quickly, I followed her orders and ran to the wagon. We then distributed the water and food with care.

"Thank you!" a little girl said.

Chase ran over, followed by Charles and Sir Frederick.

"Can you tell us what happened?" Roxanne asked a man and a woman who were sharing a piece of bread.

"Earlier this morning, two of the boys who live in our town ran into the market. They were screaming that there was a monster in the woods," the women explained.

"We didn't believe them because we assumed they were just fooling us, you know like kids do. Only seconds later did we believed them when...when the beast ran into town and...and bit one of the boys," the man said, breaking out into tears.

"We quickly fought back, but that only made it worse..." the woman answered.

"I'm going to go help Uncle William look for more survivors," Charles said, running off.

"If we supply you with more food and some medical supplies, will you be able to survive long enough for the Royal Knights to be contacted?" Sir Frederick asked the woman.

She looked unsure at first, but then she ripped off the rag she wore in her short brown hair and bandaged the large cut on her arm.

"There, now I can help the others," she said.

"Roxanne, I saw a stream back down the road; want me to go fill a bucket with water for them? They don't have nearly enough," Chase asked.

Roxanne nodded and began to quickly examine all of the adults' wounds. She had the least injured adults tend to the children. Chase came back with the water and handed the bucket to the woman whom we had spoken to. I quickly provided bread to the adults for rationing to the children. Roxanne dabbed a cloth in the water and wiped the woman's face and arm of the dry blood and ash. I was in shock from the disastrous event. It looked like a giant bolder had hit the town, leaving everything a horrible mess.

The women assured Roxanne that they were going to be fine for at least one day, which was more than enough time to get the message to the Royal Knights or any others who could help.

Uncle William waited for us in the front seat of the cart.

"We should not be far from the beast. The townspeople say we just missed the Fearhine. This means we can avenge these poor people," Uncle William said.

"Uncle William, Charles," I whispered to them.

"I wonder if the witch made the beast more violent in order to get the Prince's attention. She has to have noticed by now that Prince George is ignoring the Fearhine," I proposed.

"You might be right," Uncle William wondered.

We all jumped into the wagon.

"We better hurry!" Chase said, jumping on his horse.

Uncle William cracked the whip, and the horses raced along the road. My stomach turned into knots. In only a short few minutes, we

272

would have to face the Fearhine. I pictured the stinger and snake fangs the Prince had illustrated. I shook my head and tried to think positively. With Sir Frederick with us, this beast won't stand a chance. I felt the exhilaration of riding into battle. Then, fear overtook me again when a large woman came racing toward us with her skirt clenched up in her hands. Uncle William pulled back on the reins, and we skidded to a stop.

"Excuse me, madam, is everything alright? You look as if you had just seen a ghost," Sir Frederick asked.

She was so out of breath from running that she had to wait to speak. Pointing behind her, she stumbled over her words.

"M...m...m...mo...MONSTER!" she bellowed, running back the direction we had came, screaming at the top of her lungs.

"Get ready for a fight boys," Roxanne smirked.

"Okay, guys, this is our chance. We have to sneak up on the Fearhine in order to have any chance of beating it. I mean, we saw the results of the town's strategy," Uncle William said.

"You're right. We need the element of surprise," Roxanne agreed.

"There is no turning back now," I said to Charles. He nodded and grabbed his bow and arrow. I grabbed my sword and hopped off the wagon. It was time.

Chapter 21

"Guys, we need a plan," Uncle William said, getting down on his knees.

As Uncle William explained what our plan was, he used his sword to draw it out in the dirt. I studied the drawing carefully while at the same time keeping myself from having a heart attack. I just have to put my all into this, and I will survive.

We all dispersed from the huddle and followed each other quietly into the woods. The sun shined brightly through the leaves. At least the woods weren't dark, but it was quiet- too quiet. I began to shake in fear from the suspense.

Suddenly, Charles pointed violently at a clearing in the woods. The beast sat coiled on a rock, bathing in the sun. I noticed it stinger was covered in dried blood from its last attack. A shiver ran up my spine.

I glanced over at Uncle William and Roxanne, both of whom looked calm and determined. Charles was creeping up the side of a tree like a mountain lion stalking its prey. Chase and Sir Frederick were nowhere to be seen.

I stepped lightly, making my way to my assigned post. Carefully, I looked around, taking in my surroundings for use during the battle. On the windward side of the rock was a clearing in the trees. It was so sunny and beautiful that you could hardly believe a battle was about to take place there.

Finally, we all made it to our spots around the clearing. Charles magically had perched himself on a branch in a tree. I waited for Uncle William to give the signal to Charles. The suspense made my legs and arms feel weak. I almost collapsed as if my body turned to stone.

Abruptly, Charles raised his bow and aimed an arrow. You could see the concentration in his face. I waited in anticipation for the shot while I crouched down with my sword drawn. Charles released the arrow gracefully and hit the Fearhine in its side.

In a blink of an eye, the monster reacted and slithered down the rock into the clearing. I watched its stinger swing side to side in the air as the Fearhine slithered off its perch.

It was time to focus.

Uncle William charged at the Fearhine's chest with his sword drawn out. Sir Frederick sprinted out from behind the trees, yelling a battle cry. The Fearhine let out a long hiss from one of its four heads.

Slowly, I raised my sword and prepared for the battle of a lifetime. This was what I had wanted. This is the excitement I craved. I crept out into the battle. My eyes gazed over the Fearhine and I froze in fear. Time slowed as I watched the events unfold.

Roxanne almost reached the beast when one of its heads came out of nowhere and grabbed her sword out of her hands. Roxanne's mouth was wide open, but that did not stop her. She punched the snake right in its neck. The snakehead retreated and released her sword. She jumped back to avoid getting hit by her own weapon, falling over in the processes.

Another larger and cobra-like head was preparing to bite Roxanne when. Sir Frederick's blade pierced the Fearhine's side. This distracted every snake except for the one who was recovering from the punch given by Roxanne. Chase jumped out and held his shield up, protecting Roxanne.

"GO!" he yelled.

She retreated back into the woods to recover. Meanwhile, from in the trees, Charles was shooting arrows at the rouge snake heads. He carefully aimed each one to avoid Uncle William and Sir Frederick. Sir Frederick's sword was stuck so far into the beast that he couldn't pull it out. I could only imagine the pain the Fearhine was feeling with an arrow and a sword in its body. Hopefully, this would weaken the monster. The Fearhine lifted its stinger high into the air and came down, trying to hit Sir Frederick.

"Ahhh! Back, you beast!" Sir Frederick yelled, dodging the stinger.

Uncle William struggled to fight back three of the heads. The other heads were focused on Chase, who whacked them in defense with his shield. Chase fell backward after getting hit by a snake.

"Liam! Come on!" Charles yelled angrily from the tree.

Charles was grabbing another arrow from his quill to shoot the Fearhine. It knocked its heads down on Chase's shield, which was covering him for protection. I watched in fear. Uncle William cried out a war cry, and Sir Frederick called out in distress as he released his grasp on his sword and fell on his back. I shook my head and focused on what was happening. Time came back to normal. I have trained so hard for this, and this is what I am born to do.

They need me.

I sprinted out from the woods and aimed my sword at the Fearhine's lower body. I quickly sliced the Fearhine's side and then rolled out of the way. Effortlessly, I picked myself back up and ran toward the back of the snake.

Roxanne saw her chance and came running out of the woods. She sprinted toward the Fearhine and sliced a snake head clean off with a graceful blow. The Fearhine dripped blood down its chest. The other heads hissed in anger as they saw one of their heads on the ground.

I looked into the bloody decapitated head's cold black eyes. The beast lifted its remaining heads high into the air and whipped its body around, hitting Roxanne into a tree.

Chase ran at the monster from behind and rammed the other side of the Fearhine with his shield. I was amazed by how high the Fearhine's pain tolerance was because blood dripping from all sides of its body.

Roxanne tried to cut off another head that was distracted by Uncle William. The largest of the heads, the cobra, noticed and bit into her arm, injuring her. She screamed out in pain and dropped her sword. Chase ran quickly under the snake and pulled her out. He held up his shield for protection.

"At this rate, we will all be dead," I said under my breath, starting to panic.

An arrow shot past me and hit a snake that was right in front of me. I reacted quickly and swung my sword upward at the snake and then watched as a snake head fell right at my feet.

Uncle William cried out in victory. The cobra snapped at him like lightning. He gasped. Before the cobra could strike, Charles shot multiple arrows at the Fearhine. It retreated backward and hissed loudly at Charles. I quickly ran out of the range of the snakes and the arrows and made my way toward the stinger. I dodged arrows as they shot past me. Two shot one of the snakes straight in the neck.

I saw out of the corner of my eye that one of the remaining snakes was coming at me. I rolled to my side and then jumped backwards away from the snake head. I looked at the battle site from the side view and then saw a chance to take out one of the last two remaining snakes. Instantly, I remembered one of the moves I attempted back in Brendsworth. The images in my dad's books came rushing into my mind.

I backed up and waited for my moment. Rapidly, I pumped myself up for the most daring thing I have ever done with my sword.

Time felt as if it became slow again. Uncle William was at the front of the Fearhine with Sir Frederick, battling with the last two snake heads. Charles was firing arrows at the stinger end while Chase held his shield up for protection as he fought the stinger end. Roxanne shook her head, spit on the ground, and then stood up, ready to continue fighting.

I watched, as there was a gap between arrows and took my shot. The middle of the snake was completely clear for my attack. I ran full speed, jumped into mid-air, and turned my body sideways. In a blink of an eye, I shoved my sword at an angle into the Fearhine's back and pivoted my body around my sword. I swung myself through the spaces between the snake necks, and as I flung forward, pulled my sword out and angled it to cut into the snake head's neck. My feet hit the ground with so much speed I stumbled forward. I had actually pulled off the move!

Charles cried out cheering. It wasn't time to celebrate yet. Sir Frederick ran out of the way to the back of the Fearhine where Chase was. I turned around and looked at the blood gushing down the side of the Fearhine's back and its neck.

Charles fired an arrow at the cobra head, and Uncle William took his shot. He sliced the head I just cut clean off. The cobra head was all that was left. I took a deep breath and prepared myself for the final stretch. We were actually doing it!

Suddenly, I heard a scream of agony. I was in horror of what I saw. The Fearhine's stinger was pierced right through Sir Frederick's chest. Roxanne screamed out in terror. In a split second, her emotions changed. Roxanne stumbled over and cried out in anger. She swung her sword with great force and sliced the cobra's head off. The head fell to the ground with a thud. Chase ripped the stinger out of Sir Frederick's chest as the beast collapsed and fell to the ground. The Fearhine was dead. I raced over with Uncle William to Sir Frederick's side.

"Oh no... what do we do?!" Charles yelled, jumping out of the tree with a thud.

Chase bolted back into the woods. Roxanne rushed over and flung herself next to her husband's side. Tears run down her face.

"HURRY, CHASE! WE HAVE NO TIME!" she screamed into the woods.

He charged back with Sir Frederick's satchel in his arms. Frantically, he rummaged through the bag and pulled out a small bottle halfway filled with clear liquid and a large round bottle full of purple liquid. Potions. Chase shoved the purple one into Charles's hands. Charles began to pour a small amount on a piece of cloth and dabbed the cloth on Sir Frederick's injury. Chase poured one drop of the clear liquid into Sir Frederick's mouth.

"Don't go, Frederick! Not this time! Not like this! Please!" Roxanne begged, holding her husband's hand.

"What do those do? Will he be okay?" I asked quietly.

"This liquid is the rarest of all potions. It's Elycixuor. It can heal almost any injury, and it is only used for the most serious of injuries. An emphasis on the 'almost'. You have to pay a very large amount for this and only older, more experienced witches can create it. And that one Charles is using is an anti-poison potion," Chase said.

Sir Frederick was frozen for a minute. Sweat dripped down my face. Suddenly, his chest rose and he began to breath again. Roxanne swiftly calmed him down and he relaxed. You could feel everyone's relief when they saw him breathing normally again.

"Well, I think that went well. Chase? Any thoughts?" Sir Frederick said in between breaths.

Roxanne wrapped her arms tightly around her husband.

"Roxanne, looks like someone was scared I was gonna die," he teased her. She whacked him on the back of the head.

"Next time, I will hope you die!" she joked, helping him up.

"We did it, guys. We beat the Fearhine!" Charles said, his face filling with excitement.

"Now, what do we do with the beast? I don't exactly know how to act after killing a giant snake monster," Uncle William asked.

"I imagine something like this," Chase cracked a smile.

"We can't exactly bring it back to the Prince in a wagon," I said to Uncle William.

"Yeah, I am sure that would go really well," Charles said sarcastically.

"Sir Fredrick will gladly take it for studying purposes, and as soon as he finishes, we can just get rid of it," Chase suggested.

I did like the idea that the Fearhine would be studied, but to get rid of it for good might not be the best idea.

"Why don't you study the Fearhine and then give it to the Prince when you're done? Come to think of it…we should take a fang of that snake's head as proof that we killed the Fearhine," Uncle William said, walking over to the head of the cobra.

"I don't think the Prince would think we are lying about killing it after seeing the state our clothes are in," Charles said, pointing at the snakes blood on our clothes.

Uncle William let out a chuckle as he struggled to pry a fang out of the cobra skull. He held up the long tooth, which was in blood. Uncle William carefully wrapped it in the cloth Charles had used to tend to Sir Frederick's injury.

"There. Now we have proof. Just in case," Uncle William said.

"Good work here, probably would not do it again though," Roxanne said, helping Sir Frederick up.

Surprisingly, Sir Frederick looked healthy.

"Let me be the first to say that I really thought we were not gonna make it out of there," Chase said, wiping blood off his shield.

"Ah, we must always have hope, Chase," Sir Frederick advised.

"And maybe an army of Royal Knights next time," Charles said plopping down in the grass.

"Are you really complaining!? You got to sit in a tree!" Chase called him out.

"Oh yeah. Well, it would have still been nice," Charles admitted.

We all walked slowly back to the wagon to emptied out Sir Frederick's things.

"Well, I think we will camp here for a few days while we study the beast. It should be an interesting thing to look at. I mean, a snake with four heads and a stinger! Remarkable beast. I wonder what type of poison that was?"

"Or how it evolved to have a stinger?" Chase added.

"Why are we assuming it evolved? How do we know where it even came from?" Sir Frederick asked.

"Thank you so much for the help!" Uncle William said shaking Roxanne's hand.

"Oh, it was no problem! I mean nothing that we can't handle, but I don't think even we could have done it without you," Roxanne said.

"Yeah, that was some good bow work," Chase said, giving a thumbs-up to Charles.

"Like grandma, right?" Charles smiled.

"Just like her, except I think she was better," Chase teased.

"Pfft, thanks. Are you going to come home any time soon?" Charles asked.

"I think I'm going to continue my studies. But, I will write to Mom and Dad about where I really am," he said. Charles and Chase gave each other a quick hug.

"Uncle William, do we have to get going soon?" I asked, hoping he would say no.

"I mean I want to try and get to an inn so we can rest. I'm worn out. Welcome to the old man club," Uncle William joked, getting the wagon ready.

"I think all of us can agree on that," I said.

"Yeah, you guys were killing it out there! I mean, Liam that swing sword thing you did was incredible! And then my little brother over here was shooting arrows like crazy!" Chase said excitedly. He grabbed Charles and put him in a headlock.

"I still can't get over that we did that!" Charles said getting out of the headlock his brother put him in.

"I know! My heart is still pounding!" I agreed.

"If you like that exhilaration, you should come on the crazy adventures Frederick takes us on. Not to spoil anything for the next book, but let's just say it will include a lot on dragons," Roxanne said, butting into our conversation.

I almost exploded with happiness. The next book has dragons! That means that Sir Frederick and Roxanne have met real life dragons. Dragons are extremely hard to find.

"I can't wait for it to come out!"

"Liam, you should let us autograph your book!" Sir Frederick said, walking over to us.

"Really?!" I squealed.

That long and horrifying fight was worth all of this. I grabbed my book quickly out of my satchel and handed it over to him.

"Liam, I wish you the best of luck," he said, signing it and handing it over to Roxanne.

"Charles, next time you see Mom and Dad, can you give them a hug for me and maybe help explain why this job is so great? I still have so much to learn from Sir Frederick," Chase said.

"Believe me, I would take that job for myself! I would love to explore the Outer Kingdom!" Charles exclaimed.

"Boys, I think we have to get back to the palace sooner than later. Remember what Prince George said about our excuse having an expiration date?" Uncle William reminded us.

"Right," I sighed.

"Until we meet again," Uncle William said, reaching out to shake Roxanne's hand. She put her hands on her hips and gave him a look as if to say "seriously?" She pulled Uncle William in for a hug. She was so strong that she could probably lift him up off the ground. We all laughed.

Charles and Chase did a complicated handshake that I could barely follow. I smiled as Sir Frederick shook my Uncle's hand. If someone had told me a week ago I would be fighting alongside Sir Frederick I would have though they were crazy.

Chase walked over and held out his hand to me for a fist-bump. I smiled, and before I gave him one, I quickly jabbed him in the side for a sneak attack. He laughed.

"Good one, Liam. I can see why you're Charles's friend."

He held his hand out again, and we fist-bumped. Once we all said good-bye, Charles and Uncle William helped to prepare the wagon for departure.

I felt the same familiar feeling that I had before when we beat the troll. I feel like I belonged. As if I was born to save people and explore the Outer Kingdom! I wish I could be Sir Frederick's apprentice, like Chase. Roxanne, Chase, and Sir Frederick are such fun people; it would be a dream to have that job. However, traveling with Charles and Uncle William is just as fun.

"Remember, this is not goodbye. It's just an intermission!" Sir Frederick said.

"If you ever need us, you will find us," Roxanne said.

"Wait really? Like magic?" Charles asked.

"No not really, I just thought it sounded cool. You probably won't run into us for a while," Roxanne admitted.

"Good luck," Chase waved to us.

Uncle William cracked the reigns. He turned the wagon back the way we came. I watched Sir Frederick, Chase, and Roxanne walk back into the woods. We sat in silence, pondering the fact that we saved so many people. We were really heroes.

Chapter 22

Our wagon rolled down the gravel road at a quick speed. Uncle William was determined to get us back home by tomorrow. Charles and I sat in the back and watched the trees go by. Then, I remembered Sir Frederick's note. I quickly opened up "Sir Frederick's Adventures" to the inside cover. I began to read Sir Frederick's message. 'Liam, be brave and never stop helping people. Sir Frederick.' The message gave me strength and a new confidence in myself.

"Well, boys, … we did it… " Uncle William said, staring out into the distance.

"Even though there is no glory for us, I still feel glad we did it," Charles said.

"That's what being a hero is all about…" I said, coming to a realization.

"But hey, who knows? Maybe one day you will be walking down the street and someone will point at you and say 'Oh wow that's the guy who saved us from the Fearhine,' and then everyone will ask for your autograph," Charles dreamed.

"Maybe. You never know," Uncle William said.

Many silent minutes went by until we spoke again. We had all been recovering from the long day we experienced.

"Uncle William, how many weeks of work are left now? It's already the end of June, and when we get back, it will be the first of July," Charles said, lying his head down on his bag.

"No… don't mention work! I just want to stay here in the wagon and never leave," I moaned.

"Well, we still have about six weeks left. That is enough time to make it up to your friend for leaving," Uncle William said with a mischievous smirk.

"Ugh, don't remind us," Charles said with his face pressed up against his bag.

"She is going to be so angry that we left her alone with all that work. We are going to probably have to do twice the amount of work to make it up to her. Wait a minute… Uncle William, are you going to be in trouble for leaving for so long? You are, like, the head of the entire staff, besides the royal family," I said, waiting for his response.

Uncle William seemed calm, and he still had the same mischievous smirk.

"I have learned how to rack up vacation days over the years. You see, playing cards is not fun unless you bet something!" he said with a smirk and a crack of the whip.

"Besides, we still have the Princes excuse working for us," He said.

The ride back to the castle was boring and long. Uncle William had said he wanted to stop for the night and go to an inn, but now his motivation was just to get back in his own bed at the castle. As a result, Uncle William taught us how to steer the wagon, so we could all take shifts during the long ride. We arrived back in Trisanburg City much quicker than before because we had three people to drive the wagon. My heart warmed up when Trisanburg City came into view. It still had the same loud and busy feel to it with an occasional smell of fresh bread from a bakery, which made Trisanburg City seem almost like coming home. The ride up the hill to the castle was less thrilling this second time, but seeing it made me feel like I was coming home. I felt the summer breeze in my hair and watched as the birds flew lively around the city. Life seems so much more different than it did before. This newfound perspective has given me a new look on life. We rode past the castle gates to the front of the castle. Up in the second story window, I could see a glimpse of Queen Emily looking out over her flourishing city. She noticed me looking and walked away from the window. I shrugged and did not take it personally. I felt like a whole new man! No one can make me upset or mad unless I allow them to.

We parked the wagon in the stables, where the stableman greeted us.

"How was your trip, Mr. Rocklen? The Prince said that you and two servants were off meeting with a nobleman for staff recruitment," the older man asked.

"Uhh, it was very… refreshing. Are you close to retirement, Mr. Jones?"

"Oh yes, very exciting stuff," the old man said, placing a saddle on a horse. A knight came walking up behind us to mount the horse.

"Hey, William! Back from your trip already?" the knight asked.

"Yep. Oh, and congrats on your first patrol out of the Trisanburg City area, Nick. Was it all you hoped and dreamed it would be?" Uncle William asked him.

I assumed that Nick was recently knighted, judging by his clean and shiny armor. He had no cuts or bruises either.

"Oh yeah, it was hard, but I would say it is worth it," Nick said, mounting his horse.

"Well, we best be going, do you know if the Prince is here?" Uncle William said, walking away.

"Yes, I believe that he is either in his study or room. I don't think he is going out with the Royal Nights today to hunt," the knight answered.

"Alright, thank you," Uncle William said.

We quickly followed behind Uncle William.

"That knight is the son of my good friend, Antonio. I think Antonio is a general now- I can't remember," Uncle William said, scratching his head.

We walked into the throne room. Most of the staff was walking about, and the king's advisors were next to his throne. Right now, the king's advisors look like normal adults, but when the king walks in, they act like small frightened mice.

Uncle William led us down the hall that was lined with pictures of the rulers of the Outer Kingdom. I noticed that King Bartholomew's picture was bigger and with a large display of flowers around it.

We walked to the prince's study. The door was wide open. The Prince sat in his chair, staring down at a letter. His face lit up when we saw us. He bid us to enter, I closed the door behind me and then bowed in the presence of the prince. Uncle William bowed and extended the snake tooth up to the prince. Prince George motioned for us to stand.

"I am happy to see you were successful in your quest. Your return brings me great joy. And I see you have the beast's tooth, or if my drawing was accurate, one of its teeth. Fascinating…" Prince George said, plucking it gracefully out of Uncle William's hands.

Uncle William looked at him with great pride. The prince placed the tooth on his desk.

"I will conduct further experiments on the tooth to learn more about this animal. Your length of absence was beginning to worry me. Now that you're here, I am happy to see you alive and well. That reminds me, how long are you gentlemen going to be working here?" Prince George said, sitting down in his chair.

"Well, I'm staying all year round, and Liam and Charles are leaving in… what was it? Five or four more weeks? Just in time for school to start," Uncle William responded.

The word school sounded vulgar to me.

"Prince George, sir, did you ever figure out who the witch threatening the kingdom is?" I asked out of curiosity.

The Prince looked surprised to see me talk, but thankfully, a verbal scolding did not follow.

"I am glad you asked that, Liam. Since you have shown your bravery and loyalty, you can be sworn into the … um… one moment," the prince walked over to the window and shut it, along with the curtains, "I believe I had mentioned that I have organized a group of people that are scattered all over the Outer Kingdom. They are people who are like you, your uncle, and your friend; they want to help protect the kingdom and stop this evil witch before a war arises. This group has not become as big as I would have hoped, but I have grand plans for this group to grow and become a secret society. You must promise not to tell anyone about this," the prince ordered.

Immediately, I remembered that Charles told Sir Frederick, Roxanne and Chase about the Fearhine.

"Your highness, I have something to tell you," I blurted out.

Prince George had my attention. My face grew hot, and my palms began to sweat.

"We met Sir Frederick, Charles's brother, and Sir Frederick's wife, Roxanne, while on our travels. You see... we may have leaked out a tiny bit of your plan. But they helped us with the fight against the Fearhine but they also kinda still have the beast in their possession. But they promised it was only for studying purposes," I confessed.

I hung my head low in shame, only taking one glance up to see his stern face.

"Mr. Rocklen, boys, that was a secret mission, and this information can't be leaked all around the Outer Kingdom!" Prince George shouted. "You are very lucky that Sir Frederick is participating in my secret operation," he said in a calmer tone.

My head popped up as soon as the words left his mouth. Sir Frederick was in this secret society the whole time? My whole world just got thrown upside down.

"Wait, what?!" I said.

"Why wouldn't I recruit them? I mean they have an extensive knowledge on the creatures in the Outer Kingdom and are skilled fighters. Not to mention they are already undercover all the time for their book purposes."

"Wait, how come he acted as if he did not know about the Fearhine?" Charles asked.

"Well, sometimes you can never be too sure whom to trust. He must have been playing it safe. Sir Frederick was actually on a similar mission. He was going to be the one to capture the Fearhine at first, but after a long attempt and a lot of failure he gave up the search. He also mentioned that he needed to catch up on his book work so, I called off the mission. Right after that I began the process of recruiting you three," the prince explained.

This all began to make sense to me.

"That explains why Sir Frederick had set up his camp so close to where we found the Fearhine. He was closer to finding it than he thought," Uncle William commented.

"So, I know that he is a good fighter and knows a lot about the Outer Kingdom but, how exactly did he become part of your group?" Charles asked.

"Just like you did! I have been recruiting people for months that all share something in common. They want to save lives and the Outer Kingdom! I had trouble tracking them down at first but the man who prints their books helped me find them. When I first saw them they were studying some moths on a tree, which is something I don't see people do every day. After we met, and I pitched my cause to them, they agreed that this beautiful world we live in is worth fighting for," he said, smiling at the thought.

"So, I am thinking that we should come up with a code or way to identify your followers," Uncle William said.

"Great idea. I am positive you guys will make a great addition to this fight," Prince George said.

"Thank you, sir," Charles said, beaming with pride.

"I am going to think up a perfect code and then get back to you as soon as possible. Thank you for your service, and I will see you very soon," Prince George said, dismissing us from his study.

I felt a great deal of honor. Before coming here, I had no idea what I would do with my life. I would have to become a baker or a blacksmith. I definitely don't want to do either of those options. Now, I am a loyal servant of the prince. To me, saving the world is more important. Now, I have the option that I wanted to have.

We went down the same wooden stairs, which I have gone down a million times, leading us into the servants' area. Bethany came to my mind. I stopped not wanting to go further.

"I can't face this! She will be so upset!" I confessed to Charles.

"Come on, Liam. You took down a monster! How hard will it be to talk to our friend? We just explain that we had to go with Mr. Rocklen to recruit or whatever excuse the Prince made for us," Charles said, putting a hand on my shoulder.

I was glad to have a friend that was brave and confident. I am more nervous to talk to Bethany than to face the Fearhine!

Chapter 23

We walked into our room and put our things on our beds. It was nice to be back in the castle again.

"Remember boys, this whole time we were meeting with lords and ladies to get new servants," Uncle William reminded us.

As we exited our room, Ms. Woodround blocked our path. I jumped in fear and disgust once her face came into view. She stood with two hands on her hips.

"Well, well, well, William and his friends are back from their trip," she said with her evil, dark witch-sounding voice.

"Actually, Mr. Rocklen took the leave of absence to find servants and we were ordered to accompany him. Well, it was more like a business trip actually. Wait is that still a trip? Well, the important thing is we are back! Right?" Charles said.

I nodded in agreement.

"Pfft, you think I'm going to believe that hogwash story Prince George told me! Recruitments! Pfft! Mark my words, boys, I will figure out where you were, and when I do, I will take the job that should have been mine!" she threatened us.

"Umm, Ms. Woodround, I don't mean to ruin your little revenge story, but you can just ask the Prince if you don't believe us. Want me to go get him?" I said with a smirk.

She gave a nasty snarl.

"Nasty little imps!" she mumbled and walked away.

Her words sent chills down my spin. We had to play it off like we had nothing to hide, even though her suspicions were true. As we walked away, Ms. Woodround called down to us in a mischievous tone.

"You boys better head to the ballroom to start your work. Vacation is over! Oh, and Bethany will be very happy to see you since you left her with all of that work," she said sarcastically.

Ms. Woodround walked into the kitchen cackling like a witch. We walked quickly in the opposite direction.

"Well, that was terrifying and weird at the same time," Charles said.

"I have got to say, she is the scariest woman that I have ever met!" I said.

"Then, you have not seen my Grandma Missy when the crows get in her garden!" Charles joked.

I gave a chuckle.

"She is right though, Liam."

"Yep, Bethany is going to be angry."

We slowly opened the big wooden doors to the ballroom. Bethany was scrubbing the floor with a sponge. I looked at Charles, and he looked at me. We knew that a storm was coming.

She looked up and saw us. I cracked a smile and waved. We walked over to her, but stayed at a safe enough distance so that she would not strangle us.

"We're back!" Charles said, trying to laugh it off.

He waved his hands in the air. She gave us a sour look.

"Hooray!" he yelled trying to lighten the mood.

Bethany threw the sponge at his face, hitting him right in the nose.

"Hey! Ow, that hurt," Charles said, rubbing his nose.

She crossed her arms and scowled at us.

"Listen, Bethany, we are so sorry for leaving you with all this work. But, we have a good reason for being gone!" I said, trying to make things better.

She quickly stood up and, before I knew what was happening, she dumped the dirty bucket of water right over my head. The cold water rushed down my shirt and into my pants. My boots filled with the soapy dirty liquid. I pulled the bucket off my head.

"HEY! HE ONLY GOT A SPONGE IN THE FACE! WHY DO I GET A BUCKET OF DIRTY SOAP WATER?!" I shouted.

She put her hands on her hips.

"Bethany, we really are so sorry we left you all of this work," Charles said.

"Yeah, we truly are," I said, wiping the water off my brow.

"I'm not mad that you left me with the work! Well, I am a little, but I can handle the work!" Bethany said.

"I am mainly mad because you never said goodbye or a 'hey, we have to go accompany Mr. Rocklen on his trip, be back soon,'" Bethany yelled, getting emotional.

She was right, but I would have said goodbye if it was not a secret mission.

"Hey, can we have a truce? You dump water and throw a sponge at us, and we forget to say goodbye?" I said, offering my hand.

"Truce. But! Don't ever leave without saying goodbye again!" She said, shaking my hand.

"Thank the king that's over!" Charles said jokingly.

I smirked and took my boots off. Then, I poured the water inside of the boots all over his head. He quickly ran out of the way.

"HEY! Stop that!"

"Hay is for horses!" Bethany said, laughing.

"What kind of motto is that?" I laughed.

"I don't know, I kinda like it," she said.

We helped her clean up the rest of the ballroom, along with the mess we had created.

The days in the months of July and August passed slowly. Although my agenda appeared unchanged and boring, my life felt quiet the opposite. After our trip to kill the Fearhine, everything changed. All the secrets I had learned and knowledge I had gained was life changing. Every day, I was ready for the Prince to call me into his study so he could share any news about the secret society. I couldn't help but constantly think about how no one knew of the Fearhine, the dark witch, or Prince George's secret group of followers.

Once in a blue moon, something different and exciting would happen here at the castle to break the monotony. One day, Edward's mother sent him a package, and in it was a bottle of maple syrup, a product you can only get in Arone, where he is from. Each of us got a chance to taste the sweet, delicious treat before he ate it all by himself.

Thankfully, because the daily jobs change every day, we have the illusion that we do not live every day the same.

However, today started unlike the last dozen before. Charles and I woke early to be the first served breakfast. Never before had we gotten the freshly made hot breakfast that the earliest of risers got.

The servants' hall was empty and toast sat, fresh out of the oven, on a platter. Our faces lit up with excitement. We had never been first. The butter was still melting down the hot bread. Today, they served strawberry jam. I poured a bowl of oatmeal and drizzled the jam over it. My stomach growled for the sweet taste of the strawberry. Charles and I sat alone enjoying the warm buttery toast. When we finished our meal, people poured into the room. We fled from the crowds and headed for Ms. Woodround's room. She sat at her desk eating her oatmeal. After the prank we pulled on her with the hot sauce, she doesn't eat in the kitchen anymore. Ms. Woodround let out an annoyed sigh when we walked in.

"William's nephew and friend, Prince George requests to see you this morning. Maybe your uncle is going to get fired. Boy, would that be the day," she said, shoveling blueberry oatmeal into her mouth.

I scowled at her. My mind moved past the mean comment she made about my uncle and focused on the prince. Prince George must have news.

We found Uncle William waiting in front of the Prince's study.

"Nice of you to show up, Liam," he said.

Uncle William knocked on the door, and Prince George said to enter. When we walked in, he was writing furiously on a paper at his desk.

"Ah, hello, sorry, I am just writing to the Green Witch Carrot and Lettuce Farm. The new pay deduction that my father stupidly instituted is causing them to stop servicing us," Prince George said.

"What new pay deduction?" Uncle William asked.

"He deducted pay from the witches and people in the manufacturing and farming businesses for some reason. He said 'we need to save money'. It makes no sense because we need them to be paid so we have resources. It's all a mess," Prince George said, sounding distressed.

"Anyways, let's move on to the news. We still have yet to locate the dark witch. You defeating the Fearhine was just the beginning of our fight. The dark witch has gained many loyal followers of her own. Evidence of many new disturbances keeps coming up. I am nervous that the kingdom will slip away before I even notice. This is why I have followers like you. In order to develop and build more followers, I came up with some new things. I decided to name my group the Order of the Elk."

"Order of the Elk? But, we are monster killers and dark witch hunters," I blurted out in confusion.

I hoped that we would have a cooler name than that.

"The point is Liam, we are trying to go undercover. It's a secret group of rebellion. Not to mention this goes far deeper than killing and fighting monsters. This will affect the entire Outer Kingdom. The dark witch and her followers would have a hard time figuring out where we are and who we are if we have a name like the Order of the Elk. They will think it's a group of animal lovers who try to protect elks or something. The point of all this is to restore the power in the country back to its previous state and give it a real leader, not like this fake leader that I call my father."

"I guess that makes sense," Charles said under his breath.

"And even though we have a secret name that will be misleading, we still had to solve the problem of who to trust and not to trust. As my group will expand, moles will try to fake their way in. Which is why when you meet someone new and you need their help, you ask them this question to find out if they are in the Order of the Elk. Here is the question: 'who is the ruler of the Outer Kingdom?' Then, the answer is 'the strongest elk,'" he said.

"Very interesting," Uncle William said.

I quickly memorized the question.

Prince George walked over to a large book on his shelf. He struggled to pull it off, but managed. He placed it on his desk and opened it up to reveal the book was fake and hollow. Inside was a secret stash of money. He pulled out three small coin bags and handed them to us. I looked inside to find it was full of gold coins.

"This is for conquering the Fearhine," Prince George said.

My heart was beating fast. I am now going to serve the Prince like a real knight. My dreams were coming true! Sadly, this must remain a secret. As much as I want to go home and boast to all of the kids in school that I am basically a knight at the age of 16, I can't.

"You are free to go. I have no idea the next time you will see me again. I have to warn you though- soon this whole cold war with the witch will become very dangerous for all of us. You have to watch your backs because she will do anything to stop us," he warned.

"Don't reveal any information about the Order of the Elk to anyone but our members," Prince George said sternly. We bowed and quickly exited quietly.

"Boys, give me the coins to stash under my coat, so no one suspects anything," Uncle William said when we left.

I was curious about who else in the Outer Kingdom was a part of the Order of the Elk. Bethany's face popped into my head. Could she be a part of it? That would be the best! We found Bethany waiting for us in our room.

"Way to leave me with all the work guys, again!" she frowned.

"Sorry, we had to umm... go help my uncle with some things. You know moving things, lifting things, all that kind of stuff you go help people with," I quickly blurted out as a cover story.

Bethany looked at us with a suspicious expression. I hope she fell for it.

"Okay, then..." Bethany said, stretching out her words.

"Hey Charles, want to come play catch with me and Jeremy?" Edward asked, running into the room.

Sasha grabbed Charles's hand and pulled him toward the door. Charles looked at us for permission. We smiled at him and nodded.

"Yes! Come on guys, let's go!" Charles said, running out with the couple.

Suddenly, I remembered wanting to ask Bethany about the Order of the Elk. If Bethany really was a part of the group, we should know! Then, I could tell her the truth and maybe go on adventures with her! Prince George had said people all over the Outer Kingdom were in the Order of the Elk. I decided I was going to find out if she was too.

"Do you want to go with them?" Bethany asked.

"Yeah, but first, can I ask you a question?"

"Yeah, what's up?"

"Who is the King of the Outer Kingdom?" I asked.

"Umm… that's kind of a dumb question. King Bartholomew of course," she said.

I sighed. It was too good to be true to have both Bethany and Charles be in the Order of the Elk. A small part of me knew she could not be. She looked at me, confused by my question.

"Never mind. You are right it was a dumb question. Let's go follow Charles wherever they went!" I said, pretending to laugh at my stupidity.

"Let's go," Bethany said.

I walked quickly to the stables. Sasha had her legs up in the air and her dress over her head. Thank goodness she was wearing a pair of leggings underneath.

"Fourteen, fifteen, sixteen, seventeen… aww! Seventeen," Charles said, counting.

Sasha fell to the ground.

"Alright, Brockfur, try and beat that," she challenged Charles.

"What are you guys even doing?" I questioned, laughing.

"Handstand contest," Sasha replied.

I sat down on a hay bale in the stable and watched Bethany throw a ball back and forth with Edward and Jeremy. I looked over to Charles who was attempting to do a handstand for more than four seconds. I was lucky to have such good friends. Jeremy came running up behind Edward and knocked the ball out of his hand. Bethany broke out in laughter. Edward threw the ball at Jeremy and chased him around the field. Sasha called after her boyfriend while Charles ran to join them. With a smile on my face, I stood up and joined the group.

Chapter 24

Today is the last day of work for Charles and me. School starts in three days. When I say the word school, it is like poison in my mouth. As much as I missed my parents and Byron, I have grown so attached to my life here that it feels just like home.

Bethany ran into our rooms to wake us up.

"GET UP, GUYS! I want to spend as much time with you today as I can!" she screamed, shaking the ends of our beds.

"Whoa! Stop, stop, stop!" I said, falling out of my bed and onto the floor. Charles got out of bed himself and was already dressed in day clothes.

"How did you get dressed so quick?" I asked Charles.

"I sleep in my day clothes," he answered as if it were normal.

"Why?" I asked, confused.

"It gives me a jump start on the day," Charles responded, shrugging with a smile.

Bethany left with Charles for breakfast, so I could change. My outfit had already been picked out because all of my other clothes and belongings had been packed in a wagon that Uncle William was borrowing from a friend.

The servants' hall was bustling with life. Everyone was engaged in the regular morning conversations before work. I grabbed my oatmeal and sat with my friends. We talked about our good memories from the summer and the pranks we pulled. However, the prince's ball was the main topic of this morning's conversation. We tried to focus on the positives of that night, such as the food, the elegant people, and the dancing. My stomach growled, longing for the delicious food they served at the prince's ball. However, the conversation continued to loop back to the violent riot that occurred right outside our windows.

"Guys, we won't see you until like, next March!" Sasha realized, frowning.

"Yeah, that sucks. Now, I'm stuck with these two until then," Jeremy joked, pointing at Edward and Sasha.

"Hey!" Sasha said, punching him in the arm.

"I'm kidding!"

"You guys will still have one more week with me before they make me go back to Mrs. Opal's Preparatory School for Girls," Bethany shuddered.

"We are still here for the long run, at least for a couple more years," Edward said.

"It's gonna suck being stuck all alone with those bratty girls," Bethany complained to Charles and me.

"That's okay; we can write to each other every week! And my mom can mail you recipes since you said you wanted to try baking," I told Charles.

"Thanks! That would be awesome."

"Plus, we have spring to look forward to all throughout the school year!" I said.

"That's true," Charles said.

"Come on, let's go," Bethany said, finishing her breakfast.

We walked down the hallway into the throne room. King Bartholomew came strolling in, swarmed by his advisors. Fear struck

304

me. All of the advisors were speaking to him all at once. Charles stopped in his place, and at the same time, Bethany and Charles slid over to the wall and stood like statues. I quickly copied them. The king looked annoyed by his advisors. He sat angrily on his throne. It was as if he radiated power and fear off of himself. King Bartholomew was a fat man with a red-grey walrus mustache. His bald head was hidden under a large crown.

King Bartholomew silenced his advisors with a loud booming voice. They all cowered behind one another. The one in front, a tiny little man, spoke up.

"Your... your Highness, I really must advise you to start doing business with the kingdom's primary blacksmith. I don't know why you're cutting us off from all of our necessary resources. We have been in business with this family for twenty years. I strongly think we should stay in business," the small man piped up.

He must be the king's right hand man because his uniform was different from the rest. I could see his legs shaking. The little man waited for the king's response. Three of the other advisors were shaking their heads in agreement.

"Yes, sir, that a smart idea Mr. Jack suggested," one said.

"We should try and repair the relationships with other businesses, too!" another one suggested.

"Mr. Jack! Away with these other babbling idiots! I refuse to listen to what any of you say!" the king said.

"But!" Mr. Jack said.

"AWAY!" the king boomed.

One of the female advisors gave him an angry look.

"I QUIT!" she said, throwing down her papers and storming out.

The rest of the advisors fled up the stairs, leaving Mr. Jack alone with the king.

I looked to Charles and Bethany. They gestured to go back to the servants' corridors. We shuffled away leaving the very angry king and his terrified advisor. Bethany gave a sigh of relief.

"King Bartholomew is so scary! I'm so glad we got out of there," she said.

"Charles, do you think that there is a certain reason why the king is acting this way?" I said, hinting to what Prince George had talked about to us.

"Yes, there is, I bet," Charles said.

The day continued on as the longest day in my life. Every time I saw Bethany and Charles, all I could think about was not seeing them anymore.

I only had a few hours left with them until Uncle William gave me a ride back to Brendsworth and my parents. I got a warm feeling inside when I thought about seeing my parents again. I could not wait to go back home and brag to all the other kids about how I got to be at the castle and see Prince George and King Bartholomew. The last time anyone in my class got to go to the castle was when I was thirteen. Jeff Tomatago had gone to see his grandmother right here in Trisanburg City. Everyone in the class was so intrigued by his stories.

"Liam, do you know what time you are going to have to leave?" Bethany asked.

"Why don't we go find my uncle and ask him?" I suggested.

"Let's go!" Charles said, rushing to get outside.

We walked outside toward the garden. The wind in my hair felt refreshing. Uncle William stood in the garden with the gardener. I waited next to a bed of petunias for Uncle William to notice me. Charles came over and waved to Uncle William. Uncle William looked over and nodded. He was still busy having a conversation with the gardener.

"When will they be done?" Charles wondered.

The conversation was finishing up since Uncle William smiled and shook the woman's hand. I walked over cautiously, making sure he was done with business.

"Hey, Uncle William! When are we going to ride back to my home?" I asked.

"At lunchtime, we will ask the chefs for a sandwich, and then we will be on our way," he said.

"Wait, but lunch is in like two hours!" I frowned.

"Sorry, but that's the time we are leaving," Uncle William said, waving goodbye to the gardener.

Bethany folded up my bed sheets and blankets neatly on the end of my bed to be washed. Charles did the same for his. We sat in our room and talked one last time before I had to leave. The summer had seemed to go by quicker than I had wanted. It seemed like only yesterday I met Bethany and Charles. Uncle William walked by in the hallway. I quickly ran outside my room to talk to him.

"Uncle William, are we leaving now?" I said.

"Yep, say your goodbyes," he said.

"I don't want to leave though. I literally hate school! And what about Bethany and Charles?" I said.

Uncle William frowned. I had a gut feeling that I had no choice in the matter.

"Liam, I have to follow your parents orders. I said I would bring you back in time for school," Uncle William said.

He put his hand on my shoulder. I looked up and him and sighed. I could do nothing about my fate. It was time to say goodbye to my best friends.

"Bye, Charles, make sure you write me every week," I said.

He gave me high five.

"Make sure you bring up some of your mom's baked goods next time I see you," he said, smiling.

Bethany had tears forming in her eyes. I felt a warm feeling knowing they would miss me. Now, I will be counting down the days until I can see them again.

"Aww, don't cry. We will write each other, and it's only, let's see…six or seven months before I see you again," I assured her.

She wiped her tears away and hugged me.

"Goodbye," she said, sniffling.

"Liam, I am going to go pick up the sandwiches, and then, we can head out," Uncle William said.

"So, when do you head out of here?" Bethany asked Charles.

"Not until later tonight," he assured her.

"Well, I am not really good at goodbyes…why don't we go let Jeremy, Sasha, and Edward know you're leaving?" Charles suggested.

"Yeah, I guess so…" I said.

We walked around the servants' hall to try and find the trio. Only Jeremy was in his room.

"Hey, man! What's up? Are you leaving?"

"Sadly…" I replied.

"That's too bad. Until next time, brother." I was surprised by how much everyone was sad about me leaving.

He gave me a fist bump.

"You are just taking a little break for like five months, and then, you will be back here pulling pranks again!" Jeremy said, lightening the mood.

Uncle William came into the room.

"Time to go, buddy!" he said, handing me a paper bag of sandwiches.

We walked out with Charles, Jeremy, and Bethany to the wagon. Uncle William and I got in and started our journey home. As I rode away in the wagon, I noticed my three friends waving goodbye. I waved back as I watched them fall out of view.

The ride back to Brendsworth was not exciting. I spent the entire ride reading "Sir Frederick's Adventures". After meeting him in person, his stories are so much better. I reviewed the many fighting stances and looked into the history of witches and dark witches. Uncle William stopped only three times. When I asked why he was not stopping as much to rest, he responded, "The faster I get you home, the faster I get to some of your mother's delicious baked goods."

Soon, Brendsworth came into view and memories of the day that I had left home came back. I had left a scared kid. I returned a hero. The air felt nicer than that of the city. It smelled better because of the lack of horse and human feces. The world seemed happier. I felt more accomplished than I had ever before. My house came into view. I was home and stronger than ever before.

I am a hero.

Acknowledgements

I am very thankful for all of the people who helped me make this book possible. My editor and good friend, Michael Wei not only helped fix commas but he also made me laugh and gave me confidence throughout my editing process. My mom and dad, who listened to my stories. I would also like to thank my cousin, Elizabeth Coppes, for giving me tips on graphic design and being there to give me constructive criticism. I would also like to thank my sisters, Meika and Julia, who shared and encouraged imagination with stories and games. Lastly, I would like to thank my readers and I hope, like Liam, they will go out into the world and achieve their dreams, even if it means trying something new.

51900670R00177

Made in the USA
Middletown, DE
05 July 2019